PRIVATE DICKS
AND DISCO BALLS

MICHAEL BRACKEN, EDITOR

PRIVATE DICKS
AND DISCO BALLS

Private Eyes in the
Dyn-O-Mite Seventies

Down & Out Books
3959 Van Dyke Road, Suite 265
Lutz, FL 33558
DownAndOutBooks.com

Cover design by JT Lindroos

ISBN: 1-64396-365-1
ISBN-13: 978-1-64396-365-5

For Temple
My Love, My Muse, My Everything

TABLE OF CONTENTS

Houston, We Have a Problem   1
Bev Vincent

The Missing Delegate   21
Neil S. Plakcy

The Kratz Gambit   43
Mark Thielman

The Darklight Gizmo Matter   55
Gary Phillips

Agency   75
Laura Oles

A Woman's Place   91
N.M. Cedeño

Neon Women   109
Ann Aptaker

An Eye for an Eye   125
Stephen D. Rogers

An Evening at the Opera House   145
James A. Hearn

Cold Comfort   165
Andrew Welsh-Huggins

Stayin' Alive   185
Alan Orloff

Everybody Was Kung Fu Fighting   207
William Dylan Powell

Last Dance   231
Bill Fitzhugh

About the Editor   245

About the Contributors   247

HOUSTON, WE HAVE A PROBLEM
Bev Vincent

April 15, 1970

It was a man's world, Cassandra "Sandy" Parker thought. No doubt about it. She had been with the Wilson Bennett Detective Agency for five years, and she still struggled to get assigned to the best cases—the ones that made both headlines and careers. The ones where she wasn't simply treated like a piece of eye candy used to soften up a male suspect.

These deep thoughts were inspired by the Astrodome, which she was currently driving past. Elvis Presley had played six shows there in three days a few weeks ago as part of the Houston Livestock Show and Rodeo. It was also the site of her first-ever undercover operation, where she had seduced a murderer into confessing. Since then, she had been taking classes toward a degree in Criminal Justice at the University of Houston, but she was still mostly a Girl Friday around the office.

She had recently read a book titled *Sexual Politics*, which exposed the patriarchy and the subjugation of women in the world of literature and wondered if a similar book could be written about private detective agencies. She lamented the fact that she didn't have any female role models. All the detectives and cops on TV were men except for Julie Barnes on *The Mod Squad*, and even she was primarily window dressing, conspicuously absent whenever there were fisticuffs or other serious business.

When the Bowens hired the agency to look for Diane, their seventeen-year-old daughter, Sandy took matters into her own hands. The teenager's disappearance had been featured in the newspapers for the past few days, running a close second to the Apollo 13 crisis. Police weren't taking the situation seriously, though, according to the Bowens. The official stance was that she was just another runaway. There had been many of those in recent years—kids who thought their parents were boring, so they joined the hippie movement or a commune, looking for a more exciting life. Sandy hadn't heard if any of them had been successful in that quest.

That morning, she'd called the HPD officer supposedly working the case. The tip line had received several calls, he said, but none panned out. "She'll come back on her own in a few days," he told her. "They almost always do."

After consulting his supervisor, he agreed to send over their file by telefax. "File" was a generous term for what amounted to a few sheets of paper: the missing person report the Bowens had filed and notes about some perfunctory calls the officer had made. He was only too happy to relegate the case to private detectives so he could focus on real crimes.

While making Xerox copies of the pages for the lead investigators, she ran off an extra set for herself, as well as a copy of the file her colleagues were maintaining based on their preliminary interviews. Then she announced she was taking the rest of the day off. Woman's stuff, she told her boss, which always forestalled further discussion.

Her colleagues would, no doubt, interview Diane's family, relatives, teachers, and acquaintances, but Sandy believed she could get the girl's classmates—especially the females—to open up. The teenagers might giggle and fawn over the chiseled jaws and muscular builds of the male detectives, but Sandy was young—less than ten years out of high school—and she'd been head cheerleader during her final two years. She knew how to relate to other young women in ways her associates never could.

After calling ahead to make arrangements, Sandy drove to Westbury High School in southwest Houston. She found a place to park near the three-story building and rolled down the window. Despite T.S. Eliot's admonition, Sandy had always liked April. Today, it was cool, and there was a gentle breeze. She turned the ignition key far enough so she could listen to the end of "Bridge Over Troubled Water" on the radio as she reviewed the Xeroxed file.

What must it be like to have a child go missing? Sandy had run away when she was twelve, but only made it as far as the corner before she realized she didn't know where she was going. So, she went back home before anyone missed her. She imagined Mrs. Bowen staring out her living room window, hoping to see her daughter coming home.

Her black-and-white copy of the class photograph Diane's parents had supplied showed a smiling, bespectacled face surrounded by a mass of curly hair. Her turquoise blouse was black in the reproduction, but Sandy remembered how well it had complemented the girl's eyes. According to the file, she was an excellent student and a highly effective point guard on her high school basketball team. She had last been seen after practice on Friday, walking the several blocks home carrying a gym bag and her bookbag.

Simon and Garfunkel gave way to the new song by the Beatles, "Let it Be." The tabloids were saying Paul had quit the band and John had just released a solo single, but she couldn't imagine them breaking up. She waited for the song to end before returning the documents to the file, rolling up the window and heading into the school lobby, where she was greeted by the secretary, who introduced herself as Miss Thurston. She led Sandy to an empty classroom. "I think the students will be more comfortable here than in the principal's office," she said, to which Sandy nodded her agreement. Sandy was no stranger to principals' offices and had no desire to make the acquaintance of another. Miss Thurston also handed Sandy a copy of Diane Bowen's most recent school transcript.

After Miss Thurston left, Sandy took a few steps toward the teacher's desk but decided that might look overly formal. Instead, she pulled several desks into a rough circle. A few minutes later, the secretary returned with three students, all clutching armloads of textbooks and spiral-bound notebooks. Miss Thurston made the introductions. Melissa was blond and somewhat sullen, Crystal was raven-haired with subtly Asian features, and Jennifer had terra-cotta colored skin and high cheekbones. Until recently, HISD had been the largest segregated school district in the country. A month ago, though, the Board of Education voluntarily decided to integrate. The ensuing controversy had made national news.

The teens wore dresses of assorted designs and patterns which came to mid-thigh. Crystal and Melissa had on solid-colored leggings—orange for Crystal, red for Melissa—while Jennifer's had an interlocking black and white diamond pattern.

"Are you really a detective?" Crystal asked as she took a seat at one of the desks, her eyes wide.

"Yes, I'm with the Wilson Bennett Detective Agency. Diane Bowen's parents hired us to find out what happened to her."

"Far out," Crystal responded.

"We're really worried about her," Melissa said. She frowned to show just how worried she was, then glanced at her classmates.

"We're talking to everyone who knew her. Anything you tell me will be held in the strictest confidence, even from your parents and your teachers."

"Do you have a gun?" Crystal asked.

Sandy suppressed a smirk. She'd heard that question a lot in recent years, mostly from guys she dated. "I own one," she said, "but I don't often carry it." She ran a hand over the waist of her form-fitting pastel green bodysuit. "It ruins the lines of my clothes."

The three girls nodded as they processed this important style insight.

"Did Diane tell any of you she was planning to go somewhere?"

All three girls shook their heads, although not at the same time. Sandy made a mental note of the pattern.

"When was the last time you saw her?"

"At practice after school on Friday," Melissa said.

Sandy gave her a look that revealed how surprised she was the girl was also on the basketball team.

"I help out. Run drills, stuff like that. Kind of an assistant coach," Melissa said, blushing.

Jennifer said, "She's in my chemistry class. I'm pretty sure that's the last time I saw her."

Crystal said, "She had lunch with me."

"Did she give you any indication she might be in trouble?"

More head shakes.

"Not even boy troubles?"

Crystal shook her head. Melissa shrugged. Jennifer paused, as if she might be about to say something, but she, too, eventually shook her head. Sandy couldn't read the expression on the girl's face. Almost, but not quite, bemused.

"Arguments with her parents?"

That elicited a laugh from Melissa. Sandy looked at her and waited.

Melissa blushed again and looked down at the desktop.

Sandy waited.

When the girl looked up again, she brushed a lock of blond hair from her face. "Everyone is bickering with their parents half the time. If it's not Dad telling you who not to date, it's Mom telling you what not to wear."

"Diane, too?"

"Natch," Melissa said.

"But nothing more serious than uptight parent stuff?"

After a second or two, Melissa shook her head.

"Any recent changes in her behavior? Was she wearing more makeup than usual? Smoking? Swearing?"

Crystal grinned. "Diane could curse up a storm when she wanted to. We're bestest friends." She gave Melissa a side-eyed glance, as if daring her to challenge this assertion.

"She didn't smoke," Melissa said. "She wouldn't do anything to wreck her team's chances to win regionals."

"She was good with makeup," Jennifer added. "Not too much—just highlights."

The other two nodded their agreement.

"Did she ever have more money than she could explain?" Sandy asked.

"Do you mean, was she stealing?" Crystal asked.

"Or selling drugs?" Jennifer added.

Sandy shrugged. She hadn't considered either of those options but found it interesting that Diane's friends had come up with them.

"She was just like everyone else," Melissa said. "Sometimes she had money to buy things and sometimes she didn't."

Sandy glanced at the transcript Miss Thurston had provided.

"Her grades are good," she observed. "No recent changes there."

"Diane's super-smart," Jennifer said. "She could wind up being valedictorian if she…"

Sandy let the sentence hang in the air without supplying the missing words. She glanced at the file again but couldn't think of anything else to ask. She hadn't come up with a single clue. So much for her special bond with high school girls.

While she was rifling through her purse to find the business cards she'd ordered from the agency's printer—a purchase she'd hidden in a larger company order—Crystal raised her hand.

"Yes?"

"Maybe she was abducted by aliens."

Somehow, Sandy managed to keep her jaw from dropping.

"You hear about that all the time. Except they usually send

people back the next day. But maybe, you know, since we're sending rockets up into space looking for them, they decided to hold onto her a little longer."

Melissa and Jennifer exchanged a glance, shaking their heads ever so slightly.

"Okay," Sandy said, drawing the word out. "I'm not sure how to look into that, but I'll mention your theory to my colleagues." She pretended to write something in her notebook before handing out her cards. "Please, if you think of anything, don't hesitate to call. Anytime. I have an answering machine."

The girls gathered their books and headed out of the classroom. Crystal was telling Melissa about alien abductions. While Sandy was updating her notes, she noticed Jessica lingering near the door.

"Yes? Jessica? Was there something else?"

The girl looked nervously toward the hall, then nodded.

"Close the door, if you want," Sandy said.

Jessica did so and came back to the circle of desks. She stood several feet from Sandy, shifting her weight from one foot to the other.

"Please, sit."

Jessica placed her books on the desktop closest to Sandy and lowered herself into the seat. "You swear you won't tell anyone what I say?"

"I promise you I won't say where I got the information if it turns out to be something we have to follow up on."

Jessica inhaled deeply, held the breath, and then let it out slowly. "You should talk to Ms. Waverly."

"Who's that?"

"The basketball coach."

"I see. You think she knows something?"

"You asked if Diane had boy troubles."

Sandy nodded.

"I haven't been at this school long, but I notice things. Diane introduced herself on my first day and sat with me at lunch.

That broke the ice, if you know what I mean."

"Yes, I get it."

"Things might have been uncomfortable for me here. I'm not the only student who isn't white, but there aren't many of us, and we tend to hang out together. But Diane isn't like most people. She made the effort, and now I have friends."

"Including Diane." Sandy was waiting for Jessica to get to the point, but she wasn't about to push her.

"Yes. So, when you mentioned boy troubles, well, I almost laughed."

"Why?"

"Because Diane, she, well, she doesn't have much use for boys. If you know what I mean."

"Uh huh."

"Oh, she'll go out on dates with them from time to time, but that's just…"

"Camouflage?" Sandy said.

"That's a good word," Jessica answered. "Exactly right."

"What about Crystal and Melissa? Do they know?"

Jessica shrugged. "I'd say not many people do. People wouldn't suspect a pretty girl like her would be…" She waved a hand in the air.

"Playing for the other team?"

Jessica laughed and then covered her mouth. "I've never heard it put like that before, but, yeah."

"So, you and she were…?"

"Oh, no, nothing like that. Just friends. I could never figure out how to talk to her about it."

"And why should I speak with Ms. Waverly?"

Jessica was silent for several seconds. "I don't want to spread rumors."

"But…?"

"I've seen them together. Not just at practice or in class. She teaches algebra."

"Where, then?"

"Out," she said, with another wave of her hand. "At a coffee shop. A few times. They seemed…touchy-feely."

Sandy nodded. "Okay. Thank you for telling me this, Jessica."

"You won't say anything to Ms. Waverly about me, right?"

"I promise."

Jessica nodded. She got up swiftly, collected her books, and left without looking back.

Interesting, Sandy thought as she returned the desks to their original positions. When she was finished, she headed to the front office to find out if Ms. Waverly was available. Halfway there, she saw Melissa standing next to an open locker. The teenager waved her over.

"I had an idea," Melissa said.

"What's that?"

"Diane always said she wanted to be an astronaut. Of course, that can't happen. They don't take women. She was pretty mad about it. Said she'd have to settle for being an astrophysicist or one of those computer programmers who work on trajectories and stuff like that down at the Manned Spacecraft Center. 'Manned,'" she said with a shake of her head. "Get it?"

Sandy was sure there was a point to Melissa's story, but it was taking her a while to get to it. That seemed to be a common trait among teenaged girls, she mused.

"Well, I was thinking how upset she'd be about what's happening up there now. Apollo 13? The launch was on Saturday, right?"

"Yes, that's right."

"Maybe she went to Florida to see the rocket take off. I could imagine her doing that."

"Was that something she mentioned to you?"

Melissa shrugged, then readjusted her armload of books. "No. It was just something that came to me after we talked."

"Thank you for sharing that, Melissa. Any idea how she'd get to Florida?"

Melissa shook her head. "No clue. She didn't have a car. It's not like her to split, though. Not without telling anyone."

Sandy thanked the girl again and continued to the front office. Miss Thurston told her Ms. Waverly was in class but would be free in half an hour. She promised to leave a message for the teacher to come up when her class ended.

Sandy found a bench outside the main entrance, where she passed the time rereading her notes. The three girls had offered wildly different theories about what might have happened to Diane. She didn't put any stock in Crystal's alien abduction idea, and it didn't make sense Diane would traipse off to Florida to watch the moon launch, either. Even if she had, she'd had plenty of time to get back home. There was nothing beyond Melissa's supposition to support the idea, so it seemed like a wild goose chase. Not even worth mentioning to the lead detective, assuming she decided to update him on her off-the-books investigation.

A voice interrupted her reverie. "Miss Parker?"

Sandy looked up to see a woman of about her age wearing a powder blue blouse over a navy knee-length skirt. Her brown hair hung to her shoulders. She had chalk dust on her fingers. "Yes?"

"I'm Helen Waverly. Miss Thurston said you wanted to talk to me."

Sandy got up from the bench. "Yes. It's about Diane Bowen." She rummaged in her purse for a business card.

The teacher looked at it and shook her head. "It's terrible," she said. "We're all worried. How can I help?"

"Is there some place we can go?" Sandy asked. "It's a little... delicate."

Waverly frowned. "I have an office next to the gym," she said.

Sandy followed the basketball coach to the gymnasium, which was at the back of the school. A group of boys practicing layups stopped to give Sandy an appraising look. Their coach yelled at them to get going, although his gaze lingered on Sandy, too. Men, she thought. It was such a difficult world to navigate. Sure, she knew how to use her looks to get what she wanted, especially on the job, but there were times when she wanted to be able to turn off all the attention. Was that too much to ask for?

Waverly's office wasn't much bigger than a broom closet. Instead of a desk, she had a card table with a couple of straight-backed chairs. Basketballs were stored in a nylon mesh tube hanging in one corner. Chalkboards covering three walls were filled with sketches that looked like war campaigns, which probably wasn't far from the truth.

"Can I close the door?" Sandy asked.

"If you don't mind it getting stuffy. Not much airflow in here, I'm afraid."

"This shouldn't take long."

"I had a call from another detective this morning. I thought I was supposed to meet him after school."

"I was in the area, so I thought I'd take a chance you'd be available."

"I see."

Sitting across from the teacher in this tiny room, Sandy felt embarrassed about the questions she had to ask. She sighed. Nothing to do but go straight at it.

"You know Diane pretty well, I understand."

"She's my star player. If we win regionals, there's no telling how far she could go, and she's only a junior."

"Um, yes. I was thinking more of outside of school?" She raised her pitch slightly at the end to turn it into a question.

"I'm not sure what you mean."

"Someone reported seeing you with her on a number of occasions," Sandy said. "Having coffee. You appeared...close?"

The coach gave Sandy a long, unblinking look before answering. "I see." She looked at the ceiling tiles for a few seconds. "Diane had personal issues she wanted to discuss. Things she wasn't comfortable talking about with her parents. I've been her coach for nearly three years and, as you say, we've gotten close. But not in the way you're thinking. My boyfriend and I are quite happy, thank you very much."

Sandy didn't respond to the rebuke. "So, Diane was having problems."

The coach nodded. "Seventeen is a difficult age. I'm sure you remember—we're not all that far from those bad old days, right?"

Sandy had a flashback to some of the tortures she had endured as a teenager, even though she had been popular. "Right."

"She needed someone to talk to, and she trusted me enough to share that confidence."

"Were her problems related to her, um, who she might be attracted to?"

Waverly's eyebrows went up. "How did you know that? She hadn't told anyone else, to the best of my knowledge."

"Teenagers can be pretty observant," I said. "We underestimate them at our peril."

"Ain't that the truth," Waverly said with a sound that might have been a laugh.

"Was she involved with anyone?"

The hard look returned to the coach's face. "Now you're venturing into delicate territory. I don't have attorney-client privilege, but I respect the things Diane told me in confidence, especially since they involve another student."

Sandy nodded. "It's just that forty-eight hours is a long time for someone to be missing. Five days is an eternity, so I think you can probably make an exception."

It took the coach nearly a full minute to respond. The air in the tiny office was getting stuffy, reminding Sandy of locker rooms from her cheerleader days. Odors could be evocative, she knew—even more than sights or sounds. She waited patiently as Waverly wrestled with her conscience.

"There's another student. She hasn't a drop of athletic ability, but she asked to help with the team, so I give her things to do that make her feel useful. She runs drills, acts as a one-person pep squad during practice games, things like that."

The pieces fell into place. "Melissa," Sandy said. She thought back to her interactions with the girl, both in the classroom and afterward in the hall. She'd tried to make Sandy think Diane had gone out of town. Did she have a reason for doing so?

Waverly offered a wan smile. "It's not just teenagers who notice things, I see."

"Was it a distant longing? Unrequited love? Or were they together?"

"Together, as much as they were able. They've been best friends for years. Came up through middle school, so they've always been in each other's back pockets. At some point—not too long ago—a sleepover turned into something else. Diane was on cloud nine. Melissa...she seemed less sure."

"You've spoken to her, too?"

"About that, no. She's not easy to reach."

"I wonder what their parents would think about their relationship."

Waverly scrunched up her mouth. "The Bowdens are pretty conservative. I can tell you that much. Protective of their image."

"So, this might not sit well with them."

"Probably not," Waverly said with a shrug.

Sandy thanked the coach for being so open. As she headed back to the lobby, she considered her next move. She could summon Melissa now but calling her out of class again might make her friends suspicious. She decided to grab a late lunch and come back in time to intercept Melissa when school let out for the day.

At three-thirty, she hung out near the main entrance, searching for Melissa in the river of students streaming through the doors. She spotted the girl walking by herself near the back of the pack, seemingly deep in thought, and approached her.

"Hello, Melissa. I have a few more questions for you, if you have time. Can I buy you a cup of coffee?" Sandy had picked out a coffee shop not far from campus while she was having lunch.

Melissa frowned. For a moment, Sandy thought the girl was going to come up with an excuse to decline. Finally, her shoulders relaxed, and she nodded. They walked in silence up the street and around the corner to a place called the Black Hole, where they found a two-top table at the back. A few other students followed them in, but none sat nearby. Sandy wondered if this was the place where Jessica had seen Diane with her coach.

"I know you and Diane were close," Sandy said.

Melissa dumped sugar into her mug of coffee and stirred. "We've been friends forever."

"Really close?" She raised one eyebrow.

The color drained from Melissa's face. She lowered her head to meet the coffee cup as she took her first sip.

"Don't worry. I'm not going to tell anyone."

Melissa's hands were shaking ever so slightly. She looked up, meeting Sandy's gaze. "How did you know? How could you know?"

"Diane confided in someone," Sandy said. "I won't say who, but I believe they'll keep her secret."

"They told you," Melissa said. Now she looked angry.

Sandy nodded. "Only because it's a matter of Diane's safety."

"I don't see what that has to do with…" She trailed off.

"I'm just exploring all the avenues."

Melissa sighed. "She was at my place on Friday afternoon. After school."

Sandy tried not to react, but this was important new information. Everyone thought Diane had disappeared walking home.

"We were at each other's place all the time. Mostly hers, because it's bigger and nicer, but at my house, too. One evening, we were fooling around, acting silly and tickling each other. She had me pinned down, but instead of tickling me some more, she kissed me. It was just a peck on the lips at first, but then she did it again and it was different." She paused for another sip of coffee and looked around to make sure no one could overhear her. "I didn't know how to react. I was shocked. But it was nice. I liked it. She did it again, and I kissed her back. That's all that happened that day, but then...the next time I was at her place..." She shrugged.

"I understand."

"I was really confused about it, but she wasn't, or at least she didn't seem to be. I mean, I like guys. I've never been with one, but I think about them all the time. But being with Diane like that was amazing, like taking some kind of drug." She gave Sandy a nervous look. "Not that I ever have."

Sandy nodded.

"I never knew it could feel like that. But after a while, it didn't seem right. I could tell she wanted more than I did, and I didn't want our friendship to be ruined. So, on Friday, I told her we had to stop."

"How did she respond?"

"She wouldn't listen to me at first. Then, when she tried to kiss me, I pushed her away. That made her furious. We said terrible things to each other. Called each other names." Melissa sighed. "She grabbed her books and stormed out. That's the last time I saw her."

"Do you remember what time it was?"

It took the teenager a moment to recover from the emotional memory. "Maybe five. Before five-thirty, anyway, because that's when Dad gets home from work."

"Thank you for sharing this, Melissa. It might help a lot. I promise I won't tell anyone what you told me except the time Diane left your place. That's an important detail."

"I feel terrible," Melissa said. "What if she ran away because I was mean to her? What if she...did something to herself?"

Sandy reached over and touched the girl's hand. "You can't blame yourself for what someone else might have done," she said. She withdrew her hand and had her first sip of coffee, which by now had started to cool off. "Can you think of anyone she might have gone to see if she was upset?"

Melissa shook her head. "I dunno. Maybe Crystal? Crystal's always saying she's Diane's best friend, but she's only been here a year. She's a little creepy, if you ask me."

Sandy got Crystal's address from Melissa but didn't go straight there. Instead, she walked to Melissa's house first so she could retrace the path Diane might have taken the day she vanished. There was virtually no overlap with the route she would have taken if she'd gone straight home from school, so anyone looking for witnesses was barking up the wrong tree. She doubted the police had even tried, but her colleagues at the agency would have.

Crystal lived in an older subdivision, where the houses were rundown and the yards poorly maintained. Her place was in the middle of the street. There were no vehicles parked in the driveway or out front, so maybe Crystal's parents weren't home.

She rang the doorbell and heard it echo through the house. A moment later, the door opened a crack. "Yes? What is it?"

"It's me, Crystal. Sandy Parker. The detective."

The door opened a little more. "What do you want? I told you everything I know."

"You had an interesting idea earlier, and I'd like to hear more about it, if you don't mind."

Crystal's face lit up, and she stood back to allow Sandy in. Sandy was taken aback by how stark the place was. No wonder the doorbell had echoed. There was only an overstuffed sofa, a coffee table, and a tiny TV on a stand in the living room, and absolutely nothing on the walls. Crystal led her into the kitchen, where there was a wobbly table with a few mismatched chairs. A stack of textbooks and notebooks sat on one corner of the table. Sandy didn't wait to be invited to sit.

"I know you said you had lunch with Diane on Friday, but I was wondering if you might have seen her after school, too."

Crystal frowned, her eyes nearly closed. "You said you wanted to talk about—"

"She had an argument with someone, and I thought she might want to talk to her best friend. That's you, right?"

Crystal's demeanor eased slightly. "Yes, that's right. Bestest friends. That's what I like to say."

"Did she come by?"

The girl hesitated. "Would you like a cup of tea? I was just about to make myself some."

"Sure."

While Crystal filled the kettle, Sandy flipped through the notebook on the top of the pile of schoolbooks. It was filled with neat, crisp formulas and notes from algebra class. Presumably Ms. Waverly's class. Sandy found Diane Bowden's name and address written inside the front cover. She closed the notebook and returned it to its original position before Crystal noticed.

Crystal must have seen her, though, because Sandy observed her surreptitiously adding something to her teacup. Some kind of powder. "Milk?" Crystal asked.

"No thanks. I like mine black."

Sandy looked around, making sure she knew where the exits were. She also spotted the telephone hanging on the wall. After Crystal was seated across from her, Sandy pretended to take a sip of tea. "Did Diane lend you her math notebook?" she asked as casually as possible, nodding toward the stack of schoolbooks.

"Um, yeah, that's right. I forgot about that. She was always doing things like that for me."

Sandy pulled out the textbook underneath. Diane's name was penciled inside the front cover of that one, too. "All of these are hers."

"How's the tea?" Crystal said. "Ready for a refill?"

"Did you make tea for Diane, too? What did you put in it? Poison?"

Crystal took a deep breath. It seemed to Sandy she was never going to let it out again.

"Is Diane dead? Did you poison her?"

"It's not poison. I'd never do that. She's just...asleep. While I try to figure out what to do next."

"She's been asleep all this time? What are you giving her?"

"Not all the time. I let her wake up to eat and go to the bathroom. I'm not a monster. She was so upset when she got here, but she wouldn't say why. Something to do with Melissa. But then she looked at me funny and I knew she knew. It always happens eventually."

"What does?"

"I make it a year, maybe two, but someone always figures it out."

Sandy couldn't track what Crystal was talking about. After all, this was the girl who suggested Diane had been abducted by aliens. She obviously had a screw loose. Sandy got up from the table and went to the telephone. "I'm going to call one of my colleagues now. You won't give me any trouble, will you?"

Crystal shook her head. Before Sandy could stop her, she grabbed Sandy's teacup and emptied it in a single gulp.

Instead of calling her office, Sandy dialed 0 and asked the operator to connect her to the fire department. She told the dispatcher to send paramedics and the police. By now, Crystal was nearly unconscious. After making sure she was going to be okay, Sandy searched for Diane Bowden, finding her in a locked bedroom at the back of the house. Unconscious, but still alive.

Before long, a flurry of activity surrounded her. She called the office to let them know where she was and what had happened. Wilson Bennett himself arrived at the house twenty minutes later, where he debriefed Sandy. "Clever girl," he said, almost to himself, when she was finished.

Crystal was taken to the hospital in one ambulance, her arm attached to the rail of her gurney by handcuffs, and Diane was taken in another. Bennett called the Bowdens to let them know their daughter was safe and where they could find her.

After Sandy repeated her story to a police detective, Bennett drove her to the high school so she could get her car. On the way, he said, "I didn't realize you were assigned to this case."

Sandy remained silent for a moment. "I had some free time, so I thought I'd help out," she said at last.

"I like initiative," he said. "But don't stray so far without authorization again. Hear me?"

"I hear you."

Two days later, Sandy talked to the police detective again. It turned out Crystal wasn't a teenager. In fact, she was two years older than Sandy. Taking advantage of her unusually youthful appearance, she had moved from city to city in recent years, registering at local high schools. It wasn't a con job, exactly, the detective said. She wasn't looking to rob anyone. She'd been on her own since she was fifteen and was just looking for friends— for a surrogate family of sorts. She was recovering from the overdose of barbiturates she'd ingested and was being held at the hospital while the district attorney figured out what all to charge her with.

Diane Bowden was bouncing back from her prolonged captivity, too, and would soon be back on her feet and playing basketball again. When Sandy visited her at the hospital, Melissa was sitting by her bed holding her hand. That made Sandy happy.

Of course, the Bowdens were ecstatic, and Sandy received kudos from her colleagues—except for the detective in charge of the case. He'd come around eventually, Sandy thought, even if she had to turn on the tears and cry him into submission. That was one of her superpowers.

The crew of Apollo 13 were scheduled to splash down that afternoon. The front page of the morning edition of the

Houston Chronicle was taken up with oversized pictures of the three astronauts. Recovery of a missing teenager merited only a small item on an inside page. All credit was given to the Wilson Bennett Detective Agency, with no mention of Sandy's involvement whatsoever.

She folded the paper and threw it on her desk in disgust. It really was a man's world.

THE MISSING DELEGATE
Neil S. Plakcy

It was a hot July morning, and the air conditioner in the window of my office over Mr. Ho's Chinese restaurant on Washington Avenue in Miami Beach was already working overtime. I was considering ditching work for the day and heading to the beach when a gaunt man in a suit walked into the reception area in front of me.

It was the area where I would put a secretary, if I could ever afford one. But I was still struggling as a private eye, four years into my practice, and though I was able to pay my rent and the insurance for my lime-green Chevrolet Bel Air, I wasn't what you'd call prosperous.

"Good morning," I called to the man and waved him in.

"You're the private investigator?" he asked.

I stood up and reached out to shake his hand. "George Clay, at your service."

"John Greenhouse," he said.

I motioned him to the chair across from my desk and sat down. "How can I help you, Mr. Greenhouse?"

"You can find a missing person, can't you?"

"I can try. Who's missing?"

"His name is Jacob Abel. It's just that I promised his mother I would look out for him. His first time out of Centralia, Illinois, first time in a big city. Everything was fine. We were busy preparing for the convention until he said last night he wanted to go out for a walk."

"That would be the Democratic National Convention?" It was an obvious question—Miami Beach was swarming with delegates, taking up meeting space and hotel rooms so no other convention could be in the city at the same time. And the protesters were arriving every day, too, hippies and wheelchair-bound veterans in camouflage drab.

Greenhouse nodded. "We arrived here yesterday afternoon, and Jacob was so eager to see a big city. Eighteen years old, the youngest delegate from our state. The first time he could vote in a presidential election, and he was chosen to represent our district because he had been such an active campaigner. Straight-A student and president of the Young Democrats Club at Centralia High School. Eagle Scout. Just the best young man you can imagine."

He wrung his hands. "And now he's gone, on my watch."

"When was the last time you saw him?" I asked.

Greenhouse was sweating in his suit. He'd probably walked to my office from his hotel, and I wished I could make the room cooler, but the air conditioner was already at its highest setting.

"We had dinner last night at a Cuban restaurant a few blocks from our hotel. We don't have much in the way of foreign food back in Centralia, and Jacob wanted to try it out." He frowned. "Too spicy for me, but Jacob loved it. Then afterwards he said he'd take a little walk and meet me back at the hotel."

He stared at me, despair in his face. "He never came back. I waited up for him until almost eleven o'clock, way past my bedtime, but I didn't know what to do. I figured he'd met up with some of the delegates and gotten caught up. The boy is curious as all get-out to know other people and ways of life."

"This morning?"

"His bed hadn't been slept in. I went to the police, and the sergeant at the desk laughed and told me he'd probably found some hippie girl to shack up with, that he'd be back when he had his fill of nookie."

He said the word with a sneer, as if people in Centralia didn't engage in such things.

"The convention starts today, doesn't it?" I asked. It was Monday, July 10, 1972.

He nodded. "We've already missed two meetings this morning."

"I'm sure he'll turn up. You said he's a responsible young man. He won't want to miss being part of history."

"I need to find him," Greenhouse said. "I couldn't hold my head up in Centralia if something happened to him while I was supposed to be looking after him. Please, Mr. Clay, can I hire you to find him?"

"I charge ten dollars an hour, sir, with a hundred-dollar retainer."

"That's fine. Will you take a check?"

I agreed, and he wrote me a check. "Do you have a picture? Description?" I asked.

"I don't have a picture, but he should be easy to find. He's very tall, six-foot-three, I think, and gangly. Skinny as a picket fence, we say back home."

I was a hair over six feet myself, and I'd always felt tall. I had been skinny as a kid but filled out in the Navy.

"Hair color?"

"Blond. And before you ask, I don't know what color his eyes are, but he has a big, broad smile and his bottom teeth are a bit smashed in."

I thanked him, and Greenhouse walked out of my office. I picked up the copy of the *Miami Herald* that had come in the day before, which I'd just begun to read. As I remembered, there was a big article on the front page of the local section about the hippie city that had grown up in the last few days in Flamingo Park, a few blocks south and east of my office.

I'd been thinking of going down there to observe the antics of the Hippies, the Zippies, the People's Pot Party and all the other crazies who had flooded the city in advance of the convention. Now was going to be my chance. If a straight-arrow kid from central Illinois had been seduced into weirdness, Flamingo Park was where he'd be.

Before I left the office, though, I made the routine phone calls necessary in such a case. I called the morgue first. No unidentified bodies matching Jacob Abel's description.

Well, that was good news.

I tried the hospitals next, South Beach and Mount Sinai. Neither had any record of Jacob Abel or anyone else who looked like him.

Those were good signs, certainly. It didn't mean Jacob hadn't been stuffed in a dumpster, or drowned in the ocean, and was yet undiscovered. That meant my next stop was Flamingo Park.

I thought the police officer's idea was the right one, and that Jacob had gone out after dinner in search of sexual adventure. If that was the case, then I figured I'd find the boy shacked up with an accommodating young woman, all thoughts of the convention banished.

However, the possibility existed that he'd met up with the wrong sort of person, someone who wanted his money, or to press drugs on him. He could be lying bruised in an alley somewhere, beaten up. Or dead.

I was wearing a light seersucker shirt and khaki pants, my usual work uniform, but I opened the closet in my office, where I kept a variety of other clothes, depending on how I needed to do some surveillance. I found a sleeveless tie-dyed T-shirt I particularly liked because it showed off my biceps, a pair of denim cut-offs and huarache sandals. I looked at myself in the mirror and was satisfied—tough enough to fit in with the Vietnam Veterans Against the War, but freaky enough that I wouldn't send up alarms if I wanted to hang out with some hippies.

I left the comfort of my air-conditioned office behind and cut across Espanola Way toward the park. It was one of the odder streets on the Beach, the architecture taking a clue from the Spanish name. While much of Miami Beach was built in the art deco style popular in the thirties and forties, all straight lines and circular windows and cruise-ship style railings, Espanola had a Mediterranean influence. Pink stucco, coral tile roofs, generous overhangs to provide shade.

I kept my eyes open as I walked, but I didn't see any abnormally tall Midwestern youths, though there were more scruffy backpackers and girls in flowy dresses than I usually saw. Overhead, a helicopter in camouflage paint made lazy circles in the sky, and on the wind, I smelled the fragrance of marijuana.

I heard Flamingo Park before I got there. The voices of a gospel choir praising Jesus, and behind them some guy with a bullhorn who claimed, over and over again, that McGovern was anti-Buddhist.

Then I rounded the corner to Meridian Avenue. The normally placid street was jammed with converted school buses and VW vans painted with colorful flowers and slogans like "War is not healthy for children and other human beings."

A young panhandler with scruffy hair approached me wearing a sign asking for spare change for the community food store, and I gave him a buck. "What's the lay of the land like in the park?" I asked him.

"Resurrection City II is at that end," he said, pointing to an area of the thirty-five-acre park jammed with tents of all kinds. "That's where the cool people are. The Vietnam Veterans Against the War are at the other end. In between are the hippies and the People's Pot Party, the cafeteria run by the Green Power folks, and the medical tent."

I thanked him and walked into the park, and it was like entering the county fair back home in Tidewater Maryland, minus the livestock exhibits. The Young Socialists Alliance table was one of the first I passed, stacked with books like *A History of American Trotskyism* and flyers for Socialist presidential candidate Linda Jenness.

A young guy in a pale-yellow Indian cotton shirt approached an elderly couple and offered to share his joint with them. "No, I'm too old for that," the woman said. "But you look like you're enjoying it."

"I'll give it a try," her husband said, and he took the narrow spliff and inhaled deeply. A beatific smile on his face told me it wasn't his first puff, but then a kid in a Miami Dolphins jersey wanted to try and he passed it on.

There were people everywhere, tossing frisbees, selling balloons, playing guitar. I was interested in a handsome shirtless guy singing a Peter, Paul, and Mary song until a girl with a flowery wreath on her head draped herself over him and they began to swap tongues.

I walked on, past dozens of hand-lettered signs announcing a nude swim-in later that day at the park's pool, a McGovern rally, protests against the war, pictures of lost dogs. "Mottled gray coat, twenty pounds, answers to Trotsky," one sign read. The poet Allen Ginsberg was pontificating in front of a group of kids, with someone playing the flute behind him.

Along one edge, I found a group of Zippies, a freaky, drug-loving offshoot of the Yippie Movement, trying to have an organizational meeting. That the leaders were stoned out of their minds didn't seem to help, and then Holy Joe showed up.

He was a Beach regular, a skinny old man who carried a crucifix like he was a flag major leading a parade. It was a particularly gruesome one, a flagellated Jesus limply hanging from the cross.

In a loud, Southern-accented voice, he said, "Won't you kids accept the Lord Jesus Christ as your savior?"

"Will he give us dope?" asked a Zippie in an Indian cotton shirt dappled with rhinestones.

I walked on before I heard the answer. The olive-drab helicopter passed over, and as one, the crowd lifted middle fingers toward it.

I kept looking for an abnormally tall white kid from Illinois.

There were a few who could have been his height, but they were heavier, dirtier, or darker-haired than I was looking for. I showed my PI card and spoke to everyone I could, asking about Jacob Abel. But no one had seen him, until I approached a skinny, fey young man who was shirtless and wearing a pair of pants that looked like they had been made of goatskin.

Fake pointed ears poked through his shoulder-length blond curls. I had to admit, if you were going to pretend to be the Greek god Pan, this kid was doing a good job of it. He had a flute with him, and I waited while he tootled a few notes.

When he finished, I showed him my card and asked about Jacob Abel. "Sure, I saw him last night," he said. "Somebody had given him a beer and a joint, and he joined our dance circle in his undershirt and tighty-whities."

I was tempted to laugh at the idea of this straight-arrow Midwestern boy joining Pan's Bacchanal rites, but I worried Jacob might be sleeping off a hangover somewhere when he needed to be at the Convention Center. "Did you see him after your rites were over?"

"Yeah, he went off with a motorcycle dude," Pan said. "Mustache, leather jacket, jeans."

A motorcycle dude? Perhaps a pimp who promised Jacob a good time with a woman of his acquaintance?

Then Pan said, "I thought it was bossy that the dude wouldn't let big skinny put his clothes back on, but hey, whatever floats your boat."

Why wouldn't a pimp let a john get dressed before meeting a hooker? That didn't make sense.

"You recognize the motorcycle dude at all?" I asked.

He shook his head. "Pan doesn't play that way," he said. "But you could ask the guys at the pink tent."

I looked at Pan and realized my assumptions had been wrong. I'd been thinking like a straight guy, assuming a young man on his own in the big city would want a girl by his side as soon as possible.

He pointed down through the rows of tents to one that was bright pink. As I walked down there, I thought about my first time on my own in a city. The day I turned eighteen, I hitch-hiked from Oyster Creek, a tiny town on the edge of Chesa-peake Bay where I'd grown up, to Annapolis, the state capital.

I found the Navy recruiting office easily enough, showed a copy of my birth certificate, and signed the necessary papers for enlistment.

Walking out of there felt like an anticlimax, though. I'd spent the previous two years dreaming of that day, when I'd celebrate my freedom from small-town life. And there I was, all by myself in what I thought was the big city.

Having traveled a chunk of the world since then, I realize now Annapolis was hardly bigger than Oyster Creek, in relative terms. A few streets of houses jammed next to each other, a Colonial-era statehouse, and a waterfront that had seen better days. I wandered around for a while, desperately hoping someone would recognize the need I couldn't begin to acknowledge and take me under his wing.

I was too frightened to make eye contact with anyone I thought was remotely handsome, though I was very taken with several young men from the Naval Academy in their cadet uniforms, which somehow reinforced my decision to join them, if in a subordinate role.

What if Jacob Abel had felt the same way about his first day in the big city, and someone had accosted him in the way I wished I had been?

As I got closer to the pink tent, I saw their sign: "Fight Against the Government." FAG, in rainbow letters.

I'd been reading how a group of rights activists wanted a pro-homosexual statement added to the Democratic platform, and wondered if these were the dudes. I supported their cause, of course, but I had a feeling it would take a long time before the good people of Centralia, and the rest of the American heartland, warmed to the idea of two men, or two women, in love.

I'd been seeing a Cuban-American gentleman for a couple of years by then, but our relationship had remained casual because it was hard for either of us to see a future together. He occasionally dated women, to please his conservative family, and we both agreed "free love" meant we could be open to other encounters, though as far as I knew neither of us had indulged. Sex was better with him than with other guys, a feeling I refused to categorize and was sometimes pushed to test.

The guy behind the folding table wore a tie-dyed T-shirt like mine, accessorized with multiple chains of multi-colored love beads and a smiley tag that read "Hi, I'm Daniel." He eyed me warily as I approached, until I folded up a couple of dollar bills and dropped them into the jar in front of him.

I'd seen his type before at the Cockpit, the gay bar in Coral Gables where I worked a couple of nights a week as a bouncer. He was probably an accountant or a bookkeeper in his real life, a mousy guy who only let his real light shine on weekends, when he could ditch his corporate drag for flamboyant outfits and go looking for love.

Daniel must have seen my type before, too, because he relaxed. "Can I give you some literature on our movement?"

"Not right now, thanks." I showed him my card and said I was looking for a missing kid. "Eighteen, blond, really tall and skinny. You seen him?"

"Eighteen isn't a kid," he protested.

"Maybe not for someone like you, accustomed to the city," I said, doing my best to flatter him. "But Jacob has never been out of his small town in the Midwest. I'm worried he got himself into something he wasn't prepared for."

"I did see him falling all over a guy last night at Pan's Bacchanal," Daniel said. "Scary dude unless you're into Levi's and leather."

My heart sank. "Scary how?"

"I heard he likes masks and whips," he said.

"Sticks and stones may break my bones, but whips and

chains excite me," I repeated, something I'd seen in one of the beefcake magazines Alex liked to keep hidden in the bottom drawer of his bureau. I was flattered he saw something in my physique that reminded him of those guys.

Daniel's eyes widened. "Just a joke," I said. I leaned down and looked into his eyes. "I don't need to hold anyone down. If they want me, they stay put."

His Adam's apple bobbed as he gulped air.

"You know this guy's name?"

"What's it worth to you?"

I reached down for my wallet, and Daniel said, "Not money."

I looked up and saw him staring at my crotch. Christ, was this what my life had come to? Prostituting myself for a client? How could I explain this to Alex? Would he care, or would I be slicing a knife through our relationship?

Daniel stood up and motioned another FAG to take his seat. "Follow me," he said.

I knew it was wrong, but I followed him, and my baser animal instincts. We went around behind the table, under the shade of a tall oak tree. With all the crap piled around us, we were nearly invisible to the crowd.

Daniel leaned back against the trunk of the tree, his eyes glazed over and his mouth slightly open. "Kiss me," he said.

I leaned in and pecked his cheek, though I knew that wasn't going to be enough.

"Like you mean it," he said.

I moved in close. I cursed the part of my anatomy that reacted. This wasn't Alex. This felt wrong.

And then Daniel grabbed my shoulder and pulled me to him and kissed me, and all thoughts fled. He ground his groin into mine, and for a moment we moved as one being.

Then he pushed me lightly away. "Duane Baker," he said, breathing hard.

I stepped back, glad I hadn't done anything I couldn't admit to Alex. Damn, when had I become so conventional? Free love all around me and I was guilt-stricken over a kiss?

My voice was hoarse when I asked, "Where can I find Duane?"

Daniel began to move away. "Haven't seen him today."

I grabbed his shoulder and turned him back toward me. I struggled to control my raging pulse and the throbbing in my pants. "Here's my card. I've got an answering service if I'm not in the office. Let me know if you've seen him."

He took the card and swallowed a couple more times. I stepped around the front of the FAG table, adjusted myself in my pants, not caring if anyone saw, and walked back to my office.

I couldn't tell if the adrenaline racing through my body was from Daniel's kiss or the danger I had avoided. It would have been so easy to let him slide down, open my pants, and...

I stopped myself there. I was on a case, and I had my first real clue about Jacob Abel's whereabouts.

Once at my desk, my hormones relaxed, I called in a favor at the Motor Vehicle Bureau and got the address on Duane Baker's motorcycle registration. Since I had a Class G Statewide Firearm License, I was allowed to carry a concealed weapon, so I strapped my Smith and Wesson 9MM in a thumb holster at my waist. I didn't know if I'd need it, but I wanted to be prepared.

I drove across the Rickenbacker Causeway from the beach, marveling once again at the beautiful blue of Biscayne Bay and the private islands that spiraled off it like stars on spokes. I'd been out there a few times for cases and even after four years in Miami, it was always a surprise how the rich people really lived.

Then again, there were working-class people like Duane Baker, who lived in a neighborhood off Southwest Eighth Street, which was rapidly becoming Hispanic. Cubans fleeing Castro landed there because of the *botanicas*, selling herbs and charms and statues to serve their spiritual needs, and walk-up *ventanas*, or street-level windows, to keep them caffeinated.

Duane's home was a small cinderblock house painted an unassuming tan. A motorcycle matching the one Duane had registered was under a canopy beside the house.

I sat in my car, parked on the street, and considered my next move. It was most likely that Jacob and Duane were curled up in bed somewhere, sleeping off their exertions. But Daniel had implied Duane's interests were outside the norm, even for gay men in the loose, loving 1970s. I'd never personally experienced what some called a dungeon, where men kept all kinds of scary toys, like whips, swings, and dildos, but I'd seen enough porn to know they existed.

I decided to prowl around the house first before I approached. I walked up the driveway and touched the motorcycle. The seat was warm, but that was probably the Miami heat. The engine was cool to the touch.

I slid around the side of the house, checking for windows, but they all had their shades drawn. Even the window in the back door was covered with a curtain. The same was true on the third side of the house.

Well, not knowing what was inside, I had no choice but to ring the bell.

It took a couple of minutes, but finally Duane opened the door, wearing a stained undershirt and a pair of denim cutoffs. "Whatever you're selling, I don't need it."

"Private investigator," I said, holding up my license. "I'm looking for Jacob Abel."

"Never heard of him," he said, and tried to slam the door. I had my foot in it already, though, glad I'd swapped my huarache sandals for boots back at the office. Otherwise, that would've hurt.

"I think you have," I said. "As a matter of fact, I think he's here in your house right now."

There was a nasty look in Duane's eye as he stepped back. "Fine. Come on in and take a look. All you're going to find is empty beer bottles and come-stained underwear."

If he thought I was straight and was trying to put me off, he was mistaken. I leered at him and licked my lips. "Your come?"

That startled him enough that I could slip into the house. As he'd promised, the place was a shithole. Motorcycle leathers, crumpled jeans, empty beer bottles, and fast-food containers littered the living room. I looked around but didn't see anything that looked like belonged to Jacob Abel.

"Jacob!" I called. "Jacob Abel? You here?"

No answer.

Duane appeared next to me, holding a crusty jockstrap. "Hey, Mr. Investigator. Want to investigate this?"

"Maybe later." I glanced into the kitchen, then walked down a narrow hallway. Bedroom on the right, with a king-sized bed and rumpled sheets and the smell of sex. Filthy bathroom next to it.

The other door was locked. "What's in here?" I asked.

"Just storage," Duane said.

I knocked. "Jacob? You in there?"

In response, I heard a thump, then another. "You want to open this?" I asked Duane.

He shrugged. "Lost the key."

"No problem." The door was flimsy particle board, and it stoved in when I kicked it.

"Hey! You're gonna pay for that!" Duane tried to grab my arm, but I spun him around quickly, his face against the far wall and his hands beside him. It wasn't illegal for a PI to carry handcuffs, so I did. I cuffed his hands together and pushed his shoulders down, so he slid to the floor.

For a big guy, he had surprisingly little resistance.

Then I reached through the hole I'd kicked in the door and unlocked it from the inside. I pulled it open and saw Jacob Abel lying on a single mattress, naked and tied up like a prize hog at the state fair.

There was a dildo strapped to his mouth and a butt plug up

his ass, and he looked as scared as anyone I've ever seen. "It's okay, Jacob," I said, as I walked over to him. "My name's George, and John Greenhouse hired me to find you."

If anything, he looked even more frightened. I undid the strap holding the dildo in his mouth, and he spat it out. "Where's Duane?"

"Out of commission for the moment. Let me get you untied."

Clinically, I surveyed Jacob's body as I untied him. His buttocks were bright red, after what looked like a severe paddling and the application of a belt as well. Some strap marks on his back, too.

Delicately, I removed the butt plug and tossed it aside, and Jacob was able to roll over onto his back, though he yelped in pain. I untied his hands, which I noticed were bruised, as if he tried to fight back against Duane.

"Stay here for a minute," I said, not that I expected he'd leave and run stark naked into the street. I walked into the bathroom and surveyed the shelves, finding the right ointments and salves. Then I went back to the room where Jacob sat on the bed, his hands covering his genitals.

I handed him a tub of ointment. "Smear this on your butt," I said. "It'll help with the swelling. But don't put any on your dick—it'll sting."

"Who are you?" Jacob asked, as he took the ointment from me.

"I told you. Private eye. Greenhouse worried when you didn't come back to the hotel last night, so he hired me to track you down."

"You won't tell him about..." he waved his hand. "Any of this? Because then he'll tell my mother, and she'll be horrified. And if anyone else in Centralia knows, then I'll never be able to go back home again."

He began applying the ointment to his butt, and his three-piece set swayed. I forced myself to look away, but not until I'd noticed he had a cock ring over the base of his shaft.

"I won't tell Greenhouse, but you're going to have trouble hiding all these bruises from him." I looked around the room. "Where are your clothes?"

"Duane cut them off me," he said. "After he tied my hands up. He was so nice at first, back at the park. We kissed and touched each other. It was the first time I understood what all the other guys were talking about. First base and all that."

"I understand. I'll be right back."

Duane was still sitting in the hallway, spouting angry shit about home invasions and having my license revoked. I ignored him. I prowled through the living room and found the shreds of what looked like Jacob's seersucker shirt and Bermuda shorts. At least his sneakers were still intact.

There was no way he could wear his own clothes. I picked up a pair of denim cutoffs and sniffed them—clean enough. A T-shirt that was going to be too short and too wide for him, and a belt to hold it all together.

I carried it back to Jacob in the bedroom. "No underwear?" he asked.

"You really want to wear a pair of Duane's?"

He shuddered. "No. I'll manage."

He looked stupid in Duane's clothes, but at least I could get him back to my car without attracting attention. "What do you want to do about Duane?" I asked. "Have the cops come out, press charges?"

He shook his head rapidly. "No way. I just want to get out of here."

"All right then." I ushered him past Duane, who tried to scissor his legs to trip us, but we got away easily. You know us, light in our loafers.

I left the key to the handcuffs on Duane's sofa, nestled on top of a ratty jockstrap, and I hollered down the hall to him that's where it was. I'd have to add a pair of new cuffs to my bill to Greenhouse.

I drove Jacob to the nearest Burdine's, a Miami department store, and we went inside to buy him a new set of clothes. We couldn't match the patterns on his shirt or shorts completely, but I hoped John Greenhouse wouldn't look that closely. I also found a kids' rubber pool toy, an inflatable circle. When we got back to the car, I blew it up. "Sit on this," I said. "It'll save some of the hurt in your butt."

"How did you know how to find me?" Jacob asked.

"I'm a private eye. That's what I do." I looked over at him. "I heard you had a pretty good time at Pan's Bacchanal."

He blushed. "I never danced like that before."

"Was Duane the first guy you ever went home with?"

He nodded. "Really stupid, I know. But I was just so horny, and I felt, I don't know, bulletproof. Then when we got back to his house, I realized what a dunce I was."

"We've all been there," I said. "I could tell you some stories about shore leave that would shrink your testicles right up into your body."

"So you're…"

"Gay," I said. "Homosexual. Been called a variety of other names over the years, most of them unprintable."

"How do you…live?" he asked.

Oh, God. A philosophical discussion I wasn't prepared to have.

I looked at my watch. It was almost five o'clock by then, and I figured John Greenhouse would be finished with the convention soon. As I drove east, toward the Algiers Hotel, I tried to answer Jacob's question.

"There's no one kind of gay man," I said. "Some like the kind of things Duane does, while others are happy with kindness. Sometimes it's hard to tell which one you've come up against until it's too late."

"Which type are you?"

I thought back to way Daniel had grabbed me and pulled me toward him. Just because I'm a big guy doesn't mean I don't like to be manhandled now and then. I've simply realized I want the one doing anything with me to be Alex Reyes.

That was a hard concept to explain to the boy, though I tried as we crossed the causeway and headed up Collins Avenue. When I pulled up in front of the modern-style Algiers Hotel, I gave Jacob detailed instructions on treating his wounds.

The physical ones, that is. The emotional ones would stay for a while, and I hoped our conversation could show him he could open up to another guy someday without worrying about pain.

I said, "You're sure you're all right to go upstairs?"

"I am. I'll tell Mr. Greenhouse I got into a fight and then fell asleep." He got out of the car and grabbed the inflatable donut. "And I'll tell him I fell on my butt, which is why it hurts."

I was naïve in my small hometown, so I hoped Greenhouse would be, too.

Then I drove back across the causeway and skirted around the city of Miami to Alex's house in Coral Gables.

Alex Reyes hadn't returned from work by the time I arrived, but I had my own key. I'd been spending more of my nights there than at my own crappy apartment on the Beach, but so far, I'd resisted moving in completely.

When he came in, I was into my second Hatuey, a Cuban beer Alex had introduced me to. I had peeled off my tie-dyed T-shirt, opened the denim shorts at the waist, and kicked off my boots.

He was dressed in his work garb, a tan linen suit, white shirt, dark green tie, black wing-tips. He sat down next to me and pulled me in for a kiss, which I resisted.

"What's wrong, *mi amor*?" he asked.

The Hatuey gave me the courage to say what I had to. "I kissed a guy today and let him feel me up."

Alex surprised me by laughing. Deeply. He sat back and laughed until tears formed at the edge of his eyes. I stared at him in surprise.

"What? You don't care? I'm scared you'll kick me to the curb, and you're laughing?"

He wiped his eyes. "*Mi amor*, I am Latin. You know how we are. We kiss and hug everyone."

"But not that way," I said. "When was the last time you pressed your body up against another man, ready to do whatever he asked?"

"With you? Last night."

He saw my face, and he sobered. "George, you are a handsome, sexy man. I don't blame anyone who wants to kiss you. Or who you kiss back."

"But what about..."

"Hormones? We both have them. Do I get turned on when I see a naked man? Of course. Have I been with anyone else since I met you? No."

"I haven't either," I said. "Until today."

"Until you let a man kiss you and grope you. *Dios mio*, you are a tight-assed Anglo." He smiled wickedly. "And I mean that in the best possible way. This is the era of free love, *mi amor*. If you tasted another man, I would not be happy. But I would not kick you to the curb, as you say, over it. Would you do that to me?"

I shook my head. "You mean too much to me."

"Then there we are," he said. He stood up and shucked his jacket, then undid his tie and unbuttoned his shirt. I watched in fascination as his tanned skin and the curls of dark chest hair became visible. "You have a head start on me with Hatuey," he said. "Will you bring me one while I get more comfortable?"

I stood up. "I will."

"I'll be in the bedroom."

And then, all the cares of the day fell away. I had my handsome hombre, and nothing else mattered.

The next morning, I was surprised to see John Greenhouse and Jacob Abel waiting in the hallway outside my office when I arrived at nine o'clock.

"You're a miracle worker, Mr. Clay," Greenhouse said. "What do I owe you?"

"We'll call it even with your retainer," I said. I opened the door to the office, since they seemed intent on coming in.

"Probably more comfortable if you stand," Greenhouse said to Jacob, eyeing the two hard chairs across from my desk.

Greenhouse, though, sat and faced me. "Last night, after Jacob got back to the hotel, I recognized the source of his discomfort," Greenhouse said. "Jacob and I had a long talk. Centralia isn't as innocent a city as he thought, and those of us who live there do a good job of hiding who we are."

I stared at Greenhouse as the import of his words sunk in. He was either gay, or had some experience of penetrative sex, and he'd spoken of that to Jacob. Interesting.

"I understand you know where the police could find the man who assaulted Jacob," Greenhouse continued. "We'd like to press charges against him with the police. We'd need a statement from you, of course, detailing what you saw when you found Jacob."

I looked up at Jacob. "Are you sure you want to do this? The police will not be very nice to you, even though you're the victim."

"I can't stop Duane from doing what he did to someone else," Jacob said. "I understand that. But if he does it again, at least the police will have my evidence."

I didn't know any cops in South Miami, where Duane lived, but I did know one detective in Miami Beach I thought would be sympathetic to Jacob's story. I reached him by phone, and though he said he was due at the Convention Center soon, to help his brothers in blue protect the delegates, he agreed he could meet with us if we got over there pronto.

It was only a short walk, so we were there in a few minutes. I introduced Lou Nowak to John Greenhouse and Jacob Abel, and Jacob told his story, with admirable poise for an eighteen-year-old who was describing a sexual assault.

Nowak, a heavyset guy with white-blond hair, wasn't gay, but he wasn't prejudiced, either. He took some notes, including

Duane's name and address. Then he listened to the story of my rescue, and how I'd found the boy.

He sighed deeply. "I'm sorry to tell you there isn't much I can do. Here's the way a judge would look at this. You met this guy and willingly got on the back of his motorcycle to head to his home with the intent of having sex with him."

He pulled a tattered paperback copy of the laws of Florida, paged, through it, and read a section about "laws against fornication, sodomy, adultery, bigamy, and incest, as well as against open lewdness, or…any notorious act of public indecency, tending to debauch the morals of society."

He closed the book. "What this means, gentlemen, is that sex, even consensual, between two men is illegal in Florida. So, the only law Mr. Baker may possibly have violated is illegal restraint. And because that happened in the course of these other illegal activities, you won't get far in a prosecution."

"But," Jacob began.

Greenhouse put his hand on the boy's arm. "It's what I told you, Jacob. But you did a good thing coming here today."

"My department maintains a list of known sexual predators," Nowak said. "I'll be sure Mr. Baker is added to it, in case his name comes up again."

Greenhouse stood. "Thank you very much, detective. And now Jacob and I need to get to the convention center."

"I'm heading that way myself," Nowak said. "I'll walk with you, if you like."

The three of them headed north, and I went east, toward my office.

Jacob sent me a letter a few months later, right around the time George McGovern lost the election so horrifically to Richard Nixon.

He had decided to get out of Centralia and had gone to the University of Illinois for his second year of college. There was a gay student group there, he wrote, and though he hadn't joined yet, he was planning to soon.

He thanked me for everything I'd done, and he enclosed a page ripped out of a porn magazine. "Is this you?" he had written on it.

Alex got a good laugh out of that. It wasn't me, though I had a superficial facial resemblance to the guy, as well as a similar build. I had to admit, though, he was better endowed than I was.

I sent Jacob a postcard of the beach with a polite denial, and best wishes for his future. I was confident he'd have a good one.

THE KRATZ GAMBIT
Mark Thielman

A Ford Fairlane with its windows lowered rolled along Third Avenue North. From the 8-track, Alice Cooper blasted the chorus of "School's Out." Spilling from an NYU dorm window, Elton John sang "Rocket Man." Dimitri's transistor radio sat alongside our table. A commentator offered his analysis. I ignored the words, but the incessant noise sounded like a bee buzzing around my ear. A woman in a pink angora pantsuit, sitting on a park bench, tore small bits of bread from her lunch and threw them into the grass. The wax paper sandwich wrap crinkled with every movement. Cooing pigeons crowded around the castoff crumbs. Others clustered on the pedestal of the George Washington statue and watched. Across the park, a couple of kids hung upside down from the monkey bars, shouting that they were trapped. They played like they were the stars of the *Poseidon Adventure.* Everybody added to the cacophony. In front of me, I had Greenwich Village, then the East River. I'm sure they were making noises, too, Nehru jacketed hippies and lapping waves. I wanted to shush them all. Didn't they know I was trying to concentrate? I had a chance to win.

I advanced a pawn.

Dimitri repositioned his knight, seemingly without thought. "Is your move."

I had started reading *Chess International Magazine* to improve my game. I remembered an anecdote from a recent column written by a grandmaster. He told about the time Klinkov, the world's sixth-ranked player, started a game one day still suffering a hangover from the night before. Right off, he made a horrible move. As his opponent reached to seize the advantage, Klinkov looked him in the eye and said, "haven't you heard of the Kratz Gambit?" His opponent reconsidered and overthought his next play. Klinkov bluffed his way out of disaster. I tried my variation of the Kratz Gambit.

"What do you think of this Watergate mess, Dimitri?"

He raised a finger to quiet me while the man on the radio updated us on the game in progress. Reaching to the other board, Dimitri moved the black queen to the appropriate square, studied the board for a moment, and nodded. Then he turned back to our game. "I pay no attention to government troubles."

I almost laughed. If you asked Blackie seated over at table number one, he'd tell you Dimitri had been in the Soviet Ministry of Agriculture. He had to defect when the Russian wheat harvest failed to live up to the five-year plan. At table two, Hector pegged him as a submarine captain who had jumped ship in a Mexican port carrying a bag full of rubles and some technical manuals, which he later sold to the CIA for dollars and asylum. By table three, Everett swore Dimitri and his KGB comrades had masterminded the Kennedy assassination over vodka and rye bread. That story didn't explain how he ended up playing chess every day in Washington Square Park, but Everett never let details get in the way. Everybody agreed Dimitri had a dark past, they just differed on the specifics.

I slid queen's rook up the file and scanned the board. I winced, expecting the worst. Reluctantly, I released my fingers and cupped my chin in my palm. My fingers touched my sideburns. "Check."

Dimitri looked surprised. He drummed his fingers against his lips. His hand moved forward and then paused. His chin dipped slightly. "You play well today, Robert." He moved a knight to defend his king.

Then he said those Russian words that always sounded like he was coughing up phlegm, but I'd learned they meant "very good."

"How are your eggs, Robert?"

I attacked with a pawn. "Over easy."

Dimitri cocked his head.

"It's a way to cook eggs," I said. I knew he hadn't been asking about my breakfast. The Hellerman Gallery was about to stage an exhibit of Fabergé eggs, those treasures of Tsarist Russia. An outer shell gilded with gold and jewels; each egg opened to reveal a spherical yolk. The yolk held a surprise, an exquisitely decorated inner scene. The gallery needed a crack PI to oversee security. But they were all busy. So, they hired me.

"An American joke," he said and repositioned his king.

I snorted. "You must have a head cold coming on, Dimitri. You're not on your game."

He dipped his head toward the transistor radio. "I am, perhaps, distracted."

On the companion board, Dimitri had set up the game currently being played by Boris Spassky, the Russian grandmaster, and Bobby Fischer, the American. The Spassky side of the board faced Dimitri. I had Fischer's white pieces on my side. The Cold War was being fought by chess pieces in Reykjavik, Iceland. The contest captivated the nation. The radio station ran live updates and offered commentary. The broadcaster on the Magnavox got breathless describing the personal contest between these two men. I like chess as much as the next guy, but I had trouble picturing a board game being covered like a boxing match.

Many of the other chess hustlers in the park followed the big game as well. They each had a sideboard set up to mirror the game's progress. On Blackie's, Spassky's side was marked with the hammer and sickle flag of the Soviet Union while Fischer's showed our red, white, and blue. Everett and Hector had the commie's side marked with the letters CCCP, the Russian spelling of USSR. Fischer's side had USA, spelled the way God intended it.

I supposed Dimitri still had some warm feelings for his mother country, so I kept my opinions to myself.

He rubbed the pad of his thumb against his index finger. Then Dimitri advanced his bishop to shield his king.

I quickly reached out to make the obvious move, then stopped. "You ain't that distracted, Dimitri. I've seen you play three guys here in the park. Sometimes you make moves without even looking at the board. You're bluffing."

Dimitri frowned and shook his head. "One cannot bluff in chess. It is not like bungling political burglars in the night. The board is visible to all." He seemed to flinch.

"Something bothering you, Dimitri?"

He made a very small shake of his head. "Nyet."

I made my move. Dimitri's mouth sagged.

"I'm glad nothing's wrong, Dimitri. Because I think checkmate is on the horizon." I sat up a little straighter in my chair. "I thought you were bluffing me. Like Fischer in game two against Spassky. He didn't show up, took a forfeit. But I think he was trying to get inside of old Boris Spassky's head. That's what maybe is going on here."

"Robert, there is no such bluffing in chess."

"You can't deny that Fischer crushed Spassky in the next game."

"We will see how it plays out over time. It is long tournament." Dimitri's eyes swept the board. He pushed out his lip in a frown, then turned over his king in surrender.

"Wish I'd brought my Polaroid camera. I'd like to get a picture of this," I said.

I didn't want to rub Dimitri's nose in it, but we'd been playing chess regularly for two months. Since I moved my office to the

Village, I've been coming down to the park to eat my lunch. One day, the Russkie and I struck up a conversation. I admired his elegant chess pieces.

"It is from Jaques of London, the same type Spassky will use in World Championships." He pointed at the empty chair. "Do you play?"

He whipped me that day. We started playing regularly, and he consistently won. But I could feel myself creeping closer, the gap between us narrowing. I studied the magazines. The effort paid off. Today, I finally beat him. Can't blame a guy for savoring the success for a moment.

Still, the victory felt a little too easy. "You ain't sandbagging me, are you, Dimitri?"

He looked at me through his black-framed glasses. "I don't bag sand. I play chess. Today, you win."

I smiled. I should never forget he ain't from here. Dimitri still wears a plaid jacket with narrow lapels, a thin black tie, and a white shirt. The outfit looks like something he bought at Brezhnev's Basement.

"Something's eating you, Dimitri. I can tell."

He glanced down at his pant legs, searching for ants. He shook his head. "I am not being eaten."

"What's bothering you?"

Dimitri frowned. "In our games, I have grown to trust you, Robert." He reached into the inner pocket of his jacket. He laid it on the chessboard.

I unfolded it. Someone had cut letters from a magazine to assemble a message.

Do Not sTand op i will Shoot

I looked at him. "And you think?"

"My instincts tell me it is genuine."

My eyes widened.

The transistor announced that Spassky had made a move. Dimitri reached over and adjusted the pieces accordingly. As his hands moved, he spoke in a whisper. "I believe he is in the buildings behind me. I would assume he has rifle. The message sat on chessboard when I arrive. Folded. I thought the paper was from you, leaving a note to say you could not come today. Busy with case or whatever you American private detectives call your adventures. At least that is what they call them on *Hawaii Five-O*."

"You're pretty calm, Dimitri."

He shrugged. "It not my first time to be threatened."

I looked again at the message. "Do not stand up I will shoot. You just gonna sit?"

His eyes widened slightly. He, too, glanced at the message. "I fear I have little choice."

"What do they want?"

Dimitri shrugged. "*Ya ne znayu.* Maybe angry about the past. Perhaps mad about the present. I do not know."

"You should run," I said.

He shook his head. "Too many souls in the park. I will wait. One cannot avoid that which is meant to happen."

"Russian fatalism," I said. "Any clues at all?"

"This morning, I had call on telephone. I was told to meet a man at the World Trade Center construction. I say no, I'm not going. Then when I get to park. I have note on chessboard."

Before I could ask, he continued. "The caller did not give name. He was anonymousness."

"Looks like I'm going to the center of your trouble." It was the best line I could think of under the circumstances.

Dimitri didn't smile. He put his hand atop mine. If Dimitri wore a mood ring, his would be colored black. "Robert, I cannot allow you..."

I gestured to the board. "And I can't allow anything to happen to you now that I've got your number."

"I have no numbers."

I couldn't stick around long enough to teach him the American idiom. "I'll be back," I said and stood up from the table. "You just keep up with Fischer's moves. I want to know what's happening when I get back."

Keeping my head down, I focused my attention on the shadow George's statue threw across the grass of the park. In truth, I didn't want to alert anyone watching from the windows that I was aware of his presence. Mumbling greetings to Hector, Blackie, and Everett, I walked to the street. There, I hailed a cab and directed the driver to take me to Radio Row.

The cab had a Puerto Rican flag hanging from the rearview window. The driver rolled south, weaving in and out of cars, maintaining a running commentary in Spanish. I ignored him and looked out the window. We passed by the Hellerman Gallery. I was making good money doing background checks and providing specialized security for them these days. The gallery's paycheck was the reason I'd relocated my office to Greenwich Village. Fortunately, I was caught up with my work. The employees had been checked and the extra security was in place. I could miss a day and spend it trying to keep Dimitri alive.

The hack let loose a burst of Spanish profanity and turned sharply, cutting in front of a garbage truck. They traded angry honks.

Just a few hours earlier, I thought a chess victory represented my day's excitement.

He stabbed his hand toward the street we'd just veered from. "City closed street," he said, turning his back to the windshield to explain.

I waggled my finger, silently expressing my preference that he watch the road rather than update me on New York City's street repair. He hit a pothole with a teeth-jarring thud. The taxi's suspension creaked almost as loudly as the cussing.

Three blocks down, another blocked street had us driving back toward Washington Square. The driver let loose another fusillade of cussing. The detour again took me past the Hellerman Gallery. I watched as workers suspended banners from the nearby lamp posts promoting the exhibit of jeweled Fabergé eggs. The gallery was closed today, setting up for the opening of the new exhibit. Although focused on Dimitri's troubles, I made a mental note to mention to the director that I'd seen the men working. I needed the Hellerman's money, and I wanted the boss to know I was on the job, even when I wasn't.

At the World Trade Center, I pushed the hack a Lincoln and got out of the car. The Center, the world's tallest building, had opened earlier in the year. Construction, however, continued as parts remained unfinished. A fence blocked vehicle traffic.

Hardhats milled about the job site. I couldn't ask them if they'd seen anyone who wanted to shoot a Russian; I'd likely be inundated with volunteers. Instead, I picked my way along the fence line, looking for anything suspicious.

About twenty-five yards down, I came to a small Soviet flag wired to the fence. An envelope dangled from it.

GuESS wHeRe now—cEntrAL pArk

Again, the letters looked cut from a magazine. I studied the message, mentally comparing it to the one Dimitri had shown me. A theory formed in my head. Dimitri's assailant had to be a recent arrival in the Big Apple, new and unfamiliar with the details of Manhattan. Anybody who'd visited Central Park would know I couldn't just wander the perimeter. That search would take days. I assumed, therefore, that his adversary was an old foe, someone bearing a grudge from his Soviet past. I turned Blackie, Everett, and Hector's stories around in my head. When I got back to the park, I'd press Dimitri for the facts.

Another thought struck me. The Russian Tea Room was located just south of Central Park. As an ex-pat, maybe Dimitri frequented the place. I decided to visit there, ask if they knew him. Maybe they had an envelope taped to the samovar. It wasn't a great idea, but it beat anything else I could think of.

Still, I didn't like it. The phrase "needle in a haystack" came to mind.

To clear my head, I walked into the Trade Center. The place smelled like new paint and clean floors. The South Tower had a newsstand. The kid behind the counter chewed bubble gum and listened to Bill Withers singing "Lean On Me." I perused the magazines. I didn't want to buy anything to read. Sometimes I see best when I don't look straight at something. I was trying to organize my thoughts before I jumped into a cab and raced to Central Park.

Behind the current magazine, the newsstand carried back issues of *Chess International*. Three months earlier, the cover story featured one of the Fabergé eggs we would display in our exhibit. The yolk contained a miniature chess set, including delicate pieces crafted from ivory and black onyx. The chess pieces could be moved about the board, except you'd need a pair of tweezers and a jeweler's loupe to see what you were doing. The photographs were good. They had closeups of the egg's detail. The gallery's director would like a copy. I paid the clerk for the magazine. He popped his gum, then Bazooka Joe pushed the change across the counter.

Outside, I grabbed a taxi to take me to Central Park. I hadn't come up with a better idea than the tearoom. The afternoon sun began to dip. If Dimitri was going to make a move, he needed to do it soon.

I opened the magazine and glanced at the column by this month's grandmaster. He gushed about the Sicilian Defense. My eyes rode down the column without reading the words. I was trying too hard to think about Dimitri's problem. The story served as a distraction.

The driver cursed his fellow motorists in a linguistic mix of American and...Arabic, I guessed. I didn't know much about other languages. They confused me. Like Russian, I had no idea why they tried to spell USSR with three Cs and a P. It made no sense.

I had a sudden thought. The hairs on the back of my neck tingled.

"Stop the car!"

Maybe we'd have stopped sooner if I yelled something in

Arabic. The driver let me out half a dozen blocks from the Hellerman. I worked my way back, dodging stoned heroin addicts, their backs against walls tagged with graffiti, their legs sprawled across the sidewalk.

I ran into the gallery and looked around the floor. I hustled into the employee-only area. A few of the guys looked up and nodded. Most kept their heads down working.

I took the stairs two at a time to the second floor and stuck my head in a couple of offices until I found an empty desk. I made a call to a buddy of mine, a private dick who officed out of Brooklyn. Then I went to find the director.

I caught a ride back to Washington Square. The hack leered at a coed in hot pants, an NYU T-shirt, and a macrame vest roller skating in the park. If I was being honest, I'd admit I'd rather watch her skate than deal with Dimitri's sniper. I didn't know what would happen. I looked straight ahead and concentrated on the job.

For a moment, Dimitri's eyes widened in surprise when I sat down at the chessboard. They quickly lowered, and he looked at me. "Fischer won," he said. "He rebuffed the Nimzo-Indian Defense."

"I'm surprised you are still here."

He shrugged. "With you working on problem." Here, he paused and tilted his head to the windows behind him. "No need in trying to run. I trusted you, Robert."

"And I trusted you, Dimitri. May I see the note?"

He reached into the pocket of his jacket and fished out the letter.

I flattened it on the empty chessboard. "You looked surprised when I read the note. 'Don't stand up I will shoot.' You read the note to say, don't stand up OR I will shoot." I emphasized the 'or.' "A Russian R looks like a P to an English speaker. I read it one way. A native Russian speaker might see it differently."

"This hunter is from my past then," Dimitri said.

I shook my head. "No professional assassin would take the window facing the western sun unless he absolutely had to." I pointed in each direction of the compass. "We've got windows all around us. This was a bluff."

"A bluff?"

"You wanted me running up and down Manhattan Island trying to save you from your assassin, cashing in on the whispered reputation you have here in the park."

Dimitri grunted a laugh.

"You really going to make me spell all this out?" I asked.

"You tell stories better than Tolstoy."

I took the letter I recovered from the World Trade Center and laid it alongside his. "Notice the typeface on the letters. Someone used the same magazine to make both messages. Look at the groupings, *and* as in grandmaster, *ESS* as in chess, *AL* from international. You made both notes from a back issue of CHESS INTERNATIONAL. The same magazine with the photo spread of the Fabergé egg exhibition at the Hellerman Gallery. The same magazine, Dimitri, that was sloppy. You should have thought two moves ahead."

He looked at the notes and frowned.

"You knew I did security and background checks for the gallery. If you wanted to substitute a couple of your guys to pull off a heist, I had to be away. I'd recognize the replacements. With me walking circles around the Trade Center and then Central Park, you knew I'd be gone long enough for you to pull this job. I stopped by the gallery on my way to the park. The new employees didn't recognize me, and I didn't know them." I paused before my next move. "By the way, the director fired them all on the spot. None of them will be working when the armored car with the Fabergé eggs arrive."

"Very clever, Robert. Too bad all that intelligence is not displayed in your chess game."

I ignored the insult. "Called in a favor from a private detective who works around Brighton Beach. He says in Little

Odessa, you're known as a chess hustler who is always dreaming of the big score. You like to think you're Marlon Brando in the *Godfather* only with borscht instead of linguine. Likely you know a rich Russkie who would want a Fabergé egg tucked away in his private collection." I paused. "Hector will be disappointed to learn you're not a sub commander."

Dimitri dropped a Russian cuss word.

I wished I'd been keeping notes. After today, I'd be able to swear in four languages.

Dimitri shrugged. "One cannot avoid that which is meant to happen."

"Russian fatalism again," I said. "I hope you're as calm when all of those fired security guards come by to get paid. Or when the rich guy in Little Odessa asks whatever happened to the money he likely paid you upfront."

Dimitri dropped another word not found in most dictionaries.

"I don't know that one," I said. "But here's a phrase I do know. *Shak i Mat.* I think it means check and mate."

THE DARKLIGHT GIZMO MATTER
Gary Phillips

Passalong Pete's real name wasn't Pete. Born sixty-two years ago in the Iberville Parish in Louisiana, he came to Los Angeles with his family when he was eight years old. He'd held various occupations since then. He'd been a bootblack, that is shoeshine boy, sold the *California Eagle* and the *Herald Examiner* newspapers on street corners along Central Avenue, and even worked as a runner for the eastside bookie Carl "Straighthand" Newcomb until he died violently, rumored to have been slain on orders from the volatile Mickey Cohen.

But that seemed like a lifetime ago as Passalong Pete found himself scrambling for his life this starless night along a stretch of Main Street, identified as part of Skid Row in this part of downtown LA. As fast as he could, he ran past seamy adult bookstores. One such storefront had the lights on, its picture window grimy, as if coated by delusions of wanton sex. Near the Tiger Pit Triple X theater at the end of the block, he considered ducking inside. But he knew this would be no sanctuary. He'd be trapped and easily picked out among the mouth breathers and the other pathetic old men in their stained raincoats. On he went, praying he'd spot a police prowl car, the first time in his life he wanted to see a cop. Sadly, there were none to be seen here among the threadbare traffic at half-past one in the morning.

He did, though, spot a nearby phone booth. At the moment,

there were only a couple of bums passed out from cheap booze, sleeping it off on flattened cardboard for bedding. He ought to know. He was one of them. This flash of self-revelation goaded him to get his feet moving again. He couldn't escape, but he could leave a warning. They were out there in the stillness, and he knew they couldn't let him live. Not with what he knew.

Passalong crossed the street on leaden legs and pushed open the jointed door of the Pac Bell phone booth. He was out of breath and out of time. He couldn't run anymore, too many years of abusing his body and mind. The light automatically came on and the hunted man stared at it as if it were a lover who'd betrayed him. Using his elbow, his other arm, and hand protecting his face, he shattered the translucent glass cover and the bulb underneath to darken the interior. He was near ecstatic to find a dime in his pocket, stuck that in the phone's slot, and dialed a Hollywood number he knew because he'd had to call it more than once from the drunk tank. He didn't have her home number, but this would have to do. Sweat cooled on his warm face.

The line connected. There was a whir and click, then a recorded feminine voice with a husky quality said, "This is Nefra Adams. At the tone, please leave your message and phone number. I will get back to you just as soon as I can."

After the beep, the man said, "Nefra, it's Passalong. I did it this time, screwed up good. Yeah, well, so what's new, huh?" He swallowed dry. "Look, when you hear this, I'll be dead."

The dark-colored Lincoln came out of nowhere and zoomed down the block, its big block V8 thrumming like caged panthers under the hood.

Passalong felt more than heard its presence and yelled toward the handset he'd dropped, "Get to the Crossmore Building, that's where he—" But he didn't finish his sentence as he tried to flee along the sidewalk. The big car, outfitted with armored sheeting, clipped the phone booth, blowing it apart in a spray of metal, plastic, and projectile ribbons of glass. The stuff cut into Passalong, and he stumbled onto the pavement. He just got his face turned around to stare horrified as the Lincoln smashed into and rolled over him. By the time it cleared his body, he was a corpse. Nonetheless, its occupants stopped the car and got out to make sure their target was dead.

The two men in black suits, blue shirts, and black ties looked back. Each wore a kind of contour mask with slits for eyes and a mouth. Such precaution at hiding their identities seemed unnecessary. No police officers and no bold citizens showed themselves. One of the men walked over to the mangled, broken remains of the man born Curtis Spicer. He bent, felt for the big pulse, and was satisfied there was none. He got back in the car and drove off. In the backseat of the Lincoln was what looked like a large rectangular short wave set with all sorts of knobs, toggle switches, and two oscilloscope-like screens. Incongruously, there was what looked like a short vacuum cleaner hose with a plastic nozzle attached as well.

The man in the passenger seat removed his mask and said to the driver. "We didn't even get to use the whatzits."

"Don't you worry," his companion said, "you're gonna get to play with it again soon."

The two shared a disquieting laugh as they drove away. Back on the street where Passalong's Pete's cooling body lay sprawled across the real estate, the sleeping bums hadn't stirred once.

"Right now, the feeling at Parker Center is he was killed in a simple hit and run." Brad "Brix" Bradford hunched a shoulder and shook out a cigarette from a pack of Pall Malls. He didn't bother offering one to his friend, private eye Nefra Adams, as she didn't smoke. They were in her office overlooking the Sunset Strip. He lit up and sat back in the chair facing her desk, putting one leg at a right angle to the other.

"The cops run a check with the phone company?"

"Yep. They know he called you, but there's no recording

other than what you have."

"But I haven't been called or visited by the police, and it's been two days."

The ex-cop smiled ruefully. "A wino buying it isn't much of a priority, Nef."

She frowned, shaking her head. "I can't make out his last words on the tape, Brix. But this was no drunken accident. I get it's not a priority with the LAPD, but it is with me. It wasn't just the ramblings of an alkie."

"Yeah," he nodded, "someone should care. Which is why I did a little digging yesterday. Knowing you'd want to blood-hound this matter."

Adams smiled and was about to speak, but a scream from outside stopped her. She looked over at the window as Bradford was already there.

"Help me, somebody please help me." Three stories below, a pretty woman in a miniskirt and go-go boots ran west along the sidewalk. Her shirt was nearly torn away. Bradford moved toward the door, unlimbering a snub nosed .38 Police Special on a belt holster beneath his sport coat. The two rapidly descended the stairs.

"There she goes," Bradford said, pointing across the street when they exited the building. The woman was running toward the Pioneer Stereo store and bolted between a gap of that business and its next-door neighbor, a freestanding Chicken Delight stand. The two took off and charged through the space between the buildings. They came out into a compact court-yard. A shot echoed, and Bradford dropped to the concrete.

Crouched in the shadow of the gap, Adams quickly assessed where the shot had originated. Just as quickly and efficiently, she brought the Walther PPK into position and shot three times at an overhead sash window partly open where curtains fluttered. There was no breeze at the moment. A body fell through the pane, tearing the curtains loose from the rail as glass and wood rained to the ground. The dead ambusher hung in what remained of the window frame. His lax hand having let go of the hunting rifle he'd been holding. His rifle clattered to the ground as well.

"Find that broad," Bradford said, waving his friend off. "I'll live." His side was bloody where he clutched his wound with his hand.

Hearing an engine gun to life, she ran out of the courtyard, exiting in time to see a Camaro with a lowered front end and fat racing slicks on the rear tear away. She ran into the street, firing her pistol at the retreating vehicle, blasting the rear window to pieces. The Camaro swerved about 360 and came full bore back at her. The woman who had been the decoy in the go-go boots was leaning out of the passenger side of the car, firing a Sten machine gun at the PI.

"Oh my God," a chunky woman cried. She was carrying shopping bags in both hands from the May Co. department store. The woman ran for cover, not dropping her purchases. Adams too sought safety behind the front end of a pickup truck, calculating the vehicle's motor would stop the machine gun's rounds from puncturing her.

Rapid fire ripped bullets into the asphalt and the Pontiac Catalina Adams dove behind. Several of the high velocity rounds punched through the steel and upholstery of one side of the vehicle and out the other. Luck was with her, and Adams wasn't hit. As the Camaro roared past, Adams was able to get off several shots. One of her bullets drilled through the Camaro's driver's side window like a point of a snow axe piercing ice. It created a spider-webbed hole. The bullet zeroed into the driver's collarbone, and he lost control of the car. The Camaro twisted violently sideways and slammed against a delivery truck parked in a driveway, the passenger side pressed against the truck. The shooter scrambled over the wounded driver to get out of the car.

"Drop it," Adams ordered, her Walther steadied by both hands, the mini-skirted machine-gunner in her sights.

The other woman snarled a choice curse and attempted to

trigger her weapon. But Adams was faster and shot her in the upper body. She went over backward as if haymakered by Joe Frazier. The private investigator ran up and kicked the Sten gun away.

She demanded, "Who are you working for?"

"Screw you, baby," the wounded woman said. Blood leaked out from under her as she lay on the ground. Sirens approached.

Adams got a gleam in her golden-brown eyes. "Too bad I don't have time to be polite." She ground the toe of one of her suede boots into the bleeding wound. "You better give me a name, or I stomp you clean through to China, girl."

The gunner writhed and cried out in agony. "Colmaster, damn you, Colmaster." Blood gurgled frothily from the edges of her mouth. Her teeth ground into her lower lip, nearly breaking the skin. The gunner's smeared lipstick was called Passion Purple, Adams noted absently.

"Put the gun down now and get on your knees," a cop hollered from behind the private eye.

She voiced no argument and did as ordered. Four uniformed police officers surrounded her as she let her handgun go and complied, hands up. "Don't shoot, don't shoot," she said. Their questions came at her hot and heavy.

"You a Black Panther? This some kind of Black Power uprising?"

"You're gonna get the chair for this, missy."

"Where're your buddies? Huh? Where's the other Symbionese Liberation shits, huh?"

"Where's your Little Red Book, commie?"

"Back there behind that beige building. My partner is wounded. He's ex-Rampart Division plainclothes Brix Bradford."

They couldn't quite process these words this Afro-sporting, Angela Davis-lookin', obviously Ho Chi Minh-spoutin' Black Guerrilla Army charter member was saying as it related to the welfare of a cop, former or not. Collectively, they simply wanted to ignore her, though two of the uniforms, one named Malloy she heard, did go check behind the building. Face down on the cracked asphalt, they handcuffed her and left a cop, his foot on her back, to guard her as the others—and more squad cars came on scene—secured the area. Eventually, she was hauled over to Hollywood Station on Wilcox. She was put in a holding cell with several hag'ed out street walkers, junkies, and a possum-eyed woman who sat on the floor in the corner mumbling that the invisible tax collectors camping out at the waterbed store where she worked.

"Adams." A female uniform had come to the bars and called her name about two hours later.

"That's me."

"Come this way." She unlocked the cell door and waited, her face blank, not even registering boredom.

The PI followed her down two hallways lit in sickly yellow light as if the officers were growing strange mushrooms. She was let into an interrogation room and sat at a small square metal table on a wooden chair. The set up was such that her interrogator could sit perpendicular to her and close. Bradford had told her this was the best way to question a suspect. You didn't want the barrier of a table between you and your prisoner. The officer wanted to gauge your body posture, what you did with your hands and so on as he purposely invaded your personal space.

Adams sat, turning in on herself, employing the meditation techniques she'd learned several years ago. The guru at the retreat in Oahu where she'd studied had been an older silver-haired gentleman who called himself Norvell Stockbridge. Adams would also learn this was not always the name he went by, nor had he always been in pursuit of inner peace and cosmic understanding. During the Great Depression, he'd been a false-fanged grim-visaged vigilante known for his ruthlessness and eagerness to spill gallons of villains' blood in his self-righteous war on evil.

When the beefy detective, tie loose around his unbuttoned collar, stepped inside three minutes later, Adams was calm and centered.

"My name is McAllister." He sat, lightly, she noted, for a man of his heft. He placed a manila file folder of papers on the desk, his elbow on it.

"How's Brix?" she asked.

He lifted an eyebrow with effort. "Surprisingly, for a thirty-thirty high-velocity bullet traveling through him, barely missing his stomach and vitals, and given he's no kid, he's in decent shape. He's over at Queen of Angels."

McAllister didn't say it, but Adams knew he'd talked to Bradford, who vouched for her. That meant a lot, the okay from one of their own. Too, it wasn't as if she was an unknown quantity in law enforcement circles. "Good."

The LAPD detective folded his arms, his thick muscles straining the broadcloth of his dress shirt. "Who were the two who attacked you and Bradford at your office?"

No sense holding back, as it would corroborate what he probably heard from Brix. "I don't know, but it must be linked to the murder of Passalong Pete last night down on Skid Row. His real name was Curtis Spicer."

"And how did you know this individual? A down and outer, it might be said."

"He swept up our building, where my office is I mean, twice a week."

"You arranged that, is that right?"

"I did."

"You used him as an informant?"

"Not as your tone suggests. It was a long time since he was in any kind of racket."

"Yet he provided useful information in that kidnap case you solved last year. Getting that kid back alive and in one piece."

"Yeah." Lafayette Templesmith was a black millionaire whose only son had been kidnapped by neo-Nazis led by a wanted war criminal. They'd wanted money to finance the research on a chemical that would only react to specific concentrations of melanin.

McAllister, who'd been leaning back, sat forward some. "Why'd he call you?" His breath smelled of mouthwash.

"Brix and I were trying to find out."

The plainclothesman sat back again. He picked up the file folder and opening it, shuffled several top sheets aside, and studied an entry. Adams didn't think he was doing this for effect, as he genuinely seemed to be reading and considering something. He closed the folder, holding it in one of his large hands. "Just a second, Miss Adams." The cop left the room.

Several minutes later, he returned. He opened the door but stayed in the doorframe, one hand on the knob, leaning into the room slightly. The file wasn't with him. "You can go."

Adams frowned. She'd shot a white man and woman on a street full of witnesses and now she could go?

"What the hell's going on, McAllister?"

"Bye, bye, now." He walked away, the door remaining open.

Soon in front of the desk sergeant, she collected her belongings, though they kept her Walther pending a clearance. As she made to leave, Adams noticed two uniformed cops booking a harried older white woman in a pillbox hat askew on her frazzled hair.

"Officer, please, I assure you, I'm not drunk or crazy."

One of them said, "Then how do you explain plowing into those people on the sidewalk, lady? Lucky no one was killed."

"I...I tell you, I couldn't see to handle my car. It's so horrible."

"But you can see fine now?" The other one cracked sarcastically.

"Yes, I told you. I was blind, and now I can see again just fine."

"Then you'll be able to dial your lawyer. You're gonna need one." And with that, they led her away.

The private eye walked back to her office. At one point, she passed a wood fence. Super Bowl VII posters, the game had been played in town this past January, were mostly stripped away, replaced by placards for Tom Bradley, a black man running for mayor. From the parking lot behind her building, she collected her burgundy colored '59 Stingray and drove to Queen of Angels hospital in Echo Park.

"I've always wanted a beautiful woman to bring me flowers. Though not laid up like this." Brix Bradford was propped up in bed in his semi-private room. He was hooked to an IV, his torso bandaged.

Adams set the spring flowers on the rollaway table next to the bed. She leaned over and gave the older white man a peck on the cheek. A gray-faced, wrinkled woman glared at them from the other bed.

"My daughter," Bradford beamed at her.

"Hmpphhh," the woman huffed. Grabbing the plastic privacy curtain, she pulled it around her bed.

"How you feeling, Brix?"

"Take more than a belly-crawlin' bushwacker to put me down." He shook a finger at her. "Hey, how come you're out so soon? I talked you up good to McAllister, but I figured they'd keep you overnight at least. You've had a busy morning, dear."

"Don't I know it." She looked around the room, wondering if the cops had bugged it. Bradford might have been out of the room or knocked out after surgery if they'd done so.

"You talk to your pal, Jim?"

"Yeah, he's coming by. He had a client this morning, so didn't get my message until he was back in the office." Jim Axelrod co-owned with Bradford a pool and Jacuzzi business. He and Bradford were also lovers. Not too many aside from Adams knew the brawny, six-one-and-a-half, Korean War vet and ex-LAPD detective liked to swing for the other team, as he'd put it.

"Whoever sent those two after us had access to the phone company records," she said.

"Somebody with juice," Bradford added.

She made more chit-chat in case there was a listening device while finding a pen and a pad of paper with the hospital's logo on it. "Passalong had a sister somewhere over in Compton, I think. Guess I'll try and find her to see if she knows anything."

She wrote down her question: "You ever hear of a Colmaster?"

He took the pad and paper. "Can't say I do, Nef." He wrote down a different response and handed it over on the piece of paper.

The private eye nodded her head as she read the note. "Okay, check in with you later, Brix. Call me if you need anything." Rising, she patted his leg under the thin blanket.

"You step lightly, now, okay?"

"You know me."

He made a face. "That's what I'm sayin'."

Leaving the hospital in her Stingray, Adams picked up the handset of her radio-telephone and asked the mobile operator to make a call for her. She reached her party on the third ring. "Hi, Larry, it's Nefra. You around for the next hour or so? I need to bend your ear with a few questions about a certain someone."

"Who's that, foxy lady?"

"Elton Colmaster." Bradford had given her the man's full name in his note.

A low whistle. "Heavy dude, Nef, heavy like getting Napalmed trapped in a coffin if you dig what I'm laying down."

"That's why I need to see you."

"Come on then. I'll brew us a cup."

Popping a Tower of Power tape into her newly installed after-market cassette deck, Adams took the 101, then the 10 Freeway west out to the Venice area of Los Angeles. This was a Bohemian beach community of ramshackle apartment buildings,

Craftsman single family bungalows, and an aura that had transitioned from beatnik to hippie to whatever it was now. Like the Italian city it was named for, this Venice had its own languid set of canals—there were even gondola rides back when, but not now. Though there were still plenty of ducks.

She parked her car at a series of concrete archways in a diagonally designated slot in front of the Floating Eye coffee house Lawrence Radington owned, and entered the establishment. Inside were a few patrons, including a short-haired woman humming softly as she drank coffee while reading a Jacqueline Susann paperback. Bernard "Goldie" Hawes, a local jazz musician, was in here too. He was noodling the keys on the old Steinway in the corner.

"Soul Sister Number One," Hawes called out to Adams.

"Hey now," she said warmly to him. The swishing of beads had her head turning to the newcomer entering from the back.

"What it is, what it could be." The bespectacled Radington greeted her with a warm smile and open arms. He was in his fifties, lithe and sinewy, with a tangle of white hair. He perpetually wore vintage Hawaiian shirts and smelled of Burma Shave.

They hugged. "Come to get on the good foot," she said.

"Step right on this way, Nef. Don't know if I'll blow your mind, but as the sages say, knowing is half the battle."

"Amen." She followed him toward the rear of the establishment, stepping through the beaded curtain. In his office was an overflowing small bookcase and a surprisingly uncluttered desk. There was enough room for a Japanese tea set, and they sat cross-legged at the squat table. He poured steaming green tea into ceremonial cups from a brass teapot.

They tipped their cups to each other and sipped. Radington then said, "This cat Elton Colmaster is from unsavory money, Nef. All capitalism is dirty, but his old man made money profiteering in World War One. Then made even more on the black market dealing in much needed medicines in a post-war ravaged Europe. The son not only inherited all those rapacious qualities sitting on his daddy's knee, but he's refined them. Why you lurking around this old reprobate for?"

She told him of the morning's activities. "Brix's note said to ask you about him."

Radington sat back, resting on his hands flat on the floor. "That's 'cause I worked on a project that came to his attention when I was at Rocketgyn."

"I'm listening." Radington had once been an electrical engineer before tuning in and dropping out.

He smoothed the hair flat on the back of his head and stared for a moment into his not-so-distant past. "This project sought to create, well, for lack of a better term, a way to cause blindness."

"What?" She recalled the woman in the pillbox hat at Hollywood Station.

Radington made a funny face. "Yeah, but understand, this was a time when the CIA was pumping LSD onto subway platforms of unsuspecting civilians. The idea was they could use it as a kind of fear inducer. Our optic nerves are connected to the brain, and the brain operates on certain electrical impulses our bodies produce."

"This gadget could disrupt certain electrical impulses if you could isolate them," Adams conjectured.

"There you go. Imagine if, and this was designed to be a temporary effect, but what if enemy soldiers on the battlefield were suddenly not able to see? Not caused by a smoke screen or white-hot light, but all of a sudden, it's just black." He made a gesture with his hands like a stage magician does when they disappear a rabbit or a pocket watch.

"You can't shoot. You stumble around completely disoriented, bumping into your fellow soldiers."

Adams added, "Easy pickin's to be killed or captured. Maybe even help in interrogation if with another pass of your devilish ray, they could see again."

"Right you are."

"Where does Colmaster come in?"

Radington sipped his tea slowly, then held the cup in both hands before setting it down. "It's not headline news that there's always been a...cordial relationship between the military and business interests."

"Rocketgyn is a private company but gets lots of contracts for the Army and what have you." She snapped a finger and shook it at him. "Colmaster is an investor in the outfit."

He nodded his assent. "The Darklight Project was the official name for this particular R&D."

The private eye absorbed this. "Was the project successful?"

He shook his head. "No, we gave some test subjects headaches and spots before their eyes, but no blindness." He smiled wanly. "Five million in research and testing gone up in smoke."

"Our tax dollars at work." She looked off, then back at her friend. "But Colmaster could have continued the research, paying for off-the-books work by scientists for hire?"

"Sure. Maybe he figures to sell his results back to the government or highest bidder. Or maybe use it for himself. Like he could blind the pilot of a private jet used by one of his business rivals."

"That's worth killing for," she stated solemnly.

"Nef, I don't need to tell you Colmaster is a powerful and connected individual. He's got his hooks into the cops and having them stonewall this case."

"I need to see this through."

"Namaste."

"Namaste." She rose, trying not to let the enormity of the situation weigh her down. Back outside, she fired her Stingray to life. Given it was a sunny day, she decided to take the streets back to her office.

Now heading east on Venice boulevard on this sunny day, she let her mind leap ahead, figuring out her next steps. She came to a red light, and, shifting out of gear, applied the brakes.

The pedal felt spongy, and she realized she'd better get the car checked soon. Driving several more blocks, there seemed to be no further worry. But just as she was coming to a major intersection, the brakes failed completely. Adams clicked on her cool and downshifted, made the clutch groan. She maneuvered around a slowing station wagon and was heading right into the intersection against the red light. She tried the parking brake and got no resistance. That cable had been cut. Drivers honked at her. Looking to her right, she saw a tanker fuel truck barreling at her even though the driver was standing on his brakes, creating a cloud of white smoke and ear-splitting screeching. This happened in milliseconds, signaling her sure demise.

Adams shifted out of gear. At the same time, she turned off the ignition and cut the wheel sharply. Her Stingray fishtailed violently and slid sideways along the sidewalk as she hoped it would. Pedestrians scattered. The car slammed into a fire hydrant, ripping it free of its bolts. The hydrant's trajectory was like that of a runaway rocket. It arced upward, then came down hard, right onto the hood of a Ford Falcon, bashing it in. The Stingray's momentum halted upon impact. Water geysered with force from the now-exposed pipe, and the intersection was flooded by the time the police and fire trucks arrived. Nefra Adams had already been on her car phone to her attorney.

Finally released on a sizable bond and facing several lawsuits from disgruntled drivers, particularly the owner of the ruined Falcon, the private eye called a friend over at the *Herald Examiner*. He owed her more than one favor, and he planted a false story, complete with an indistinct black-and-white photo from the archives of a woman covered up on an ambulance's gurney. The piece that ran in the late edition stated Adams had been injured in the crash and was recovering at an undisclosed location. This lie had been sanctioned by the reporter's editor on the promise from Adams that she'd have a juicy exclusive for the paper—or so she hoped.

* * *

Access to the Crossmore Building on Olympic Boulevard in west Los Angeles during business hours was no big deal, as it housed various offices, including two optometrists and a talent agency specializing in juggling singers. Colmaster owned the building and had a penthouse on top. A disguised Nefra Adams entered the lobby the following day. She was dressed in modest office clerk type clothing and wore a straight hair wig over the large Afro she'd tamped down under a tight cap. She also had on cat eye glasses and flat heels.

There was a security desk with a bored older gentleman in a rent-a-cop uniform planted behind it. But far as she could tell, at least not during daytime, no one was required to sign in. She went about unmolested. Adams also reconnoitered the exterior, noting a metal door out back where the dumpsters were. Out front, she spotted a Burger Land drive-thru across the wide expanse of Olympic from the office building. She walked over there, then went back to see Radington.

Adams returned that night. She'd discarded the disguise. The private eye was now dressed in a black, form-fitting zippered jumpsuit and boots with composition soles. A stylish equipment bag was slung across her torso. She waited in the near gloom at the rear of the building. Sure enough, eventually one of the janitors came outside for a smoke break after dumping some trash. She slipped past him and through the door he'd left slightly ajar. Crossing the lobby, a different security guard was in his cubby, watching a portable TV. She crept unnoticed past him too and entered the stairwell. She went up steadily to the top, eighteen stories above. She was barely breathing hard when she reached the locked door leading to the penthouse level.

Looking up, she saw the wiring leading to an alarm on the door. From her equipment bag, she extracted a device made by Radington about the size of a transistor radio. It had a heavy wire with an alligator clip and wire on the other end. This she attached to the alarm wiring, enabling her to bypass the alarm. Essentially fooling the circuitry that it was unbroken. She then picked the lock, a skill Bradford, the former robbery-homicide detective, had taught her.

The exit didn't let out on a hallway but an open expanse. The penthouse was its own structure, taking up a good portion of the flat rooftop area. It was glass walled on one side, but heavy curtains prevented a look inside. Stationed on a chair in front of a set of double doors into the penthouse was a man in slacks and dress shirt with a gun in a shoulder holster. She wondered if he was the only guard. His legs were stretched out in front of him, and he slumped, his snap-brim hat low on his forehead. From the angle she was at, she came up behind him quickly and silently. Hand over his mouth, a specifically placed karate chop with the other hand sent him to slumber land. Behind her, the door was unlocked, and she stepped inside.

Adams found herself in a living room replete with a sunken conversation pit. A well-endowed woman wearing a cave girl outfit like you'd see on a *Flintstones* cartoon wiggled and gyrated in the pit area. A Lex Baxter lounge music LP played on a stereo. A man in an expensive suit, sans tie, sat on the couch. He was in his fifties, thickset with workman's hands, and smoking a stubby black cigar. He clapped and guffawed, animated by the woman's grindhouse performance.

"Oh, baby, you're the greatest there ever was," he said excitedly. "Dimitri and his buddies are gonna dig you."

The cave dancer, gyrating her head about, noticed the intruder. The man turned his large square head, following her gaze.

"You," Elton Colmaster said. He gaped, barely catching the cigar as it fell from his hanger of a mouth. "What does it take to stop you?"

"I guess this chick ain't here to party," the cave dancer concluded. She seemed sad about that.

"Marty, Francois, get your asses in here," Colmaster yelled. He was off the couch, quick for a man of his size.

Rushing through a doorway at the side of this area came two of his henchmen. One of them had a partially eaten sandwich in his hand. He threw this aside and reached for the .45 in his shoulder rig. The other one held a revolver, already barking bullets.

The private eye dived behind a stacked stereo system, which included a receiver, tuner, dual cassette tape deck, and turntable. Rounds tore into the works, sending shards of metal, plastic, and glass everywhere. On her belly, Adams shot from underneath the table the stereo was on, blasting open the gunman's guts. Cave girl screamed in horror as pieces of entrails and blood splattered her. She cursed and ran toward the side doorway. Her action momentarily put her between the other hood and Adams, who was in motion as well.

"Stupid, broad, get the hell out of my way," the one with the .45 bellowed. He clotheslined her, and she went down hard on the carpet. Simultaneously, he cranked off shots from his cannon, and the reverberation boomed in the enclosed space.

But Nefra Adams had gotten to relative safety behind one of the couches in the conversation pit. Not that the furniture stopped the bullets, it was just he wasn't sure where she was as the couch was more than six feet long. Then the lights went out. No, not the lights, she understood. She was blind, the Darklight gizmo at work, she concluded. That must have been what Colmaster had run to operate.

"What the hell?" she heard the hood proclaim.

"That's okay, Marty," Colmaster said. "I've got my mask on, I can see. I'll come to you and get your gun and deal harshly with this nosy bitch."

Adams quieted the panic bubbling in her. Calling again on what sensei Stockbridge had taught her, she visualized the layout of the room. She channeled energy into the four senses left to her. The lighting had been subdued to better set the mood for the woman's sexy dance. There were two table lamps on, and she pinpointed them in her mental schematic. She looked to the left, sightless but not defeated. She detected Colmaster's shuffles as he trod mouse-like over the thick carpet. She shot with her replacement Beretta, and he laughed scornfully.

"Dumb dame," he jibbed.

She shot again and was rewarded with the tinkling of glass and plaster breaking as the struck lamp fell over.

"How the fuck...," Colmaster growled, now running to where his henchman was before she could shoot out the other light and put him into darkness too.

She blasted two more shots, locking in on his heavy breathing. He was not a man who had salads for lunch. Years of thick steaks, martinis. and little exercise had its effects on his constitution and corresponding girth. She brought him down like a charging bear. His wheezing, dying body crashed hard onto an end table, splintering it apart as he exhaled a death rattle.

"Boss, boss?" the one named Marty hollered as he stumbled about, knocking into all manner of furniture. "When the whatzit's blindness wears off, you're gonna get yours, girly." He wanted to sound defiant, but it came out as hollow bravado.

It wasn't hard for Adams to locate him and, ducking his punch, put the muzzle of her weapon to his chest, silencing him for good when she squeezed the trigger.

"Ughhh," the hood sighed as he expired.

He sagged against her, and she eased him to the floor. She then sat cross-legged, as if meditating, and waited. In less than an hour, her vision returned. She was alone with the two dead men. Colmaster's protective mask of mouth and eye slits was comically askew on his face. The one she'd knocked out she'd bound with his climbing line. Adams studied the Darklight machine, a low rectangular metal box that used what looked like a short vacuum cleaner hose to aim its invisible beam at the intended target, she surmised.

She called her lawyer first. He in turn called a contact in the Defense Department, getting him out of bed back in DC. What followed was a lot of back and forth, Adams being threatened with legal action from Colmaster's board of directors. Eventually it was uncovered that Colmaster had made overtures to certain foreign powers to sell his prototype to—foreign powers considered the Cold War enemies of America. All that went away. She wasn't officially thanked, nor was she sued.

"I guess Passalong must have seen something about what Colmaster was up to one night cleaning up at Burger Land." She'd found out he worked there a couple days a week in addition to cleaning her building.

Adams discussed her recent case with a recovered Brix Bradford. "The burger joint owner told me he'd gotten that second job and was looking forward to getting a decent place to live." She shook her head sympathetically.

"That louse Colmaster had his henchmen out on the streets using the device randomly to test the results," Bradford added. "Though the scientist who worked on the device, we haven't identified who that was yet."

"Whoever it is, I'm betting he's going to make himself known." Adams paused, then, "Real soon, I'm thinking."

"Yep," Bradford agreed.

AGENCY
Laura Oles

Minerva Kline downshifted into second gear as she slowed toward the light at Staples and Sorrell. It was still considered summer in Corpus Christi, even though it was edging toward the end of September. The air conditioner in her Maverick was as reliable as her soon to be ex-husband, and the rolled-down window did little to ease the heat enveloping her. On the radio, Lou Reed's silky voice encouraged her to take a walk on the wild side. She pressed the cigarette lighter in and waited for it to pop while she reached for her Kools.

Minerva pulled into her reserved parking spot by the dumpster and cut the engine. She took a final drag from her cigarette and stubbed it out in a small ashtray that threatened to spill over. Empty coffee cups and takeout paper bags were scattered in the backseat. Housekeeping wasn't her strong suit. Bob got that right, at least.

She reached across the passenger seat and grasped the handle of her shoulder bag, scattering her collection notices. Bills continued to pile up. Money was tighter than David Bowie's pants.

Schuller Investigations was a short hop from the side alley. The day's *Caller-Times* had been delivered on the front porch, crammed into the corner between the concrete step and the front door. She picked it up and made a mental note to have the cracked glass on the entry door replaced.

Directly inside, she spotted her boss, Alan Schuller, sleeping on the waiting-room couch. His crumpled dress shirt and matted hair served as clues he'd spent the night.

Again.

Minerva reached over and tapped him on the shoulder. Alan snored deeply and simply rolled over, giving her an unfortunate view of his backside. She tapped him a second time. Harder.

"Alan, maybe it's time to work things out with Darlene so you can sleep in your own bed." She leaned towards him and sniffed. "Tied it on pretty good again last night?" She unrolled the paper and took a glance at the front page. "Looks like Spiro Agnew might resign as VP. About damn time," she said before tossing the paper on the corner of the receptionist desk. Her desk. She glanced at the stack of papers waiting for her attention.

Alan rolled back over, reached for his eyes, and rubbed them as if doing so would help him see the error of his ways. He pulled himself up into a sitting position. He'd have looked more put together if he'd been thrown out of a car.

"Alan, if you're going to meet your ten o'clock this morning, you better get moving. I'll get the coffee going and then start logging your notes."

"Speaking of sleeping arrangements, what about yours?" he asked.

She hadn't been aware he was listening. An old detective trick of his—always let people underestimate you, he had said.

"Bob's parents own that house, and I'd rather spend a month doing summons deliveries followed by attending a Donny Osmond concert than stay there." Minerva gestured to the office space her boss had turned into his makeshift bedroom. "At least my RV has a beach view."

"You sound like your dad," Alan said, drawing a cross across his chest. "Good PI. Great friend."

Minerva agreed on both counts, but those roles put fatherhood as a distant third. Still, Alan had given her a chance once she'd earned her PI license. She was six months into the job.

She turned her attention to the desk littered with papers behind her. "All this needs to be transcribed and filed?"

The idea that she needed Alan's presence to have a stab at credibility on the job frustrated her no end. But Alan was a good detective, and not many clients trusted a woman to assist in a case. And while her looks didn't turn many heads in high school, being able to get in and out of most any building unnoticed had its advantages. For a girl who didn't have the coin for college, working for Alan gave her the freedom few careers could.

Her boss stood and tucked his crumpled shirt into his pants and smoothed his hair. "You can take lead on the ten o'clock."

"Me?"

He ignored her. "It's a basic cheating surveillance from what she said on the phone."

"What's her name?"

He yawned and waved his hand toward her desk. "I wrote it down somewhere."

"You sure you're ready to hand one over?"

He gave her a look. "You're ready. And besides, I need a break from these women's issues."

"I don't think you understand the term 'women's issues,'" Minerva replied. "Job equality, access to capital. Those are women's issues." At least the Supreme Court had finally given women the right to govern their bodies. Dominion over their financial autonomy still fell short. Virginia Slims may have thought she'd come a long way, but the banking system for single women proved otherwise.

Alan shrugged. "I'm tied up on the Faldo case for the next few days. Call in if you need help," he said before disappearing into his office. "And don't forget the coffee," he added before closing the door behind him.

Minerva sat down at her desk and triaged the stack of papers. The squeaky twist of the doorknob caused her to glance up. A woman entered. She wore a navy shift dress, and the way it hung perfectly on her petite frame indicated some expense. A leather frame handbag dangled from her grasp. Her blond hair grazed her shoulders, and her face needed no makeup, although her lashes and lips hinted at cosmetics. Traditionally beautiful and expertly accessorized with some financial resources. She represented the wifely perfection Minerva's own husband so desperately wanted.

Minerva glanced at her appointment book to double-check the client's name. She stood from her chair and extended her hand. "You must be Kaye Stratton." She gestured to the coffeemaker on the cart in the corner of the room. "I was about to put a pot on..."

Kaye raised her hand. "I'm fine. I've already had two cups this morning."

She glanced around the small waiting room. "Is Mr. Schuller in?"

"He is, but I've been assigned to handle your case."

She blinked at that. "You?"

"Yes. Me."

"I'm confused. Aren't you the secretary?"

Minerva took a deep breath and pointed to the plaque on the wall. "I'm a licensed and certified private investigator. And considering the circumstances, we think I'm the best fit for the case." She gestured Kaye to the seat in front of her desk. "So, how can we help?" She reached for her notepad and wrote the date, September 17, 1973, at the top of the page.

Kaye sat, studying her handbag. "As I told the man on the phone before, I need some surveillance done." She paused a beat. "On my husband." She briefly made eye contact before her gaze returned to her lap. "I think it's been going on for a few months. Maybe longer. You know those little signs you ignore?"

She did.

"I need proof, of course, so I can figure out what to do next," she said. "He's a powerful man, so I need leverage. He holds all the cards, has all the money, and I'm pretty sure he's hiding some…illicit earnings…which could factor into my settlement." She pulled a matchbook from her bag and placed it on the desk in front of Minerva. "I think this is where he's spending his time. I find them now and then around the house." Her gaze focused just over Minerva's shoulder. "He doesn't seem worried enough to even try to hide it anymore."

Minerva held the black matchbook cover with a bunny head logo in the middle. The White Rabbit. She knew the place. Booming nightlife, some of the best disco dancers in the city. A known gathering spot for movers and shakers of local industries.

"We can start surveillance if we can get a few details. Our rate is one fifty a day, plus expenses." The woman didn't flinch. "Can I get some names?"

Kaye hesitated, her fingers working the strap of her handbag. "His name is William Stratton."

"And what does your husband do?"

"He's in commercial real estate development." She continued to fidget with the strap of her bag. "My friends keep telling me I should just stay put, especially since I don't have any money of my own. Dropped out of college to get married. He was so charming, so attentive back then…" Her voice trailed off as though disappearing over a cliff of marital regret.

Minerva knew the feeling.

"If you can give me some details about his schedule, where his office is located and such, I can get started on this," she offered.

"I overheard him say he had a meeting at the Bayfront at three o'clock today. I don't know with whom." She then handed a wallet-sized family photo to Minerva. William Stratton was as handsome as Kaye was beautiful. The All-American couple. On the rocks.

Minerva continued making notes on her yellow pad.

"There's one more thing I need to mention," Kaye said.

"There's a ledger he keeps. It's extremely valuable."

"What's in the ledger?"

Kaye smiled for the first time. "My freedom."

Minerva drove down Chaparral in search of William Stratton's office. Warm air filtered through her open window as the Texas sun beat down against her windshield. She located Stratton's office as she made the block. Surveillance would be tricky due to parking and busy traffic, but less of an issue in the evenings when businesses closed shop and people went home for the day.

Chaparral street was known for jewelry stores like Zales, Missions, and Cizon's—although Alamo Loan and Jewelry was close by for those who didn't care about a piece's provenance. Minerva had already developed contacts at Alamo from past cases. She'd also picked up a birthday gift for her sister there last year.

Minerva cruised the block once more and pulled into an open space a half block shy of Stratton's office. A small walk down Chaparral revealed a payphone. She pulled a reporter's notebook and pen from her bag and then rifled around the inside pocket until her fingers grazed the cool ridges of a quarter. A glance at her watch told her it was almost two in the afternoon.

"Development Services Department. This is Lucia. How can I help you?"

"Hey, Lucia, it's Minerva. Got a minute?"

Lucia Alvarez was one of Minerva's closest friends. Tight since sophomore year at King High, she was one of the few people Minerva would trust with her life. Not that she hoped it would ever come to that.

"You should have called me sooner, and you could've taken me to lunch." Lucia's throaty laugh filled the receiver.

"I'll cover your drinks Thursday night at Monroe's for the King/Riggs match."

"Did you get your bet in with Slay? I've got fifty riding on Billie."

"Yes, and yes. Put fifty down on Billie." Minerva cleared her throat. "Hey, have you ever heard of a guy named William Stratton?"

Lucia let a low whistle slip from her lips. "You got a case?"

"You know I can't discuss that."

Lucia's voice softened to almost a whisper. "Word is he and one of the zoning officials are arguing about a new Six Points project. I heard my boss talking about it when I brought him his coffee yesterday morning."

The afternoon sun penetrated the booth glass, and Minerva took a step back in hopes of catching a small breeze. Drops of sweat rolled from the nape of her neck down the back of her blouse. "Anything else?"

Her whisper continued. "He's got more grease on his hands than my mechanic husband, but him paying people off don't make him special around here, *mija*."

"I owe you one, Lucia."

"You got it, love. One more thing."

"Yeah?"

"Be careful. He may not be tough, but he knows some tough people. You dig?"

Minerva returned to her car and continued down Chaparral, taking note of *Papa en Onda* playing at The Tower theater. Palm trees waved in the distance as she traveled toward Shoreline, the yellow brick road that turned into Ocean Drive. Money people built big houses and soaked up the Bay views. At least the parks department had protected some of the prime views for the average joe, but who knew how long that would last.

The Bayfront Hotel claimed an entire block of prime downtown real estate, its rust-colored first floor arches serving as the foundation for several rows of beveled glass hotel room windows. Minerva stepped out of her Maverick and ran her hand down her slacks to straighten the seams. Her outfit proved professional enough to be seen at the Bayfront Hotel, although the climate and the location drew people dressed in all manner of fashion.

She strode through the sliding front doors with purpose and a burst of cold air rushed over her skin. The lobby for the Palms restaurant was off to the right. The hostess, a young brunette in a navy uniform, greeted her and Minerva requested a table for one in a corner.

"I'm sorry. We only seat parties of two or more. Except at the bar."

"How about I leave a big tip, and you have double vision for the next half hour?"

The hostess cracked a smile. "Right this way." She escorted Minerva to a corner table.

Once seated, Minerva scanned the room. Several duos. One party of four. No sign of Stratton yet, although she'd timed her arrival to be at the restaurant first. The hostess returned with a glass of water and a menu.

Just shy of three, William Stratton appeared, beige suit and white shirt, a brown hard-shell suitcase in his hand. The hostess guided him past Minerva's table to a man waiting at a two-top close to the window overlooking the water.

Soon after Stratton's ass hit his chair, the man across the table leaned forward and spoke with an intensity that included clenched fists and narrowed eyes.

Her water glass perched in front of her lips, Minerva considered who this man might be in Stratton's life. Maybe the business partner on the Six Points project? Someone from local government? A gun for hire? Was there more to this story than Kaye knew? Stratton's attempts at placating the man with his open hands and reassuring demeanor provided a temporary salve.

The two men parted ways, and Minerva took in the man's features as he walked past her table. Lean and polished, expensive suit, dark brown hair feathered with a center part—the kind of man who didn't do his own dirty work but maybe paid someone else instead.

She named him Mr. Bad Business.

She left a cash tip on the table and left.

Minerva tracked Stratton back to his office. She walked down Chaparral until she found a shaded bench with a view of Stratton's office door. She pulled a copy of *Ms.* magazine from her bag, lit a Kool, and killed time until the sun set. She then returned to her Maverick and waited for Stratton to show himself.

She almost missed him when he finally left a little past nine. Stratton wore a denim leisure suit with a black and white check shirt underneath, the lapels stretching across his jacket like landing strips for his shoulders, briefcase in hand. He slipped into the driver's side of his Bahia red Porsche 911. Fifteen minutes later, The White Rabbit Disco came into view.

Had Stratton chosen The White Rabbit as his evening entertainment because it was located close to his new construction project? After he disappeared inside, Minerva reached behind her seat for her duffel bag and pulled out her red halter top, black flares, and white ankle boots. No Peeping Toms in sight, she squatted low and changed quickly, and then walked into the disco.

Arched windows lined the side walls and met with the parquet floor. A large silver disco ball threw squares of light into patterns across the room. A crowd formed on the outskirts of the dance floor, watching the top peacocks twirl to Barry Blue chanting "Do You Wanna Dance?" through the speakers. Minerva stood back, scanning the room until she spotted Stratton sitting with a group of men. A tall blonde, in a white crop top and matching shorts that left little to the imagination, stopped at Stratton's table. She balanced a tray of highball glasses on her cocked palm. Minerva watched as Stratton reached his hand towards the back of the waitress's thigh as he spoke to her. She didn't flinch. They knew each other. Either that, or the waitress was used to men putting their hands where they didn't belong.

Minerva moved to the bar and waved her hand until she got a bartender's attention.

"What'll it be?"

"Hey, that waitress over there?" She pointed toward Stratton's group. "Isn't that Diane? I'm pretty sure we went to school together."

"Nope."

She held up a ten spot. "Are you sure?"

He smiled at the bill, tucked in his tip jar. "Nah, sweetie. That's Jenny Boyd. Hottest ticket not on the dance floor here. Some of the guys call her The Body."

Minerva cocked a brow. "I can see why."

The bartender held his hand out. "You want something to drink or just dish on my waitresses?"

"I'll have a rum and Coke, thanks."

The bartender delivered her cocktail and Minerva dropped an extra bill on the bar before she disappeared into the crowd. After a half hour of watching Stratton's hands read Jenny's lower half like a relief map, she returned to the parking lot and waited for Stratton to leave.

Surveillance wasn't nearly as exciting as Barnaby Jones made it out to be. It required long stretches of focus and a bladder of steel. It was almost midnight when Stratton left the White Rabbit. And he wasn't alone. Jenny "The Body" Boyd walked arm-in-arm with the straying Stratton, not a care in the world.

Minerva held her Leica M3, her elbow perched on the car windowsill for stability, and took several photos. Once Stratton and Jenny settled into his Porsche, Minerva started her engine and waited. She trailed them a short distance away to the Summer Sands Motel. They parked, Minerva did the same a solid distance away, and focused her Leica on the two in an embrace, the motel sign serving as the nail in the coffin on the divorce case. The couple disappeared inside room 138, and Minerva packed up for the evening.

She needed a shower.

For a variety of reasons.

Minerva arrived at Schuller Investigations just shy of ten in the morning. Allen had a morning consult, but he normally handled his primary cases alone and then met with her on secretarial tasks once a new case file was started. The day's *Caller-Times* in hand and her bag dangling over her shoulder, she dropped both on her desk and glanced around the office. Alan banged around behind his closed door. Minerva needed coffee, which meant she needed to make it. Alan would rather wait for her than do it himself.

Once the pot was started, she slipped into her chair just in time for Alan to appear from his office. A new file folder had appeared on her desk, likely for transcription and hours billing. Sleuthing generated substantial paperwork.

"Oh, good, you've got coffee going," he said, sniffing the air. "How did your surveillance go?"

"Standard like you said," Minerva replied. "Got the goods on the husband. Found the girlfriend at the White Rabbit. Some photos from there and the hotel. Going to drop them off at Paul's for processing once he's open." She turned to the paper. "You watching the Billie Jean King match Thursday night?"

Alan shrugged his shoulders. "Why? She's going to get clobbered."

She flipped through the paper. "Well, the match only made the back of the paper, so I guess the patriarchy agrees with you. Can't wait to see it on page one come Friday. But, hey, the deepwater port proposal for Harbor Island made top billing, so the battle between ecology and economics continues."

The phone rang just as Minerva rose from her chair to fetch coffee for the boss.

"Schuller Investigations."

"Hello, this is Kaye Stratton."

"Good morning, Mrs. Stratton. I was going to call you later today after my findings yesterday, but I don't have the file together yet…"

"William's been shot," she said, a small quiver in her voice. "They found him this morning."

"I'm sorry. Who found him where?" Minerva reached for her pen and pulled her notebook towards her.

"CCPD came by the house this morning. William was found inside the Summer Sands Motel." She then whispered, "He's dead." She paused for a moment before uttering, "I don't know what to do."

"Are you okay?" Minerva asked.

"I'm not sure."

"Where were you last night?"

"What do you mean by that?" Kaye's tone turned terse. "I was with the kids at my sister's house. We just watched TV all night."

"I didn't mean anything by asking," Minerva said. "Wanted to make sure you were safe. I'll call you back once I consult with Mr. Schuller."

Minerva hung up the phone and explained the situation to Alan.

"You got photos of Alan with the girlfriend?"

"Yes, but just arriving, not leaving. I went home once I had the money shots."

"Maybe a lover's spat?" Alan said, "Women get crazy sometimes, you know."

Minerva stifled the urge to respond. "I don't think so. They looked lovey-dovey to me."

"You better get those photos processed pronto. See if Paul can put a rush on it."

* * *

Minerva picked up the prints, double sets, from Paul's before eight o'clock and returned to the office to meet with Kaye. She was waiting in her Mercedes, parked close to the dumpster, when Minerva arrived. Alan's car was gone.

"How are you holding up?" Minerva asked as they walked inside. She gestured to the seat in front of her desk.

Kaye gave a small shoulder shrug. "I'm okay, I suppose. I don't know if it's sunk in yet. I can't believe he's gone."

"Are you sure you're ready to look at these photos so soon? You're taking in a lot right now."

Kaye crossed her arms in front of her chest. "Did you confirm my suspicions?"

Minerva nodded.

Kaye held out her hand. "I'll look at it when I'm ready."

Minerva slid the manilla envelope across her desk. Kaye tucked it underneath her arm, stood from her chair, and then left the office without another word.

Alone, Minerva pulled the duplicate set of prints from her bag. At first glance, the photos told a simple tale of infidelity. She placed the half dozen eight-inch by ten-inch glossy images on her desk and scoured them for any clue as to what might have happened. And then, on photo five of six, in the top left corner, half clipped from her Leica lens, she saw it. Mr. Bad Business standing by the ice machine on the first floor of the Summer Sands.

She'd missed him, but her camera hadn't.

After a night of fitful sleep, Minerva returned to the Bayfront Hotel. She entered the lobby, smiled at the hotel clerk, and continued toward the restaurant. From the open door, she recognized the hostess from her previous visit. She hoped the woman would have Stratton's lunch partner's name in her records. As the hostess turned away from the table, Minerva had a clear view of the diner.

Mr. Bad Business.

But this time, his dining partner wasn't the ill-fated Mr. Stratton.

It was his wife.

Kaye Stratton bore little resemblance to the shell-shocked, newly widowed woman Minerva had met with the night before.

She moved to the corner of the entry door, out of view. The two talked over coffee—signaling it would be a short meeting. Kaye pulled a black, legal-sized ledger from her tote, resting on the floor and placed it in the center of the table. Mr. Bad Business took it and reciprocated by moving his briefcase close to her feet. He then stood and tucked the ledger underneath his arm.

Minerva darted from the doorway and scrambled to sit on a couch located behind an array of decorative greenery in the lobby. She pretended to read the *Ms.* magazine she pulled from her bag until Mr. Bad Business left the hotel. A few minutes later, Kaye left the restaurant and Minerva trailed her outside.

"So that's it?" Minerva called out to Kaye's back as she moved toward the parking lot.

Kaye stopped, waited several seconds before turning around, and fixed her eyes on her investigator. "So, that's what?"

Minerva glanced down at the briefcase dangling from Kaye's grip. "Must have been some pretty incriminating information in that book to warrant that payday. I suppose you're set for life now."

A simple shrug from Kaye. "Women are always told to work harder, and we do, but we should be working smarter." A glint in her eye. "You should open your own agency instead of working for Schuller."

Minerva ignored the career advice. "You know that man you were meeting with? He might have killed your husband."

"I don't know any such thing," she said. The chill in her voice cut through the warmth of the humid air. "Detective Varelo called to tell me they found a gun in that waitress's car, hidden underneath the seat. They have her in custody now."

Gulf winds tousled Minerva's dark hair, the strands sticking to her neck, flush from the realization this was anything but a simple surveillance case. "You can't let an innocent woman go to jail for something she didn't do."

"She isn't innocent. She ruined my marriage."

"William ruined your marriage."

Kaye shook her head as if the truth had threatened to stick. "He was going to leave me with nothing. I built my life around him. He didn't care about us, the kids. Just himself." She glanced down at the briefcase. "I'm the only one looking out for me."

"You knew photos would give you motive," Minerva said. "Aren't you worried about that?"

A small smile emerged on the widow Stratton's lips. "That ledger has a lot of details our local law enforcement would prefer to stay hidden. It won't see the light of day. This case will be closed. No one cares about a cheating disco hall waitress."

Minerva knew she was right.

The *Caller-Times* offices had the good fortune of residing in the heart of downtown on N. Lower Broadway. Prime location for the Fourth Estate, and rightly so. Minerva parked her Maverick on the side of the building, a trio of palm trees providing proper south Texas scenery against the stoic multi-story brick building. Several cars remained in the lot even though it was past normal business hours.

Minerva surveyed the area before walking toward the side mail drop, manilla envelope in hand. She'd heard Alice Montoya was an up-and-coming reporter, so she hoped the photos of Mr. Bad Business might help Jenny Boyd's cause. Worst-case scenario, Minerva would jeopardize her job, but Jenny's stakes were exponentially higher. Besides, the photos could be evidence in a murder. That ended her obligation to Kaye Stratton.

With a flip of her wrist, the envelope disappeared inside the mail drop.

No going back now.

She checked her watch.

Lucia would be waiting for her.

Monroe's Tavern on Ayers was already hopping at eight o'clock. She found her way through the crowd and spotted Lucia nursing a Coors Banquet. She glanced at the television propped up on a shelf behind the bar. Apparently, the Battle of the Sexes didn't get priority viewing at Monroe's. Still, a steady stream of women came by the television to check the match. A screen was perched on each end of the bar. Minerva squinted at the score.

"Billie Jean won the first set?"

"Don't act surprised," Lucia said. "We know she's going to deliver."

"It's not that," Minerva replied. "Just not used to good news these days."

Lucia low whistled at the bartender and held up two fingers before pointing to her beer. He brought two additional Banquets over. Minerva felt the wet chill of the can and put the metal rim to her lips. It was half gone before it met the bar top again. They watched the match, intermittent cheers and boos echoing in the crowd behind them, as they witnessed Billie Jean King beat the snot out of Bobby Riggs in straight sets.

Minerva lit a Kool and surveyed the crowd. Some men were already crying foul before the court cleared. The women hugged and high fived, a few offering some well-deserved jibes. Lucia smiled at the scene.

"Look at this, love," she said, her arm waving across the room. "We know we're equal to the men. This proves it. Things will change now."

A WOMAN'S PLACE
N.M. Cedeño

I shouldn't have let the young woman get the drop on me while I was staking out that warehouse. When I encountered her earlier in the day, she appeared to be running her own parallel investigation, which was no skin off my nose, but I still should have kept an eye open for her. Between fighting to stay alert while watching for my target and mulling my impending unwanted early retirement, I'd dismissed her from my mind.

She wasn't the first female investigator I'd encountered, but she was by far the smallest at less than five feet tall and barely one hundred pounds. And I'd let her sneak up on me in the shadow of a brick wall I was using for cover at the edge of a parking lot across from the warehouse. That it was a dark night with few lights around was no excuse. As I turned slowly with my hands raised, I caught sight of her for the third time in so many days. She was a petite Mexican-American girl, young enough to be my daughter.

The look in her wide brown eyes was resolute, and she held the Smith & Wesson .38 Special in her small hand like she meant business. Her light jacket, worn over her yellow blouse and striped miniskirt, almost swallowed her petite frame. The top of her head, with a wide orange scarf tied around shoulder-length black hair, barely reached my sternum, even with black platform boots adding a few extra inches of height. She looked fragile and deadly, an impressive combination.

In my defense, I was out of practice with women, having decided they were irrelevant in my life, which was less painful than moping over missed opportunities. After five years in the Army during World War II, I joined the police. Patrolmen earn chickenfeed, so I set aside marriage for when I moved up the ranks. Then a car wreck destroyed my left hip and my police career. I threw myself into my own private investigation business to avoid brooding over my losses. By the mid-1960s, my business was stable, and I was in my mid-forties with chronic hip pain and graying hair. Looking around, I found the only available women in my age bracket were divorcées with long-haired, hippie children in the midst of adolescent rebellion. No thank you.

On that night in Houston, Texas, in September 1973, most of my generation was anticipating becoming grandparents, and I was a fifty-two-year-old, confirmed bachelor. How was I to know this girl might be important to me?

"Greetings," I said. "I should have introduced myself earlier today outside Caleb Jones's house." She'd been driving a yellow VW bug, making her easy to spot. "You must have spoken to him right after I did."

"Who are you?" she asked in a low growl.

"I'm Jerry Milam, private investigator." I gestured toward the back pocket of my black trousers without lowering my hands, cognizant of the gun still aimed at me. "My identification is in my pocket."

"Show me. Slowly!"

Her husky voice held only the barest hint of a Texas accent, suggesting she'd probably grown up in Houston. Texas accents broaden in small towns, but nearly vanish in the big cities.

I slid two fingers into my pocket and pulled out the wallet. Flipping it open, I showed her my credentials.

She lowered the gun a fraction.

The longer I stood, the greater the pain in my blown-out left hip. Sitting was most comfortable, but I couldn't stay at my desk and do my job. Walking was less painful than standing, but still contributed to ever-increasing levels of pain throughout the day. It was late, eleven p.m., and I'd spent much of the day walking. I shifted my feet to take some of the pressure off my hip. "Now you know my name. What's yours?"

She didn't answer my question. Instead, she raised one sculpted eyebrow and leveled the Special again. "Why are you watching this warehouse?"

"If you talked to Caleb, then you know his brother Billy's friend, Mose Mitchell, works here. I need a word with him regarding Billy's current whereabouts."

"Listen, Gramps, stay out of my—"

I pounced forward and grabbed the gun, twisting it upward so if she did manage to squeeze the trigger, we'd be momentarily deaf, but not dead.

The gun didn't go off.

"I'm not your gramps. You can call me Jerry, or Mr. Milam, if you're feeling formal." I placed her .38 Special into the right front pocket of my suit coat as I released her. "I'm guessing someone hired you, like someone hired me. Now, I need to talk to Mose."

She gritted her teeth and glared at me.

I peeked around the brick wall. Parked by the warehouse was a white Chevelle that hadn't been there before Miss What's-Her-Name interrupted me. "He's here. Are you coming with me, or do you want to stay here?" I didn't wait for her answer as I rounded the corner into the unlit parking lot.

The case had started simply enough. A security guard named Jamison Cockrell died in a warehouse fire. His boss refused to pay his widow her due for Jamison's death on the job, claiming Jamison had started the fire and killed himself. The warehouse owner, Painter-Mason Company, had received a massive insurance payout for the loss of the building, and the boss didn't want to share any of it with a grieving widow, no matter what company policy or employment contracts said.

Cockrell was working two jobs, trying to earn extra money before the birth of his second child. He did maintenance work for the Austin Independent School District while moonlighting as a security guard at the warehouse. His distraught, pregnant widow came to me, and I took the job of determining who started the fire at the P & M Warehouse that night in Austin.

From the police and fire investigation reports, I learned only one of two security guards had clocked in for work the night of the fire. I was hunting for the other man, Billy Jones. In researching Billy, I'd discovered he was also wanted in connection to warehouse fires in Houston. His brother Caleb, fed up with Bill's activities, said if anyone knew where he was, it was his friend Mose Mitchell. Then he directed me to a Port of Houston warehouse where Mitchell was employed.

I heard the quick steps of the young woman hustling behind me as I crossed the parking lot toward the warehouse.

"Who hired you?" she asked as she scurried to keep up.

"The victim's family."

"What victim?" The pitch of her voice rose.

I turned and found her stopped a few feet behind me. The change in her voice suggested she intentionally lowered her pitch to keep from sounding childlike. "Jamison Cockrell, the man who died in the Austin warehouse fire."

"The guy who helped Billy Jones start the fire?" she said, her voice husky again.

"No, the innocent guy blamed for starting the fire so the company wouldn't have to pay death benefits to the widow."

"The widow needs money and doesn't want to admit her husband was involved."

"Look, miss, I've met the family. They're law-abiding, hard-working people. No criminal ties of any kind."

She snorted in an unladylike fashion. "But look where he lived. He needed money. And besides, he and Jones are both—"

"So, he lived on the poor side of Austin. That didn't make him a criminal. The fact both Cockrell and Jones are Black doesn't make them automatically friends either." I shook my head. "Being Black just made Cockrell a scapegoat."

"How do you know he had no criminal ties?" She put some scorn into her carefully modulated voice.

"Because I've been a private eye for twenty years. I was a cop for five years before that. I know how to check someone's background. Jamison Cockrell did his duty by Uncle Sam in Vietnam, married, started a family, and worked hard to support them. He didn't have a criminal bone in his body. Billy Jones, on the other hand, owes loan sharks who will eat him alive if he doesn't pay and has a lifelong criminal history as a hired thug."

She tossed her dark hair and frowned at me. "I was told Billy and Jamison were in this together. Jamison needed the money for the new baby."

"Look, miss, clearly, no one gave you the autopsy details. The *victim*, Jamison Cockrell, was hit over the head and died of a skull fracture before the fire. No smoke in his lungs. Dead men don't start fires. However, security guards who interrupt arsonists do get murdered." I watched her process the information I'd given her. She was out of her depth. "Have you ever worked a murder case before?"

She put one hand on her hip and tilted her head. "I've seen death."

I glanced back at the warehouse. The white Chevelle hadn't moved. "That's not the same as investigating murders yourself. Do you even have a license?"

"I'm an apprentice. My boss has the license."

I rolled my eyes heavenward. "Of course. Miss, go home. You're going to get hurt. This is no simple skip trace."

Her button nose flared, her chin came up, and her hands clenched into fists. "I am not a child. I am perfectly capable of doing any job you can do, you male chauvinist pig. You middle-aged white guys are all the same, just like Bobby Riggs."

"I may be middle-aged and white, but I'm not a loud-mouthed misogynist. I hope Billie Jean King whips the pants off Riggs when she plays him at the Astrodome tomorrow. Some of the best private detectives I know are female. They went private when the police departments refused to promote them. But you"—I eyed her tiny frame and stubborn jaw—"you've got the spirit, but not the training. You're a danger to yourself and others. Join the police. Get some training, even if they don't let you use it. Then switch to private investigations."

Her dark brows came together. "I tried. The police academy told me I'm too short and don't weigh enough."

I could hear the bitterness and frustration in her voice. "Tough break, kid. I'm out of the police because I can't pass the physical either."

"Because of your limp?" She gestured toward my left leg.

"Yep."

"War injury?"

"No. Car accident. Enough prattle. I need to see Mose." I limped across the parking lot, wondering if she was ever going to tell me her name.

Then, I was blasted off my feet.

I found myself on the ground in the parking lot with my ears ringing, wondering who dropped a bomb on Houston. Groaning, I took a moment to assess my limbs for damage before I pushed myself up onto one elbow. Part of the warehouse had exploded, and burning debris was raining down around me. My black suit coat was torn at the elbow and my navy-blue tie had a cinder on it. The girl was gone.

After picking myself up, I hobbled to a parking block at the top of a parking space, dusting cinders from my clothes as I went. I sat, found the aspirin I always carried in my breast pocket, and popped a couple into my mouth.

Despite constant hip pain, I never took strong painkillers. I'd discovered after my accident that morphine made me want to scratch my eyes out. The doctors decided I was allergic to opiates. I'd tried newer pain medications, but found they incapacitated me, leaving me tired and my brain fogged. Alcohol had a similar effect on me, which is why I'd long been a teetotaler. Dull senses and mental sluggishness were incompatible with working investigations, so I lived with the pain by popping aspirin as needed.

Eventually fire trucks came roaring down the street, their shrill sirens startling my already shocked ears. An HPD police officer approached me. "Do you need medical assistance?"

"No, thanks."

"What are you doing here?" he asked.

"I was walking by when the building exploded."

"May I see your identification?"

I produced my wallet. That bought me a trip to headquarters so the detectives could ask me what a PI was doing next to a building that exploded. I left the girl out of my explanations because I never got her name, which left me with a niggling itch on the brain. Why wouldn't she give me her name? What was she hiding?

I wasn't from Houston. Austin, my home base, was where I knew all the local police. It took a few calls to reach my friend, Sergeant Mutt Prichard, with the Austin Police Department, to ask him to vouch for me. Even then, I still had to explain my presence at the warehouse before HPD detectives Smyers and Locke stopped looking like they wanted to knock me around to see what shook loose. At least they let me sit down while they interrogated me.

Once they decided I wasn't a suspect, I obtained some information from Detective Smyers about the other fires connected to Billy Jones.

Smyers, twenty years my junior, well-muscled, and with a scar across one cheek, lit a cigarette as he lounged against the edge of his desk. "This was the third warehouse fire in the last few months. No one died in the first two, but tonight we lost a night watchman, an accountant working late on the books, and some poor guy who was driving by when a chunk of concrete came through his windshield."

I said, "The Austin fire, where cannisters of compressed gases were stored in the warehouse, killed a night watchman, Jamison Cockrell. Billy Jones was the other night watchman at the Austin warehouse, and his friend, Mose Mitchell, worked at the warehouse that exploded tonight."

"That links Billy to all the warehouse fires," Smyers said. "Maybe he rotated over to Austin and then used Mose Mitchell for access because we were already looking for him. Tonight, he outdid himself. Did you hear what he ignited?"

"What was it? It felt like a bomb went off." I'd been wondering what had caused a blast strong enough to knock me on my keester and destroy half a building.

"You remember that explosion in Texas City in '47?"

"Ammonium nitrate fertilizer?" I was horrified. For those of us who remembered the 1947 blast in Texas City, ammonium nitrate was the stuff of nightmares.

"Yep. Tonight's situation was extra explosive. He poured gasoline on sacks of ammonium nitrate fertilizer and ignited it with dynamite. Cooked the accountant in the building. As for the night watchman, well, only thing worse I've seen was done by napalm."

As he inhaled from his cigarette, Smyers's focus turned inward. I suspected he was remembering events that equaled my memories of the war in the Pacific.

Releasing a puff of smoke, he said, "We have everyone looking for Billy Jones. He's moved up from arson to explosives. We have to find this bastard."

I reviewed what the police had on the other warehouse fires before calling it a night.

In the chilly, wee hours of Thursday morning, I limped back to a cheap motel room that reeked of stale cigarettes. The room's threadbare sheets, lumpy mattress, stained orange carpeting, and dirty yellow walls didn't meet my usual minimum standards. Business was good, so I could afford a better hotel, but vacant rooms were hard to come by because reporters and spectators had flooded into town to see that day's tennis match dubbed the Battle of the Sexes.

After popping a few more aspirin and cleaning my scraped elbow, I settled onto on the lumpy mattress to look for any commonalities between the burned warehouses, other than that they all stored flammable commercial substances, beginning with butadiene, turpentine, and motor oil, moving to cannisters of compressed gases, and finishing tonight with ammonium nitrate. But it was late, and I kept thinking about the girl detective.

If it hadn't been for her, I'd probably have gone into the warehouse and been blown to oblivion. Where others might have resorted to drink or pills to forget the girl, the pain, and the close call with eternity, all I could do was wait for my aspirin to work and try to sleep.

Late the next morning, I awoke with my body aching and pain stabbing through my left hip. The day my hip injury would force me to retire felt closer than ever. My notes lay strewn around me. I was still missing something. Billy Jones had no history of arson before these fires. He had to be working for someone, but the destroyed warehouses had nothing linking them. So why burn those particular warehouses with those particular flammable materials? Standing in the shower, an idea came to me.

After donning my spare black suit, I drove back to HPD to request the files on local fires. What if other locations were involved? What if someone was practicing igniting substances he knew were found elsewhere?

Outside HPD headquarters, I spied my young colleague sitting in her yellow VW bug again. She was staring at the building, pursing her lips. Her dark hair, parted in the middle, covered half her face. A silky gold scarf was knotted around her throat.

Deciding it was easier to keep her close than to monitor her as she followed me, I limped toward her car. My limp was decidedly worse today.

She shrank into her seat when she saw me approaching. When she recognized me, the tension left her body, and her shoulders dropped as she sighed in relief. "Thank God. You're alive."

"No one will work with you if you leave people for dead. You might consider how you'd want others to treat you and act accordingly."

She flinched and dropped her eyes. "I came here to find out what happened to you. I was trying to figure out how to ask about you without having to admit I was at that warehouse last night." When she raised her head again, her hair fell away, revealing bruising around one eye and a scrape on her cheekbone.

I leaned against the VW's left front fender. "Is that from last night's explosion?"

Her hand went to her face. "Yeah. I landed on my shoulder and my face. Then, I got up and ran. I wanted to get as far away as possible, but I should have stopped for you." She cleared her throat. "I'm sorry."

My chest tightened as I observed her remorseful expression, but I ignored it. "Live and learn. Come on. I'll let you tag along while I search for Billy Jones, but only if you tell me your name."

She exited her car, straightened her brown and gold, paisley-print minidress, and extended her hand. "Maria Salvadora Garza Muñoz. Call me Dora."

"Pleased to meet you, Dora," I said. Her child-sized hand vanished in my larger mitt, but her handshake was firm.

I walked her into the police station and persuaded Detective

Smyers to allow us to review every arson case and every fire of undetermined cause from the previous twelve months.

At a scratched table in a stifling, windowless interrogation room, I handed Dora a stack of files. "Look for fires similar to the ones we already know about. The warehouses that burned all contained flammable materials." I listed the chemicals involved in the previous warehouse fires. "Check if these other fires align in any way with the warehouse fires. Are the dates close together? Were similar accelerants or chemicals involved? Look for any commonalities." I placed a chart I'd created showing the date, location, time, and flammable materials involved in each fire on the table before her.

While reviewing files, I also evaluated Dora. She was thorough and efficient, asking pertinent questions and eliminating files quickly based on my answers. She never asked the same question twice. After two hours, I reached the end of my stack. I dropped my last file and said, "What have you found?"

She held up two files. "These fires occurred within a few days after the warehouse fires and involved similar accelerants: motor oil and cleaning solutions, including turpentine. But the exact cause of the fires is unknown, possibly accidental. One fire was at a car dealership and the other was at a janitorial service company."

I tapped files by my elbow. "I found two: a dentist office and a manufacturer. The dentist's office had cannisters of compressed gases like the Austin warehouse fire and occurred two days after that fire, but the cause of the fire is classified as unknown. The manufacturer fire involved butadiene which lines up with the earliest warehouse fire."

Dora had a thoughtful look as she leaned her chin on her hand. "Do you think Billy Jones is responsible for all these fires?"

"He's involved. Is he working alone? Probably not. He doesn't have the brains. Billy has a long record of criminal activity, but someone else has always been the brains of the outfit, and he doesn't have a history as a firebug until recently."

She pushed the files in front of her into a neat stack before tucking her dark hair behind her ears. "Who do you think he's working for?"

"Someone methodical. Someone who practices on a warehouse before burning down his real target. He uses accelerants already present in the businesses to make the fires look accidental. We need to find out what the companies that burned have in common and see if we can tie Billy Jones to them."

I placed the four files we'd found in front of me. Parson Manufacturing, Great Smiles Dentistry, Go Clean Janitorial Services, and Hensen Auto. I pulled a pad of paper and a pencil from my pocket and opened the first file, Parson Manufacturing. The owner's name was Margaret Bunt. The details on her were typical of most business owners: educated, financially solid, involved in the community on various boards and committees. I flipped through each file and collected details about the other businesses, their owners, the fires, and any victims.

I said, "An employee was caught in the fire at the janitorial service company and died."

Dora cleared her throat.

"What?" I asked, glancing at her across the table.

"Nothing." She looked away from me.

"Here." I handed her my notepad. "What do these businesses have in common?"

She studied my notes. "All the owners are women?"

"Successful women, running businesses, who are active in their communities."

Dora returned my notepad. "The Equal Rights Amendment was passed by both houses of Congress last year. It still has to be ratified by the states. Title IX was enacted last year too, right before the fires began. Could someone be angry enough about women's rights to start fires?"

"Maybe. Bobby Riggs isn't the only sexist out there. Let's get out of this airless room. I need a telephone."

I borrowed a phone at Smyers's desk and called all four business owners to ask if they'd ever heard of Billy Jones. Each owner confirmed Jones had been hired in some position—security or janitorial—right before the business burned. He had provided a fake birth date and a different social security number with each job application, making it unlikely a cursory background check would identify any problems.

I said to Dora and Smyers, "If the fires hold to the pattern, the next one might be any time in the next few days, possibly at a fertilizer factory owned by a woman. That could cause an explosion and blaze worthy of Red Adair."

Dora hovered near me with her hands on her slim hips, ready for action, but wanting direction. "Where do you want to start? Are we going to call fertilizer factories to see if one hired Billy?"

Nodding to Smyers, I said, "We'll let the police deal with tracking down the fertilizer companies. I can think of another place to start searching for Billy Jones." We left Smyers to deal with his end and went to continue our search.

As she followed me down the sidewalk outside police headquarters to the parking area, Dora asked, "Where are we going? I've been looking for Billy for ages and haven't found him."

"Mose Mitchell's house, right after we grab some lunch."

We agreed on hamburgers.

Then, while Dora devoured a burger with cheese, I excused myself, but not to the bathroom. I swallowed an aspirin and found a pay phone. I had to verify a few suspicions and do my due diligence on Dora. My gut told me she wasn't who she pretended to be.

We arrived at Mose Mitchell's rundown house in South Houston in my black Buick Centurion. The treeless yard was overgrown with dandelions. Shingles were missing in patches. A cinder block replaced a broken step to the tiny front porch. The house was silent. When no one answered my knock, I led Dora around the side of the house to a weathered gray shed standing at the end of the gravel driveway. It wasn't big enough to be a garage, but it was the right size for a workshop.

"Are we breaking in?"

"We're looking for any signs of bomb-making or arson."

The shed's barn-like door wasn't locked, only latched. I swung it open on squeaky hinges and stepped inside the dim workspace.

The odor of gasoline slapped me in the face as I flicked on a light and closed the door behind us. Twenty empty gas cans, a pallet dusted with a scattering of white granules and powder, and a heap of empty sacks lay on the floor. "Well, that's not a good sign. Check the workbench for papers or notes of any kind," I said as I limped over to pick up one of the sacks. I read the label. "Damn. Ammonium nitrate fertilizer. If last night's explosion was the practice, then the bomber went out and bought a pallet full of fertilizer to use on his next target. He must not be targeting a fertilizer factory, or he wouldn't have had to buy the stuff."

Dora called out, "I found a rental agreement for a truck and some newspaper clippings about the Astrodome and the Battle of the Sexes."

A sense of foreboding washed over me. "What time does the tennis match start?"

"Seven p.m."

I glanced at my watch. Three o'clock. "We have four hours to find the rental truck with the ammonium nitrate bomb in it before someone tries to ignite it at the Astrodome."

She stared at me in disbelief. "By ourselves?"

"We call the police, and they put every officer in town on it."

"We have to hurry! They might not find the truck in time." Her voice rose from husky to bell-like tones as she forgot to modulate it. She bounced on her toes like she wanted to bolt out of the shed.

Then our luck changed.

I reached out and grabbed her arm. "Shh. Do you hear that?" I said. A vehicle pulled into the gravel driveway.

Dora whispered, "I could really use my gun right now."

"We need people alive if we want to identify everyone involved." I grabbed a pipe wrench from an array of tools on the wall and handed it to her. Then I selected a crowbar for myself and moved to take a position beside the door. Dora moved opposite me without hesitation. The girl had guts. Pain surged through my left hip, causing sweat to break out on my forehead. "You hit the first guy who enters. I'll take any after that."

We listened as the engine cut and vehicle doors opened.

A weaselly, young man's voice said, "There's a car in front of the house. Is someone here?"

"Look around. Do you see anyone? Now, get your ass inside so we can go over the route," said an older man with a gravelly smoker's voice.

"Don't worry, boss, I got the hang of driving this truck now. How many people do you think this will kill?" the weaselly voice asked with barely suppressed excitement.

"Lots. But only if Billie Jean King wins. If that happens, then the whole world has gone to the dogs and deserves to be blown up."

I heard footsteps approaching and raised my crowbar, ready to strike. Dora mirrored me with the wrench.

The footsteps stopped. "Did you leave the light on again?" the gravelly voice asked.

"No, not me. I swear." The younger man didn't sound certain.

"You're an idiot, Billy."

The door to the workshop opened.

Billy said, "I'm sorry, boss—" as Dora crashed the wrench down on his head.

Over Billy's collapsing body, an older white man surged toward Dora. I swung the crowbar down, missed his pale, bald head, and connected with his left collarbone. The bone broke with an audible crack. Then, Dora hit him on the right shoulder, cracking the other collar bone. The man fell to his knees, howling in pain. I pinned him to the ground with one knee in his back.

After a minute spent searching the workshop, Dora found twine to tie their hands and feet. Billy was down for the count, but the boss cursed a blue streak when I tied his hands behind his back.

Once that was done, I left Dora to keep watch while I rousted a neighbor to call the police. Awaiting reinforcements, I opened the back of the rental truck and smelled gasoline. Inside were barrels rigged with dynamite, probably containing ammonium nitrate soaked with gasoline. I didn't envy whoever had to dismantle that mess.

Eventually, an array of police cars arrived, and I, once again, had some explaining to do. Billy regained consciousness swiftly, but an ambulance had to be called for the boss, who turned out to be a loan shark named Andrew Smith. He sat ranting to anyone in range about how Title IX caused his son to lose his wrestling scholarship because the university had to cut the men's wrestling program to create a women's tennis program. He blamed women for taking men's jobs. He expected the Equal Rights Amendment to destroy civilization. "If women knew their places and stayed in them, the world wouldn't be falling apart!"

As the police led Billy across the weed-choked lawn to a patrol car, whining about his aching head, Dora looked at me wistfully and said in a gruff voice, "I've learned more from you in the last few days than during the months I spent searching for Billy Jones. Do you need an apprentice, Mr. Milam? Someone to do the legwork when you need a break?"

Arranging my expression into a look of annoyance, I said, "I can't have someone driven by revenge working for me. I do things the legal way. Besides, you would have to leave the steno pool and become an actual apprentice."

She inhaled sharply. "You knew?"

"That you wanted to kill Billy Jones that night at the warehouse? Why else would a secretary go through the trouble of acquiring a gun and tracking Billy? It was simple to link your aunt's death at the janitorial business to you. Her last name was Muñoz Diaz; yours is Garza Muñoz. I'm not likely to miss a connection like that. I knew you were hiding something when you refused to tell me your name and when you asked me what victim's family had hired me."

Her brown eyes blazed at me. "My *tía* deserved justice. The police weren't even investigating. Billy was the security guard that night. I saw him when I dropped my *tía* at work. But then I found they thought he wasn't there, because he didn't punch his card. I knew he was involved." The pitch of her voice rose, as it always did when she was angry or surprised.

"Justice and revenge are different things. If you'd killed him, we wouldn't have caught his boss."

The anger seeped out of her. "I know that now. I'm sorry. I really did try to join the police. That wasn't a lie. And, I did try to become an apprentice, but no one would hire me."

"I know." I shifted my feet as my hip began to throb.

Dora was holding her breath, waiting for me to give her the brush off, which was what I had planned to do. But she was brave, persistent, and a quick learner, and I could use the help. "So, do you want the job or not?"

"Yes! Thank you, thank you," she squeaked, her voice back to bell-like tones.

"You'd have to move to Austin."

"I will!" Her eyes glowed, and she reached out to shake my hand with a level of enthusiasm I hadn't even possessed in my youth.

I wondered what I had gotten myself into. My colleagues, especially Sergeant Mutt Prichard, might accuse me of having ulterior motives when word leaked out I'd employed Dora, but she needed a mentor. And as much as she needed a mentor, I needed a protégé. My hip pain was only getting worse with age. Without help, I'd have to close up shop and face an unwelcome early retirement. With Dora to help with legwork, the future looked rosier.

We spent the next few hours at the police station where we learned Andrew Smith had written sexist, vitriolic letters to every major newspaper in the state denouncing the Equal Rights Amendment and Title IX. He thought a woman's place was beneath a man's foot. By the time the police finished taking Smith's statement, I had more than enough evidence to complete my case for Jamison Cockrell's widow.

Smyers informed me that the police captured Mose Mitchell at Intercontinental Airport trying to leave the country ahead of what he expected to be a night of explosions, followed by riots, and the complete breakdown of society. Smyers's partner Locke was busy tracing the source of the dynamite, since Smith couldn't have obtained it legally.

Finally, the police chief called me into his office to talk to him. His face was pale. "Ammonium nitrate, fuel, and dynamite in a truck. A mobile bomb. And the target was the Astrodome. The carnage would have been unthinkable. Can you imagine if one of these radical groups promoting some crackpot cause thought of this? The exact details are not going in the report file or to the press. I don't want anyone getting ideas from this."

I nodded my understanding, but deep down I knew what one perverse criminal could imagine, another one would, too. History had shown people on opposite sides of the world had invented the same things, without the knowledge someone else had done it first. I only hoped I didn't live to see the day when someone trying to promote their own bizarre ideology or to send a message to the government succeeded in exploding a truck full of ammonium nitrate near a building full of innocent victims.

NEON WOMEN
Ann Aptaker

He's just a junkie, a scabby-faced loser, the kind of guy life or a fed-up God kicks to the curb, which is where the junkie is now, dead in a puddle at the curb of Forty-second Street at the edge of Times Square.

His face looks weirdly alive in the red and pink neon of the street's all-night sex joints. The guy's long, ratty brown hair is matted with gutter gunk. His bell-bottom jeans and denim jacket are soaked through, shiny with water reflecting the night's neon glow. The red and pink light makes the slimy gutter soot staining his floral shirt look like streaks and blobs of blood.

But there's no blood on the body. The guy's dead of an overdose of smack.

A handful of uniformed cops keep the rubbernecking crowd of underdressed hookers, fancified pimps, scuzzy drug pushers, hopped up hippies, and terrified but smug out-of-towners back from the action while the police photographer snaps away. The camera's flash lends a gaudy glamor to the dead junkie. The Medical Examiner's boys busy themselves setting up a body bag and a gurney to take the stiff to the morgue.

Homicide cop Lieutenant Sal Barone stands over the junkie. The narrow brim of Barone's hat throws a slim line of shadow over his sourpuss face, obscuring one of his dark, scowling eyes. He pulls a cigarette from the pack in the pocket of his coat, a gray plaid that tries to look hip but has *cop taste* written all over it. He lights his cigarette and exhales the smoke while he flips through the soaking wet wallet he'd pulled from the back pocket of the junkie's jeans. There's nothing in the wallet except two limp bucks, an expired driver's license listing a drug-den address, and an unopened condom packet.

Standing next to Barone is a woman in a black leather coat and green platform shoes. The coat hides a .38 tucked into a shoulder rig. The woman's not a cop. She's a private investigator. Her name's Gussie Diamond. Her shag cut brunette hair, tinged by the neon light, frames a face whose eyes are hip to the Forty-second Street scene. She's been around the Forty-Deuce and Times Square since she was a kid hanging out in her dad's private investigations office above the Rialto movie theater. The theater used to feature classy Hollywood fare. It's a porn house now.

Barone says, "Stay outta this, Gussie. For chrissakes, it's one o'clock in the morning. Don't you ever go to bed?" Despite his cool way with her, Barone can't ignore how the belted coat clings to her body, the way the red and pink neon of the sex parlors slithers like probing fingers along the black leather. If she wasn't a pain in the ass private eye, and one of those crazy bra-burning feminists to boot, he might even consider giving her a tumble. Gussie Diamond might be a foxy mama, but she's a cop's worst romantic nightmare: a woman too snoopy for her own good.

"You know I can't stay out of it, Sal," Gussie says, her Noo Yawk tone and delivery as aggressive as Barone's. "I'm getting paid to deal with it." She lights her own cigarette, not waiting for Barone to do the gentlemanly thing, which she doesn't give a damn about, anyway. She has no use for chivalry. Too many strings attached.

"Paid? By who?" Barone says. "Who'd give a damn about a dead junkie?"

"If his name's Darryl Wickers, my client gives a damn. She hired me to find him."

"She? There's actually a she in this loser's life?" Barone's snicker rides on a stream of exhaled smoke, tinted pale red in the neon light. "And just who is this she?" He takes a pen and small notepad from his coat pocket. "Where can I find her? I'll need to talk to her."

Gussie answers Barone with a *tsk*, her hand going to her hip in a this-woman-doesn't-take-any-crap posture. "Don't you own a calendar, Barone? It's 1975, not 1875. I'm not on this earth to fetch and carry for you. Do your own legwork. And I don't have to give up the names of my clients, either. You worked with my dad often enough to know that."

Barone gives her the size-up from head to toe, making a macho point of lingering from the above-the-knee hem of Gussie's coat and down along her legs. "And your father was just as much a pain in the ass buttinsky as you are, Diamond, except his legs weren't as nice."

"How would you know?" she says. "Dad always wore pants. Listen, Barone, just tell me: is the guy in the puddle Darryl Wickers? Age thirty-six? Small time dope peddler?"

Annoyed at the brushoff, annoyed, in fact, that she's even here, Barone gives her a terse, "This is police business, Gussie."

"I take that as a yes," she says. "So, next question: what's homicide's interest in what looks like an overdose case? Dead junkies are a dime a dozen on the street, so why does the NYPD send in a gold shield homicide cop to write up a loser like Darryl Wickers?"

"Again, this is police business, Gussie."

"So you said. C'mon, Barone. You know I'll see the autopsy report five minutes after it's outta the typewriter."

Barone's smile has more leer in it than cheer. "Just how many people owe you favors, Diamond? And how'd you rack up those favors, anyway?"

Gussie wouldn't mind smashing her cigarette in Barone's sourpuss for his sleazy put-down, but she keeps her hand in check. She knows damn well that after his howl of pain his rage would only make him clam up even tighter, and certainly get the cuffs locked on her. So, she swallows Barone's insult, though it sits like a stone in her throat. Like every woman who makes her way in what's still a man's world, she's been on the receiving end of so many put-downs that only the chutzpah she inherited from her pushy broad of a mother and the discipline she inherited from her PI father kept her from getting squashed on the pavement.

But she doesn't shrink from Barone, either. "Spare me the tough-guy crap, Barone, and fill me in," she says. "Something's not kosher with the OD, right?"

"How many times do I have to tell you to stay out of this, Diamond?" Barone's scolding-the-pesky-little-girl tone brings Gussie dangerously close to giving him that poke in the puss with the burning tip of her smoke. She'd be willing to go to the slammer just for the pleasure of hearing this caveman yelp.

But it's clear standing up to the guy is getting her nowhere. If she wants information from Barone, she'll have to come at his soft spot. Much as she hates the idea, Gussie figures it might be a good time to stroke Barone with a female feather. Gloria Steinem might not approve, but Steinem doesn't have to deal with neanderthal cops; well, not regularly and not in the middle of the night on Forty-second Street's carnival of drugs and sex.

Gussie puts on her most girly-girl smile and gives Barone a friendly, slightly seductive poke in the ribs with her elbow.

Her poke rattles him, makes him fumble his cigarette, crashing it against his teeth.

Her tactical mistake reminds Gussie she'd broken the first rule her father ever taught her when she joined him as a licensed PI: never try to be palzee-walzee with a cop.

With each slide up and down the stripper pole, with each toss of her wild blond mane of hair, with every kick of her leg, every bend over, every rehearsed caress of her pastie'd breasts,

Marsha St. Clair dies a little more. Inch by inch, disco beat by disco beat, Marsha writhes and shimmies toward the final death of her soul, a demise that will come long before the death of her body.

K.C. and the Sunshine Band's "Get Down Tonight" blares through the Hot Nights Club's amped up speakers. The song pounds against the clatter of whiskey glasses, beer bottles, talk and guffaws in the smoky room, creating a noise that's neither music nor laughter but a deafening throb of desperation. The glare of a twirling disco ball makes the noise feel even louder.

Marsha's due for a break at the end of the Sunshine Band's number. She lives for the breaks, when she can give her aching body a rest, wipe the sweat off her face, grab a smoke or a joint in the alley and get free of the stench of sweaty flesh and cheap booze clogging the air of the club.

The Sunshine Band eventually bleeds into James Brown's "Papa's Got a Brand New Bag." It's a crowd favorite, eliciting whoops and hollers as Chi Chi LaRue sashays onto the stage, her black hair piled atop her head in a hair-sprayed mountain, her red thong and pasties shimmering like flashing danger signs in the disco ball's glare. After Chi Chi's routine of seductively sliding around Marsha to take her place at the pole, Marsha shimmies into the shadows and off the stage.

She heads to the dressing room, a dingy slice of space shared by six other women in various states of undress and inebriation. Marsha grabs her coat and her pack of smokes and heads out to the alley, where she can shed Marsha St. Claire, wrap herself in her coat, pull a joint from her pack of Newports, and just be Marsha Clunie, ex-high school cheerleader with big dreams, ex-waitress with smaller dreams, ex-wife with no dreams left.

It's the ex-wife part that greets her in the alley.

"I found him," Gussie says. "Or rather, the cops found him. Sorry to have to tell you this, Marsha, but Darryl's—"

"Lemme guess: dead?" There's no sadness in Marsha's voice. There's barely any surprise. When she lights the joint, the match flame reveals no tears in her eyes or any emotion at all. "Well, ain't that just groovy for him. The no-good slob probably offed himself with a hot needle in his arm."

"You're not far wrong," Gussie says. "Yeah, Darryl OD'd, but there's something fishy about it. The cops aren't saying, but something's not kosher."

"Huh. That doesn't surprise me," Marsha says, her face scrunched in disgust. "I don't trust any of those badges. Those guys come around here and rough us up, haul us in just because we make some extra dough turning a trick or two, and *then* they come to see the show and have the nerve to ask for, y'know, freebies. Oh yeah, I've seen plenty of cops. Wouldn't give you a nickel for the lot of them." Marsha finishes her rant with a strong drag on the joint.

"Yeah, well, every job has its perks. You know the game, Marsha."

"It's a rotten game if you ask me. The cops win and everybody else loses."

Maybe it's the dope talking, maybe the high is chipping away at Marsha's stony spirit, but this time, Gussie hears plenty of emotion in the woman; it's the frustration of a bruised life, of a soul kicked around so much it's black and blue.

Gussie lights a cigarette, looks at Marsha through the flame. "The cops are playing a high-stakes game on this one, Marsha. They sent a big-time homicide guy to handle Darryl's case, and he's keeping the lid on it pretty tight. Can you think of anything about Darryl that might interest the cops?"

Marsha pulls another long drag on her joint, holds the smoke in, and takes her time about letting it out. At the end of the exhale, she smiles. It's a sneery smile that cancels the dose of sympathy Gussie felt for her a minute ago. "The only interesting thing Darryl Wickers ever did was marry me," Marsha says. "And now you can add dying." She takes another hit off the joint, offers a toke to Gussie.

Gussie waves it away. She's not against the stuff, even likes to indulge now and then. But not with clients, and especially not with a client who might get her mixed up in a murder.

It's not the first time Gussie's dealt with nasty babes. Her line of work brings her into the company of any number of cold or sour spouses looking to get the goods on their no-good husbands or exes: suburban housewives with nothing exciting to do but go to the beauty parlor every week to have their hair teased or tied high or feathered; Park Avenue types who consider dancing the Hustle with coked-up celebrities at Studio 54 slumming; and hard-luck types like Marsha, women who want more dough squeezed from the pockets of their deadbeat men. "You know anyone who'd want to knock Darryl off?" Gussie says.

Marsha snorts a laugh, a sound sharp as cracking glass. "You mean, besides me?"

"I wouldn't advertise that attitude when the cops come around, Marsha. Cops always look to the spouse first. An ex-spouse isn't off the hook, either."

Marsha gets the message. The snarky attitude dissolves into mere amusement. Another drag on the joint keeps it that way.

Of all the unhappy spouses Gussie's run up against, the ex-Mrs. Darryl Wickers is turning out to be among the most annoying. Maybe she's not snooty like Park Avenue's genuine socialites or phony like the suburban ones, but she's right up there among the coldest. As far as Gussie is concerned, getting rid of her can't come soon enough. "Listen, Marsha, Darryl's been found, which makes the business between us closed. Since I had nothing to do with finding him, I'll just bill you for the consult, and we can forget about the fee for the search. So, see you around sometime." She starts to walk away.

Marsha grabs Gussie's arm, pulls her around to face her. "Just a minute, Gussie, our business isn't over. You saying that lousy ex-husband of mine was maybe murdered? Well, if that's what went down on the stupid slob, I want you to find out who did it. I'll get you the money, okay?" She didn't have to say she'd turn a trick or two. Gussie knew.

"It's not the cash," Gussie says, and peels Marsha's fingers one by one from the sleeve of her leather coat. "We're done because the case doesn't need me. You don't need me. The cops are already working it. They'll fill you in."

"And when they find whoever did it, they'll arrest the poor schmo and let him rot in prison, if they don't fry him first. No, I want you to find whoever killed Darryl, Gussie, before the cops do."

Marsha says it like she's trying hard to sound like a loving wife, but it still comes out on a giggled marijuana sneer. It gives Gussie what her dad used to call the creepy crawlies, a feeling along the spine like a line of ants on a death march. "What's the story, Marsha? I didn't think you gave a damn about the guy. So, what's your hurry to find his killer?"

Marsha pinches out the joint, puts the roach into her pack of Newports. "That's my business."

"Then it'll have to stay your business, Marsha. I'm—"

"Hey, St. Claire!" It's Chi Chi LaRue. She's come through the alley door, the sudden chill of the night air making her shiver in her thong and pasties. She wraps her arms around her body. "Get your tits and ass moving, Marsha. You're back on the pole for the 'Jive Talkin'' number. The other girls are already up there. And who's this you're yammering with?"

"Never mind who I talk to. None of your business, *Miss* LaRue," Marsha says, hissing the *s* in Miss like a snake. The dope's heavy on Marsha's tongue now, her words slurring. But Gussie also hears the sharp edge of Marsha's attitude, the sort of bitchiness she's afraid might end up in a hair-pulling fight.

"Just get your ass on that fuckin' stage, St. Claire."

Marsha gives that a shrug, says to Gussie, "See the trash I gotta work with?"

Gussie answers, "See you around, Marsha. Just go do your job."

"And you do yours. Get it?"

* * *

In the PI game, if you want to earn a living, you take most of the cases that walk through your door. Some cases, though, you run from; cases with dicey clients or cases so down and dirty, you'd emerge with so much mud all over you your reputation would be shot, you'd never get a respectable client again, and you might even have your license lifted. But there are some cases you can't outrun, cases that follow you around like a sick and needy dog no matter how fast you run from them.

Gussie could feel the case of Darryl Wickers and Marsha St. Claire running right behind her, running so close she could feel its breath on her neck. It gives her the shivers. Marsha gives her the shivers.

The creepy crawlies join the breath on Gussie's neck. The breath grows colder. Gussie tightens the belt on her leather coat.

The neon-lit action on Forty-second Street is still going strong by two-thirty in the morning when Gussie finally finds a phone booth that isn't busted, the phones smashed by junkies or teenage runaways scrounging for change. In the space of two blocks, from Times Square to Eighth Avenue, she'd seen three drug deals: nickel bags of grass to a couple of sandal-footed hippies, glassines of smack to two guys barely able to stand up, and to a mini-skirted woman too jittery to sit down. She saw half a dozen hooker pickups, a pimp in a chrome-encrusted Cadillac pull up to a line of hookers at the curb, and a pair of cops who ignored all of it.

Gussie drops her dime into the phone slot, dials the number for the morgue. It's too soon for the full autopsy report on Darryl Wickers, but her night-shift pal might have some preliminaries.

She asks for Marty Nash and gets right to the point when Nash comes on the line. "Anything you can tell me about the

Darryl Wickers's death? It was murder, yeah?"

"Don't I even get a 'Hello, how are you?'"

"Okay, hello, how are you? How's the family? How's the Wickers case treating you?"

"Don't be such a smart-ass, Gussie. If I didn't want to get under that leather coat of yours so bad, I'd hang up. By the way, there's a new disco opening on Fifty-third. How's about you put on your go-go boots and hit the floor with me this weekend."

"Only if you get me the ME's stuff on Wickers."

Marty's "Uh…" is low in his throat, barely a whisper. "No can do."

"Why not? Who's squelching this, Marty? Is it Sal Barone?"

"Let me know about the weekend, Gussie. You'd look swell in go-go boots." He hangs up.

"Here's a dance you can do, Marty, you spineless piece of crap," Gussie says into the empty air and slams the receiver onto the cradle. "It's called the Drop Dead."

If you want to know what goes on anywhere in Times Square and who's doing it, you talk to a newsie.

Sonia Ortiz's newsstand is in a hot spot, right next to the entrance to the Times Square subway station and in the bright lights of Broadway. She sees who comes, who goes, and who's just hanging around looking for a mark to proposition or rob.

Sonia's selling a guy a girlie magazine when Gussie walks up to the newsstand. "I don't judge," Sonia says when the guy's gone and she sees Gussie. "Guy wants to jerk off lookin' at nudie pics, well, it gets him through his lousy night, y'know? I just take his money and send him on his way. I'm too old and too short to give him any trouble." Sonia's worked this news-stand for forty years, ever since she got off the boat from Puerto Rico. Her English has a juicy music, a combination of San Juan lilt and New York snap.

"Who you kidding, Sonia?" Gussie says. "You're strong as an ox. I've seen you lift bundles of Sunday papers like they're just so many feathers."

Sonia just shrugs her meaty shoulders, made even bulkier by her big wool coat. "So, chica, somethin' tells me you're here to ask me about all that commotion down the block a coupla hours ago, yeah? All them cop cars and everythin'? Wouldn't be one of your cases, would it?"

"You know that junkie I asked you about yesterday? Darryl Wickers? I asked if you'd heard any chatter about where he keeps himself?"

"Yeah, sure, I remember. He get picked up?"

"More like scraped up. He wound up dead in a puddle."

That just gets another shrug from Sonia. "Junkies die. They're good at that."

"But there's something wrong with this one, Sonia. They put that big-time homicide guy, Sal Barone, on this two-bit overdose case and he's got it clamped down tight. Makes me wonder what the NYPD's hiding."

Along with shrug number three, Sonia lights a cigarette. "That's what cops do best. Hide things. And that Lieutenant Barone is real good at it. Most other cops on this beat, sure, they hide the big stuff, but they like to yammer about the little stuff. They like to shoot the shit; y'know, show me pictures of their kids, bitch about their wives, their girlfriends, bitch about the job. But Barone? I wonder if he's even got any family to take pictures of."

"I wouldn't know." And Gussie wonders, too, what with Barone's sourpuss face and attitude, who'd want to make a family with him, anyway? "So, you've heard nothing about Wickers?"

"Nah, nothin' important. The guy was strictly small po-tay-tas. Smack addict and nickel and dime pusher. Why Barone is treatin' this like a state secret beats me. But you never know with cops. One minute they're bustin' the hookers and strippers around here, next minute they're buyin' 'em drinks. Barone, too. I once seen him walkin' outta that Hot Nights Club, though I couldn't tell ya if he was bustin' the girls or fuckin' 'em. Look, I like you, Gussie, and all that, but I gotta make a livin'. You buyin' somethin' or not?"

Gussie takes her wallet from inside her leather coat, peels out a fiver. "A pack of Marlboros."

"You're givin' me a five for a sixty-cent pack of cigarettes? I don't like makin' that much change."

"Keep the change, Sonia. Consider it a tip for your wisdom."

After her dad told her never to get too friendly with cops, the next piece of advice he gave Gussie was, "Amateurs look for clues. Professionals listen for them."

That's why she's walking back through the alley outside the Hot Nights Club. She heard a clue, or at least the possible location of one, in Sonia's chatter about seeing Barone leaving the club. Whatever he's sitting on in the Wickers case, she figures the secret just might be hiding in the pasties and feathers of the Hot Nights Club. The key to that secret might even lurk in the mind of Marsha St. Claire, whether she knows it or not.

It's a few minutes before three a.m., the weeknight closing time for the city's nightspots, when Gussie walks into the club. Backstage, tired strippers saunter into the dressing room, ready to exchange their thongs for panties, their pasties for bras. A few shady looking guys in shady looking flashy clothes hang around. Gussie figures them for pimps, here to pick up any strippers who are part of their crib, ready for middle of the night work. Gussie thinks, *"Jeez, ain't this life tough enough?"*

Inside the dressing room, Marsha's tucking a ribbed purple turtle-neck sweater into her black bell-bottoms, finishing the outfit off with a wide black belt. Seeing Gussie, she says, "So, you have anything new for me? I don't pay without results, Gussie."

"What's Lieutenant Sal Barone's interest in this place?"

"He the cop who's handling Darryl's killing?"

"That's him. I hear he's been a visitor here." The dressing room goes quiet. The other women stop their chatter as they put on their street clothes. No one looks at Gussie.

She says to everyone in the room, "So I'm guessing some of you know Lieutenant Barone. I'm guessing he either roughed you up, hauled you in, or maybe he wanted to play a little footsie. Look, I'm happy to grease palms for what you know, and as one woman to another, I won't spill your secrets. You don't even have to tell me your real names."

Chi Chi LaRue, now in a pink pullover instead of pasties, unpins her piled-high hairstyle, lets the black tresses fall to her shoulders. She says, "And just why do you want to know? What's your nose in this for?"

"Because he's sitting on a murder."

That doesn't even get a gasp from the Hot Nights ladies. Some just shrug their shoulders, some don't react at all. None of them are strangers to the wily ways of cops.

Marsha says, "Now listen, you bitches, she's talking about my ex-husband's murder, I'll have you know. Yeah, that's right, my Darryl's dead. He owed me a bundle, and then the SOB goes and gets himself knocked off. Ain't that just like a man? And now this Barone is hiding it under a rock. So cough up, damn it, and spill what you know about the high and mighty Lieutenant Barone."

The ladies gasp now, though not because of Marsha's rant but because while Marsha rattled on, Chi Chi LaRue quietly got up from her chair, stepped close behind Gussie, grabbed her around her waist and put the needle of a loaded hypo to her neck. "Leave your hands where they are, Miss Nosybody," she tells Gussie. "If I even feel them twitch, I'll pump this needle and fill you full of so much smack you'll sleep the long sleep, the kind where you never wake up. And then I'll take that nice leather coat of yours."

"In front of all these witnesses, Chi Chi?"

A redhead in a striped sweater says, "None of us sees a thing, do we, girls?" The only response from the other women in the dressing room is to turn back to their mirrors, resume getting dressed, combing their hair, fixing their makeup.

Only Marsha starts to get up.

Chi Chi snaps, "Keep your ass in that chair, St. Claire, or your nosy lady friend gets it in the neck."

Every muscle in Gussie's body tightens, every nerve coils, ready to spring if she senses even the smallest chance to make a move. The odds are slim, and any sudden action might get that needle stuck in her neck. She figures her best move is one that keeps Chi Chi talking, keeps her distracted. "What's your play here, Chi Chi? You going to press that plunger, anyway? What's your plan? Walk me out into the alley? Pump me full of smack and push me behind a dumpster for the rats to feast on? They'll die of heroin poisoning, too, y'know, when they swallow my blood. Now why would you want to do that to poor innocent rats?"

Marsha's hands grip tight to the sides of her chair, her eyes go dark with anger. "So, Chi Chi, it was you who gave Darryl the hot shot? What did he ever do to you?"

Marsha's remark causes Chi Chi's body to stiffen along Gussie's back, the woman's breath hot against Gussie's neck. "Hah!" Chi Chi snaps the laugh. "Look who's asking! You know what a two-timing rat he was, Marsha. You divorced him for it. Well, I wasn't married to the guy, so I couldn't divorce him, couldn't get whatever dough he had. I guess you could say I divorced him in my own way. Nobody gets away with double timing Chi Chi LaRue."

"But what's Sal Barone got to do with it?" Gussie says, keeping the talk going, keeping Chi Chi distracted and that needle out of her neck. "Why is he—? Wait a minute, what's Barone to you, Chi Chi? You and he make time between the sheets? He knows you killed Darryl, or at least suspects it, but he's nuts about you? Is that why he's protecting you?"

"Yeah, he's nuts about me all right," Chi Chi says with another wild laugh. "He's been nuts about me ever since we were kids. He's protected me from all sorts of trouble, and when he became a cop, he kept on doing it. After all, isn't that what big brothers are for?"

"So you're a Barone," Marsha says, as if the idea is common as dirt. "I never did believe that LaRue moniker."

"St. Claire ain't exactly on the up-and-up either."

Marsha shrugs, says, "We're two of a kind, Chich. I tell you what. I'm not nuts about the idea that you killed Darryl before I could soak him for more cash. Oh, I know he was dealing, so I know he had the dough. But I also know he was a no-goodnik, so I'm not real sorry he's dead. But I don't want to get on the bad side of a cop, especially a gold shield like Lieutenant Barone. Nobody here wants that, do we ladies?"

Hair-sprayed heads nod, shoulders shrug.

Marsha's on a roll. "So, Chi Chi, whaddya say we just drop this whole bit. Nobody here's gonna turn you in—not that it would do any good, anyway. Your big brother would see to that. But if you kill my friend here, it'll draw the kind of attention none of us wants. Barone might protect you, but the rest of us will get lots of other police eyes on us, know what I mean? So, here's how it's gonna go down—"

"No!" roars out of Gussie as she flings her arm up fast, knocking the hypo from Chi Chi's hand. In one smooth move, Gussie pulls her .38 from inside her coat and puts it against Chi Chi's cheek. "*Here's* how it's going to go down. First of all," she says over her shoulder to the other women, "all of you get the hell out of here. And take your pimps with you."

They waste no time making the big scram.

"You, too, Marsha."

"I don't think so," she says. She's picked up the hypo from the floor. "What were you going to do, Gussie, turn her in? Her cop brother would only bury the case, probably even pin

Darryl's killing on someone else, someone like me. So, if I can't get money from Darryl, I can at least get justice for him. And protect myself." Marsha, grinning, grabs Chi Chi's arm and plunges the needle of the hypo into a vein. "In a few minutes, she'll be just another junkie who OD'd."

"You'll never get away with it, Marsha. I'm a witness. Barone will come after me to spill, and he'll come for you with everything he's got."

Marsha's smile spreads slowly as she watches Chi Chi fall to the floor. "Maybe. But he can't make a case on just your word. In this state, he needs corroboration, and there isn't any. By the way, good job, Gussie. You solved Darryl's murder. Send me your bill." Marsha walks out of the dressing room, her laugh scraping Gussie raw.

It's never dark in Times Square. Even in the pre-dawn hours, when the sky can't make up its mind if it's black or murky gray, the lights of Times Square throw neon colors all over the street and the people on it: the last of the night owls, the bodies sleeping it off on the pavement.

Gussie Diamond, her black leather coat bathed in neon light, her green platform shoes splashed by a puddle, walks away from the Hot Nights Club, away from the dead body no one will care about except her brother, who'll mourn her but will go to his grave who knows how many years from now never having the satisfaction of jailing her killer. It will eat him alive. Gussie knows it because it will eat her alive, too.

A pimpmobile drives by, a big metallic blue Cadillac heavy with chrome. Its windows are down, the radio blasting James Brown's "It's a Man's World."

Gussie thinks, "Not tonight, it wasn't."

AN EYE FOR AN EYE
Stephen D. Rogers

ELIZABETH

Father parted the curtains. "It's your ma."

Leaving my toys behind, I ran to the window and looked down.

A yellow car. Did she get to ride in a taxi?

The driver opened his door and walked around the vehicle. A man wearing a black hat and a green shirt.

He stepped up onto the curb and opened her door.

He motioned her out. Offered a hand.

A woman rose out of the taxi. Stood next to the car, stood in the open door, her golden hair covering her shoulders.

After a minute while I willed her to look up, he touched her arm, and she flinched.

A murmur of voices tickled my ears until a siren in the distance drowned their conversation.

She stepped away from the taxi, and he closed her door. He hurried around the car, opened his door, climbed in, and drove away.

After what felt like forever, the siren growing louder, she crossed the street and disappeared, the glass cold against my cheek.

* * *

On second thought, I transferred the gun to the silver bag before slinging the strap, reinforced by piano wire, over my shoulder. Then I went out into the living room, smiled at the sitter, and leaned into the crib to kiss Susie on the forehead. I spread the blanket over her sleeping form.

As I straightened and turned around, the sitter jumped up off the couch. Teri? Carrie?

"She should sleep until I get back."

"I'll defend her with my life." The teenager's pimples raged as she blushed.

"I'd rather you stay alive long enough to feed her if she wakes screaming. You do know how to warm up the bottle in the refrigerator?"

The sitter nodding vigorously. "If I have any questions, my mom's just down the hall."

"Bring your mother to Susie. Don't bring Susie to your mother. Understand?"

"Yes."

She didn't, and that was okay.

I smiled as I pointed to put her at ease. "There's an extension on the table next to the couch."

JOSEPH

I pulled to the curb on the corner of Washington and Beach, leaned across the passenger seat, and rolled down the window. "How much?"

"Ten dollars."

"Get in." I straightened, looking around to see if anybody was paying attention, but having lost me as a potential customer, everybody quickly lost any interest in me at all.

A smell of cigarettes, cheap perfume, and mouthwash as she bent towards me, slamming the door shut.

"How's Cherry?"

She fluffed her stole. "The Red is always shining."

"Good to know." I rejoined the stream of cars that never stopped flowing through the Combat Zone. "You can kick off your heels if you want. Relax."

"Bare stockings on a floor mat?" She shook her head. "That's wicked unhygienic."

Not bothering to point out the irony, I asked, "Petey treating you all right?"

"He loves me."

I laughed, and a second later, she joined me. "Okay, so he loves I'm still an earner."

"And you don't give him any trouble."

"Not for a long time."

We drove in silence until I parallel parked my Torino deep within Chinatown.

Cherry glanced up at a neon sign. "I sure could use a Bi-Centennial eggroll."

I handed her a ten, knowing I'd never see change.

"Thanks." Just like that, she was gone.

Cherry Red could exit a car faster than anybody I knew. One of the skills you mastered if you wanted to survive, I suppose, and Cherry had been in the life longer than most of the other girls in the Combat Zone had been alive.

She slipped into the car with a wax-paper bag and the twin aromas of Fryolator and cabbage.

I waited while she pried the lid off a plastic cup she balanced on the dashboard, crinkled open the bag, and dipped the eggroll in the duck sauce before crunching off a bite.

Good thing she still had her teeth. Not everybody out there did.

"I'm looking for a girl."

"Who isn't?"

"Fifteen. A runaway. I've talked to her friends, her teachers. Her parents who hired me. Nobody had a clue she was going to bolt."

127

"You think she's tricking?" Cherry dipped and crunched.

"She left behind a little sister who said she caught Kathy looking at a map of Boston. The kid burst through the bedroom door, and Kathy couldn't fold fast enough to hide what she was doing."

"Kathy probably wasn't being abused if she left her little sister in the house."

"My thought exactly. The consensus is Kathy doesn't know a soul in Boston. She never even went on any of the school field trips. That made me wonder if maybe she was being abused by a teacher, but I couldn't uncover any evidence of that."

"And so, you decided she must have come to the big city to realize the dream of selling her ass."

I shrugged. "I've run what leads I have to the ground. How's the eggroll?"

"Hot. The duck sauce helps."

"You could wait until it cools."

"Time is money." She dipped the last of the eggroll and popped it into her mouth.

Recognizing she was finally ready for me, I reached under my seat and came up with an oversized envelope.

Cherry snapped the cover back on the cup and wiped her hands on a small napkin. "What do you got?"

I handed her the envelope, told her to shield her eyes, and flicked on the overhead light. "Some Polaroids and family pictures. I'm afraid I'll have to ask you to fix her in your mind because I've run out of copies."

"That's okay. I left my briefcase at home next to the Jacuzzi." Cherry closely examined the first Polaroid. "I don't remember ever seeing her."

"She probably looks different now."

"Don't they all." Cherry continued going through the pictures, spending longer on some than others, but never stopping until she was done.

"Anything?"

Cherry slid the pictures back into the envelope, which she handed to me. "Sorry."

"Give me a call if you see her?" I handed her a fresh business card.

She tucked it into her bra. "Drop a dime, turn a twenty."

"A twenty Petey knows nothing about."

Cherry shook her head. "I never hold out on Petey."

"That's probably best."

"Speaking of Petey, I need to get back."

I dropped Cherry where I picked her up, glanced over my shoulder to see if it was safe to pull out, and saw someone I recognized.

Liz. Liz Perkins. We worked together once on a sting at the Sheraton Tara in Framingham, right after the hotel opened, formal invitations to an opening ceremony on official letterhead sent only to a hand-picked few.

The client hired six of us from across Massachusetts, a regular private-eye convention.

I made a U-turn and stopped in front of Liz, leaning over to roll down the window. "How much?"

"More than you—" Her expression changed.

Liz opened the door and jumped in.

ELIZABETH

Joe looked like shit. Deciding to give him the benefit of the doubt, I asked, "How you been?"

"Burning the candle at both ends, trying to keep up with inflation." A quick glance. "Inflation. That why you're tricking?"

I laughed. "Oddly enough, I'm working for an owner of one of the strip clubs. The dick and duck has been scaring off some of the suburban crowd, cutting into his profits."

"Dick and duck sounds like something you'd order in China-town, and I should know because I just came from there."

"There's girls working the Zone, not whores. They lean into the vehicle, grab the guy's dick, snatch his wallet, and duck into a bar with a bouncer outside. The bouncer stops the guy to collect the cover charge. She slips out the back."

Joe nodded. "Dick and duck."

"I'm trying to identify the members of the ring, after which the owner will pass the information on to the cops, or at least the cops who will do something about it."

"Groin and gone. Maul it and wallet."

I ignored his stab at poetry. "What are you doing cruising the Zone, the price of gas being what it is?"

"Dip and rip."

"What the girls are doing already has a name."

"Mash and cash."

"You sure it's a candle you're burning at both ends?"

Joe smiled. "Sorry. I've taken on a case or three too many. Anyway, why I'm here, I'm looking for a runaway. Maybe you can help."

"How young do I have to appear to be to fool your client into thinking you found her?"

"Her parents probably know her too well, Liz."

"I'm not exactly a master of disguise, but I'm good enough to fool them here."

"How's this strike you? I'll give you half my hourly rate to keep an eye out for my girl while you're already keeping an eye out for yours."

"I assume you have pictures."

He reached under his seat and handed me an envelope. "She was last seen studying a map of Boston."

"The Zone is just one tiny part of the city. That's the whole idea. Confine the adult entertainment to a small area. What's to say she's not elsewhere in Beantown?"

"Her mother said Kathy recently asked about the Combat

Zone. A fifteen-year-old kid from the suburbs, more than an hour from the city."

"Did the mother ask what prompted the question?"

"Kathy said it was just something she overheard. With a teenager, the interaction might mean nothing, or it might mean something."

"It might mean everything."

"Which is why I'm hiring you to add another set of eyes. A fifteen-year-old? This place will swallow her whole."

I opened the envelope and shuffled through the pictures. "She doesn't look familiar, but that doesn't mean I won't see her ten minutes after you drop me off."

"If we're lucky, she's staying with a boyfriend the parents don't know about. If we're not, the clock is ticking."

"You said Kathy."

Joe nodded. "Kathy Harper. Short for Katherine."

"She have any other nicknames?"

"The mother said not that she knew about."

"You keep mentioning the mother."

"Sandy. I talk with her more than the father, but only because he's a short-haul truck driver, and he gets home late."

"On purpose?"

Joe shrugged. "They both met with me that first time. Tom, that's his name, he brought up the subject of the retainer himself, wrote me a check without bothering to negotiate."

"You see those as good omens?"

"Sometimes he's there when I visit, mostly not. He says it's not a problem. He doesn't have anything useful to add to what his wife knows, how little he sees of his girl."

"How little he probably sees of his wife. Sandy have a boyfriend?"

"Not that I could find."

So, Joe had checked the possibility someone close might have snatched Kathy. "What about uncles?"

"Two on mom's side, and two on dad's. All of them out of

state, and none of them sounded dodgy on the phone."

"Better than the alternative."

"Exactly. Three of them have never even met the girls. The uncles, all the relatives for that matter, are just people who send the girls cards containing money."

"You've been thorough."

"I've worked this case seven ways since Sunday, Liz, and now I'm of the belief the Combat Zone is our last remaining chance to locate the missing girl."

"When this den of iniquity is your best hope, you know you're in trouble."

Joe sighed as he pulled to the curb. "Roger that."

I joined the girls on the sidewalk, thinking Joe needed to get some sleep before he made a deadly mistake. Looking for a runaway in the Zone wasn't the same as looking for one in New Hampshire.

Kathy wouldn't be sighted sitting at a picnic table smoking with her boyfriend, the girl wearing a cut-off T-shirt advertising Hampton Beach, the boyfriend slipping her sips of beer from a souvenir cup.

If Kathy were here, and if she could pass as older, she'd be plainly visible trying to entice customers. If she looked her age, she was probably handcuffed to a bedframe somewhere.

One thing Joe hadn't mentioned was how long the girl had been missing.

A pimp would have her standing out here within a day of her arrival. If she'd left home more than forty-eight hours ago, she would never be found.

JOSEPH

I took the Natick exit off the Mass Pike, followed 30 until it merged with 9, and then banged a right at Trolley Square to head north into Sudbury.

While I hadn't promised a daily update to Kathy's parents, they'd also acted as though I would leave their house, check in hand, and return with their daughter that evening.

I figured the least I could do was provide the personal touch, remind them not to give up hope.

Two more people were now looking for Kathy, at no additional cost to my clients. That was good news, right?

That I'd found her would be better, but being able to report additional eyes beat reciting all the leads I'd followed, only to turn back empty-handed.

Maybe it wasn't them I was trying to reassure.

Maybe it was me.

Today being Sunday, they were both home, Kathy's little sister at a friend's, and I described all the avenues I'd pursued since the last time I made a report, ending on a positive note.

"So that's two more people looking for Kathy in Boston."

Tom frowned. "Why would my little girl be in Boston?" As usual, he'd remained standing my entire visit, as if a show of force could keep away bad news.

I splayed my arms. "In my experience, runaways do one of three things. They follow the lead of the person they're with; as far as we can tell, your daughter left alone. They head for a distant friend or family members; I've checked every possibility, unless you're haven't told me about an estranged branch of the family."

I paused until they both shook their heads. "Finally, they head to the excitement of the big city, a place they can easily hide."

"Kathy never liked the city."

"Kids change."

Tom shook his head. "When she was younger, I would

sometimes ask if she wanted to go to work with Daddy. Before she let herself become excited, she always asked first if I was going into a city. It didn't even matter which one: Boston, Worcester, Providence. She would never come along on those trips."

Sandy nodded, her eyes red. "Kathy is a homebody."

"I understand, Mr. and Mrs. Harper." I shifted on the couch, the cover crinkling. "What do the police say?"

Tom sniffed. "If I had any faith in the police, I wouldn't have hired you."

"Still, they have resources."

Sandy smiled. "They're searching for her."

Tom waved, exasperated. "They've notified whoever it is they notify. Kathy's description is posted to the daily log. She's staying with a classmate and will be home when she realizes she doesn't have it so bad."

"Is that a direct quote?"

He hung his head. "They see this all that time. That's what they say."

"It's true it's possible she's sleeping in a friend's brother's treehouse. That today or tomorrow she'll show up on your front stoop. Unfortunately, I don't think we can count on that happening."

"I already hired you once." He grinned through the pain.

I turned to Sandy. "I'm sorry, but could I trouble you for a cup of coffee?"

She shot up out of the rocking chair, her hands automatically smoothing her skirt. "Of course. Cream and sugar?"

"Just sugar, thanks. I've still got a lot of calls to make before I can finally crash tonight."

As soon as Sandy left the room, I motioned Tom closer, lowering my voice. "There's another possibility we haven't talked about yet."

"What's that?"

"You're a short-haul truck driver."

"That's right."

"Have any loads recently gone missing, been hijacked?"

"What are you inferring?" He cupped his fingers to touch his chest. "Are you suggesting this is my fault?"

I raised my hands. "I'm just asking if your daughter could have been snatched as a hostage, someone holding her until their goods were returned."

"I'm not a crook."

"Second possibility. You could have been loading, or unloading, and seen something that has someone nervous. They might want to make sure you don't talk."

He stepped forward. "If I thought my daughter was in physical danger, don't you think I would have told you that?"

"I would hope so, and I would also understand if you didn't, because so many clients leave things out. Partly self-protection, partly denial."

"My delivery record is impeccable." He took a moment and calmed himself. "Yes, there are drivers whose loads come in a little light, who are robbed at gunpoint by assailants who can only be vaguely described, but I'm not one of them. I'm not a crook."

"In that case, I don't have to waste time pursuing those avenues."

"No, you don't."

"Of course, there's still that second possibility. You don't have to be doing anything wrong to witness something."

"I didn't."

"Are you sure? Maybe you saw something but didn't realize the significance at the time. Maybe now, in retrospect..."

"There's been nothing like that. I mean, I once saw a guy get the piss kicked out of him in a back alley, but that was ten, twelve years ago. Kathy would have been three." His expression hardened. "Before you ask, she wasn't in my truck that run. This isn't my fault."

I nodded as the smell of fresh coffee wafted into the room.

"What about Kathy's little sister?"

"Sandy told you. She's at a friend's house. We're trying to keep her distracted from what's happening."

Go to a friend's. Forget your older sister has disappeared. "Has Kathy been in touch with her?"

"She says not."

I paused. "You've made it clear you don't think much of what the police are doing. Have they told you any specifics?"

He glanced at the doorway to the kitchen before answering. "They checked the hospitals. They checked the morgue."

ELIZABETH

I'd talked to about a third of the girls, small snatches of conversation between cars pulling to the curb. Johns didn't like when we congregated. I think it made them nervous.

Nobody had seen my "niece." Nobody had heard anything about a new girl that young. There was Princess, but that was last month, and she'd already died of an overdose.

Or maybe it was the month before that. And she might not have been fifteen. But she was definitely dead.

Satisfied I'd fulfilled my obligation to Joe, that I'd hear if Kathy was sighted, I returned to my own case.

While a fifteen-year-old with Kathy's description would stand out, I couldn't even come up with a count for the dick-and-duck ring. Every sighting had produced a different description. There could have been dozens of women involved, or only one with a wardrobe and collection of wigs.

The only words I hadn't heard were "black," "Hispanic," or "Asian." So, one white girl or a trove of them.

Assuming the Johns were clear-headed enough to be credible witnesses.

Furthermore, the attacks took place randomly, often with days between them, any time between noon and midnight.

I couldn't even be sure those responsible weren't also street-walkers, maybe ripping off Johns when sex-for-money lost some of its appeal.

Perhaps I should have turned around and hired Joe.

Of course, if I was going to use him as bait, I had to know how the dick-and-duck ring picked their targets. My client hadn't told me if there were any similarities to the men robbed, and neither had any of the girls to whom I'd mentioned the situation.

If the never-ending stream of whores made them anonymous, they were less invisible than the never-ending stream of Johns they serviced.

I let myself into my apartment to find the babysitter asleep in front of the image of a waving flag. Debbie. I was fairly sure this one's name was Debbie.

After locking my gun in my bedroom safe and checking on Susie, I returned to the living room and touched Debbie's shoulder.

She jumped and immediately apologized.

"There's no need to apologize. You don't think I'd be asleep if you weren't here."

"Thank you, Miss Perkins. It will never happen again."

"Did the baby give you any trouble?"

Debbie visibly relaxed. "No, she was an angel. She only woke twice. I changed her diapers, fed her, and played a little peekaboo."

"She loves that game."

"Do you still need me tomorrow?"

I counted out her money. "If you're still available."

"Thank you, yes. I'm saving up for a bike."

"It's never too early to learn how to start managing money." The last one had been saving up for her wedding. Didn't even have a boyfriend yet.

Debbie covered a yawn. "Have a good night, Miss Perkins."

"You too, Debbie."

The sitter frowned. "Dani."

"Yes, sorry, that's what I meant, Dani." I leaned forward and whispered, "It was a very long shift. I'll probably be asleep by the time you get to the elevator."

I walked Dani to the door, locked it behind her, and slid the deadbolt into place.

I'd checked with my client before leaving the Zone, and he confirmed my understanding that the ring hadn't struck today. That made four days since the last attack, three days since he hired me.

Even if I hadn't managed to identify the members of the ring, maybe I was doing that one better by serving as a lucky charm.

I went into the bathroom to remove my makeup.

Then again, maybe not so lucky. Maybe of the ring members recognized me, and thus they were lying low until I went away, which wouldn't be much longer if the drought continued.

After all, why would my client keep paying me to stop crimes that weren't occurring?

JOSEPH

I shouldn't have had that second cup of coffee when I was with the Harpers, even if Sandy did make a mean cup of java. After getting home, I'd read every local newspaper I'd picked up while driving around, and now I watched the minute hand tick towards dawn.

My brain wouldn't let me sleep.

It also wouldn't let me think. Or to capture the experience more accurately, it wouldn't allow me to keep my thoughts in any semblance of order.

I would remember a snatch of conversation, attribute it to Tom Harper, and then realize the information came from somebody else regarding some other case.

Current cases. Old cases. Cold cases.

I jittered from interview to interview, bounced from couch to kitchen to office to bar. My car, the traveling office. Route 20. Route 9. Sixteen and one twenty-six. The Pike. A thousand back roads.

Cruising the Combat Zone. Sighting Cherry. Sighting Liz. Hiring both, the prostitute and the detective.

Dick and duck. Biscuit and gravy. Sleazy in the CZ.

Religious paintings.

The Harper residence?

No, the paintings hung in the office of my client who managed Shrewsbury Savings and Loan.

He thought one of the tellers was stealing, but he didn't know which one, or how. "Keep your investigation quiet. We don't want to make the depositors skittish."

Nobody should know how fragile things were. Nobody should know, no matter how we pretended otherwise, that we were all only human. That innocence was merely the absence of awareness, the waiting for the flaws to emerge.

Kathy, asking about the Combat Zone.

How did she even know such a place existed?

Why would she care?

I must have slept because I woke, my mouth dry, my lips splitting as I yawned. Perhaps I would have been better off not sleeping a wink, but then how would I have known it was a new day?

After going to the bathroom, I wandered into the kitchen and snapped on the small black-and-white that sat on the counter. Watched the network news show people beating on each other while I ate dry cereal with my fingers.

A new day indeed.

* * *

ELIZABETH

It was a cold, gray afternoon to stand on a cold, gray sidewalk.

The evocative costumes, which seemed flashy at night, polished to a sheen by neon, now appeared tawdry, the girls clutching at the jean jackets and the fake furs as a sharp wind sliced through the city streets.

I could only imagine how the girls must fare during the bleak midwinter, their shoulders hunched against the sleet, their heels cracked by salted slush, their heavy makeup the only thing protecting them from the elements.

Those images in my head, my gaze fell on a woman whose costume looked like a costume on her, just before she approached an idling car.

I broke the rules when I sidled closer.

She leaned on the edge of the door. Reached inside. Leapt back and bolted.

She broke for a strip club, and I set off in pursuit.

As the bouncer looked away, she slowed to open the door, and I tackled her at the waist, bringing her down in a fury of pink feather boa.

I wrapped her hands behind her back with my reinforced purse strap. Drove my elbow up into the crotch of the bouncer trying to pull me up off her.

Hissed in her ear before whistling for the cop I saw smoking on the corner.

Maybe I could have settled for simply making a note of her description if it weren't such a cold, gray day.

If Susie, bouncing in the babysitter's arms, hadn't seen me slipping out of the apartment and screamed.

JOSEPH

Looking for Cherry, I spotted Liz and pulled to the curb.

She sauntered over and climbed in. "You want to party?"

"I'd rather take a nap."

"Maybe I can help you with that."

I chuckled. "You've been undercover too long. Any sight of Kathy?"

"No, but I caught one of the dick-and-duck ring. Maybe the whole operation. It's not like the cops are updating me on their investigation."

"Congratulations." I pulled out into traffic.

"My client still wants me out there. Now that the girls know who I am, he says it sends a message he's looking out for their best interests."

"In other words, it's good for business."

"And I'm cheaper than what he was losing." Liz paused. "I had a thought earlier."

"Thoughts are good. Unless they keep you up at night."

"Is that why you look more like shit than usual?"

"At least I'm improving. You had a thought?"

"Do you know if Kathy babysat?"

"For her little sister and the family next door. Why do you ask?"

"The money adds up at an age when bills don't exist. Could seem like a fortune for a teen."

"Her relatives sent her money. Birthdays. Christmas."

"Watching for Kathy, watching for the dick-and-duck ring, I wondered if Kathy was watching."

"Watching what?"

"Watching the street. Maybe the reason we haven't seen her is she's hiding behind a window."

I dipped my head to look up at the apartment buildings we were passing. "Why would she be doing that?"

"You said the mother told you Kathy asked about the Combat Zone. Maybe she asked at home because she heard it at home."

Joe grunted. "Sleazy in the CZ. Mom accuses Dad of maybe

not turning around as soon as his truck is unloaded in Boston."

"Kathy overhears."

I shuffled the pieces into place. "Kathy decides to investigate. She gathers her money and rides the train inbound from Framingham. But, hating the city, scared of the city, she doesn't venture from the room she rents. Which is why no one here reports seeing her."

"Instead, she waits."

"Watching."

"Watching for her father's vehicle. Not wanting to see it, because that would make him wrong. But also wanting to see it because that makes her mother right. Either way, Kathy loses."

"The theory makes sense, Liz. Nicely done." I chuckled. "First you took down the dick-and-duck ring, and now this. You've had quite the red-letter day. Kudos to me for hiring you."

"Did you interview landlords?"

"The thought never crossed my mind, because why would I need to? If Kathy were here, she would want to be seen. That's how the girls get clients. That's why they're called streetwalkers."

"But Kathy wasn't a streetwalker."

"My mistake, jumping to that conclusion. I didn't once consider the possibility she was using the Combat Zone as a surveillance blind."

Liz shrugged. "It's not the usual story, the missing kid searching for a parent. You can beat yourself up after we find her."

I smiled. "Or not."

"As you wish." Liz pointed. "There are the apartment buildings. The rooms for rent. We could split the list."

"A fifteen-year-old with a pair of binoculars. How many tenants can there be who match that description?"

ELIZABETH

We located Kathy that very day, probably within the hour, renting a room above an adult bookstore.

I think she was relieved when we told her it was over, and she was young enough to believe the lie.

Joseph called her parents and drove her home.

Mailed me a check.

My own mother only returned once for some faded family portraits and a high school yearbook, mementos of a time before I was born.

Father pried me from her leg, the blue silk pantsuit slipping through my fingers, the fabric cold.

Spotted with my tears.

AN EVENING AT THE OPERA HOUSE
James A. Hearn

July 23, 1977. Fort Worth, Texas

"Fifty across, seven letters. Extreme lassitude, first letter M."
Harvey Lisch sat in his Chevrolet Impala, windows rolled
down, and battled *The New York Times* crossword. He tapped
the tip of his pen against a scruffy cheek, forgetting once again
the cap was off. The ink, now damp from sweat, left a smudge
below his right dimple as a dark bead inched toward the wattle
of his neck.

The forecast called for another cloudless day, and the Texas
sun was baking Harvey inside the sedan like an overcooked
turkey. When today's stakeout was over, he suspected firemen
would need the Jaws of Life to extract his posterior from the
vinyl seat.

Just feed me to Jaws and get it over with, Harvey thought. *At
least I'd have a nice, cooling swim before dying.* He bit into a
sloppy Big Mac, somehow cold in his oven of a car, and looked
up the street to the house. He'd parked well away from the
target, in front of a dilapidated residence with a FOR SALE
sign. No neighborhood busybodies bothered him, probably
because any sane person was inside with the air conditioning on
full blast.

Harvey had been on this stakeout for five days, but it felt
more like fifty. His forty-year-old back ached from sitting too

many hours in the car, and his normally immaculate midnight blue suit (once worn by Frank Sinatra himself, or so the tailor back in New York had claimed) was a rumpled travesty.

When Harvey adjusted the visor to block the sun, a creased photograph fell in his lap. He put down the newspaper and picked it up. In front of his childhood home, he and his older brother played Flash Gordon in a cardboard box painted like a spaceship. Stanley always played Flash, of course, forcing Harvey into the dual roles of Dr. Zarkov and Ming the Merciless, while Betty the Border Collie played Dale Arden.

Brother, you're a real mess. Stanley's voice rang clearly in Harvey's mind, though his brother had been dead for twenty years. "Mess" was the catch-all term Stanley used to describe any suboptimal condition regardless of severity. *My Cheerios are a soggy mess, can I eat yours?* And: *I have the cancer like Dad, aren't I a mess?*

Stanley had the mind of a child and couldn't read or write, and many people had a difficult time understanding him, even Mom. But not Harvey; he perfectly followed the meandering pathways of Stanley's mind. His brother wasn't "the poor idiot" (the charitable term used by the neighborhood matrons) or "the retard" (the pejorative that merited a punch in the nose, no matter how big the bully). Stanley was just Stanley, all the way to the end.

Harvey wiped special sauce from his walrus mustache and remembered the disapproving tug of his brother's fingers on the whiskers. When they were older, Stanley teased him about the mustache, calling it a "fat, hairy caterpillar" and always wiggling away from Harvey's hugs. Except the day he passed away, when he'd been too sick to move, but not to say I love you.

Harvey kissed the photo and tucked it into a pocket, wondering what'd become of the family photo albums he'd been forced to abandon when fleeing New York. Probably thrown out by his landlord and rotting in a New Jersey landfill with Jimmy Hoffa for company.

Speaking of smells, his fleabag motel on the south side of Fort Worth had no running water. For the past four nights, after a fruitless day watching the house, Harvey would slink back to the inappropriately named Traveler's Delight, eat a fast-food dinner, read *The Times*, and watch Johnny and Ed yuck it up on *The Tonight Show* until he fell asleep in a sweat-drenched bed.

"Eight down, six letters. Paul Terry's blank mouse." Taking up his pen, he scratched in *mighty* and thought, *Oh, how the mighty have fallen.* Harold Lipper, once Wall Street's favorite private detective and the toast of the Upper East Side, had escaped his beloved New York with only the clothes on his back, a mere hop, skip, and a jump ahead of the SEC and their overzealous investigators.

Insider trading, they'd called it. As if what he'd done was any different than what happened in every corporate boardroom across America. But if the common man dipped his beak for a taste of the good life, the powers-that-be mobilized the National Guard.

Now Harold Lipper was in hiding among heathens as Harvey Lisch in the purgatory called Texas. Houston, the base of operations for The Lisch Detective Agency, had a decent symphony and a few museums, but these rednecks were more interested in football than the finer things, and the local opera house wasn't a patch on The Met. Houston aspired to be a great city, but where was the art and the music? Where was The Culture?

And where was the cowboy in the cherry-red El Camino with stolen plates?

Harvey's eyes flicked to the house up the street. The brick ranch-style rental with pecan trees was an unlikely place to harbor any criminal element; in fact, the quiet neighborhood of middle-income homes was the definition of wholesome suburbia. What would the honest, hard-working residents say if he told them 917 Garden View Drive was a drop house?

The burly cowboy with the El Camino and his blond girlfriend—Harvey didn't know their names, so he called them Buster and Kitty—usually came once a month with their Samsonite luggage and stayed for a few days before dashing off to the next city and the next drop. As for what they carried in those black suitcases, he didn't particularly want to know. Plausible deniability was good, but outright ignorance was bliss if the police got nosey. Harvey had learned this lesson the hard way, as he had another guiding principle: the richer the client, the worse the case.

Millionaire Elmer Gaddis was living proof of that. Harvey's current client was a self-described "man of business," like a long-lost offshoot from the mythical Corleone Family who, instead of disembarking at Ellis Island, had ended up in Houston. And like the Corleones, Elmer fiercely protected his territory from interlopers.

"Harvey, I want photographs of the impudent scum making drops on my turf," Gaddis had instructed.

"Certainly, Mr. Gaddis."

"Clear ones, mind you. Let it not be said Elmer Gaddis ever punished the wrong parties." Elmer had the unfortunate habit of referring to himself in the third person. Harvey would've found the affectation comical had the businessman not been so deadly serious about, well, *everything*.

Back in New York, Harvey would've refused any work from a client like Gaddis. It was exactly the kind of blue-collar investigation he detested; stakeouts, cheap motels, bad food, and trailing disreputable characters for unsavory clients whose only redeeming quality was their money.

But beggars couldn't be choosers. Gaddis's tedious assignment had carried Harvey all over Texas, and he'd photographed over a dozen persons, except for the elusive Buster and Kitty. He felt no remorse over the fates of these strangers; they were career criminals who reaped what they sowed.

Buster and Kitty were young, though, and in these hard

times, even people with the best of intentions might find themselves on the wrong side of the law. Did they deserve to die because of Elmer Gaddis's greed?

Harvey shook these thoughts from his mind. So, what if criminals came to a bad end? He was snapping a camera shutter, not pulling a trigger. His face grim, he checked the telephoto lens on his Pentax K2, then placed the camera on the passenger's seat amid wadded-up hamburger wrappers and dirty napkins. The K2 had almost caught the cowboy and his girl in Waco, but a trip to the Fotomat revealed only overexposed prints from a melted roll of film.

Some people were born lucky, Harvey supposed. He glanced over the crossword, returning to fifty across: seven letters, extreme lassitude, first letter M. He knew this word, but his brain couldn't function in this infernal heat, and tomorrow's forecast promised more of the same.

More of the same. More Big Macs when he should be dining on filet mignon. More watered-down domestic beers when he needed a cooling Pavillon Blanc du Chateau Margaux, more Willie Nelson when Wagner soothed his soul. What Harvey really needed was the Opera; what he got was the Grand Ole Opry.

With a defeated groan, the private detective folded the sports section of his newspaper into a funnel, glanced around to be sure he was alone, and proceeded to relieve himself into a moldy milk jug. He knew he shouldn't have ordered the large Coke, but then what did it matter if his blood pressure was skyrocketing? He was in hell, and the rest of the country was doing its best to catch up with him. The peanut-farmer-turned-President, while a nice gentleman, seemed powerless to stop the nation's descent into the maelstrom.

The headlines Harvey consumed daily were all depressing— the war was over, thank God, but new problems sprang up like weeds in the garden of humanity—runaway inflation, gasoline shortages, high unemployment, and an endless parade of political scandals. It left Harvey with the feeling there was something *fundamentally wrong* with America, a nagging sense of...fifty across.

"Gotcha," Harvey said. A jogger, in defiance of the heat-wave, eyed him askance as she passed his open window. He called out, "I'm not a masher," but she only quickened her pace. *Oh well.* With a self-satisfied grin, he picked up his pen and wrote *malaise* into fifty across.

Up the street, a shimmering mirage of candied cherries re-solved into the long-awaited El Camino, its throaty engine growling beneath a hood scoop. Harvey, about to pour out the milk jug, almost dropped it as he reached for the Pentax.

Everything's fine, Buster. A crazy coed is out jogging, the Rain Trains are watering the lawns, and your cozy rental is ready and waiting for you and Kitty.

But to Harvey's dismay, the El Camino didn't turn into the driveway, nor did it stop at the curb. Like the world's slowest bullet, it was coming toward his Impala with a deliberate speed that made him nervous.

The worst thing would be to panic. Harvey set down the Pentax, covered it with the newspaper, and started the engine. *No, I haven't been sitting here all day. Even though it's hotter than Hades, I'm going for a drive.* He placed his hands on the steering wheel and kept them there, though it burned his palms.

Behind the wheel of the El Camino, Buster's expression was murderous. Kitty, in the passenger's seat, was giving him an earful. Were they having a lovers' spat, or was she vexed about something else?

The El Camino passed without incident, and Harvey relaxed. They'd seen him; that was certain. But had he registered as a threat? As anything?

It's better to be safe than sorry. Harvey put the car in drive and pulled away from the curb. He'd come back tomorrow in a rental car, snap his photo when they went out for the day, and be done. He was passing the drop house when the El Camino reappeared up the block. They were coming back, but why hadn't they stopped before?

Harvey had about eight seconds before they passed him again, but it would be enough. He eased up on the accelerator, let go of the steering wheel, and snatched up his Pentax.

The shutter snapped twice, once for Buster and once for Kitty. *It's time to go home to a hot bath, a bottle of chilled rosé, and Wagner's* Tristan und Isolde *on the gramophone.* He concealed the Pentax beneath the newspapers and returned his hands to the wheel, all smiles beneath his walrus mustache.

But Harvey's hackles rose when he noticed the El Camino's windows were rolled down instead of up. Either Kitty's yammering had increased to an uncomfortable volume, or Buster was going to pull a gun and start blasting. Harvey, betting on the latter, was prepared to duck and hit the accelerator for a hasty getaway.

Instead of gunplay, Buster chose a different tack as the El Camino swerved in front of Harvey and braked hard. Harvey slammed his brakes and felt the seatbelt bite across his waist, their bumpers coming to rest mere inches apart.

The other vehicle's doors sprang open, and both Buster and Kitty marched toward the Impala. Though they carried no guns openly, it was clear they were armed; beneath Buster's denim jacket was a noticeable bulge, and Kitty's right hand was in her leopard-spotted purse. The cowboy took up a position by Harvey, while the woman stared at him from the passenger side with languid blue eyes.

"What's the problem, friends?" Harvey called.

Buster leaned down, his hands on the hips of his faded jeans, a huge belt buckle flashing in the sun. With his Clint Eastwood squint and protruding chin, his facial expression came to a point somewhere beyond the tip of his pinched nose.

"The problem, amigo, is you. I've seen you before." Buster tipped up his cowboy hat for a better look, the squint increasing. "Austin, maybe."

"Waco," Kitty said from the other side. "I've seen this car in Waco."

"I've never been there," Harvey said affably. "As for my Impala, Chevrolet has sold a million of them. If you'll kindly move, I'll be on my way."

Buster was staring at something on Harvey's face. The cowboy pointed to his own cheek and said, "You've got a little something-something right there."

Harvey touched his left cheek. "What? Here?"

"No, the other side."

Harvey stroked out his mustache, wondering if there was more special sauce from his Big Mac stuck there.

"Not in your soup-strainer," Buster said in irritation. "Oh, forget it. Rose, what's inside the car? All I see is a jug of lemonade."

"A bunch of fast-food wrappers and a crumpled newspaper with a crossword puzzle," answered the girl. "Guy's more of a slob than you."

Thank God. "Mistaken identity," Harvey said. "I have one of those faces."

Buster's smirk revealed the stains of chewing tobacco. "If by one of those faces, you mean ugly, I agree. And you've got a raging case of BO to boot."

"Could be one of those, whatchacallits?" Rose said.

"A coincidence?" Harvey offered.

"Right. A coincidence. Look at him, Parker; he's a harmless little fellow."

Parker and Rose, not Buster and Kitty. Harvey filed the information away.

"Move along, Mr. Crossword," Parker sneered. "And if I see you again—" He left the rest unsaid.

You won't, since I have my photos. Harvey muttered something obsequious in reply, thinking he'd escaped the encounter unscathed, when Rose's voice cut across his nerves like a knife.

"Parker, he's got a huge camera. We've been made."

The cowboy whirled, his hand reaching underneath his jacket. Harvey didn't see what they did next, as he was too busy throwing the car into reverse. The Impala raced backward, swerved 180 degrees at an intersection, and righted itself in one smooth maneuver that would've made Gene Hackman in *The French Connection* proud. Behind him, he heard the roar of the El Camino and the screech of tires.

If Harvey couldn't outrun Parker's souped-up car, he'd grab his film and ditch the Impala in a densely populated area. Some place like a shopping mall would do the trick, anywhere with a large crowd. Pulling into a police station was the final option, to be exercised only at extreme need. His new credentials were flawless, produced by the best of the best, but nothing good ever happened at a police station.

Harvey turned onto a busy street named University Drive and headed north, toward what looked like an entertainment district of medium-sized businesses. The Impala slipped among the rush of cars and sped onward, the El Camino trailing behind.

For the next hour, Harvey played cat-and-mouse with Parker through the streets of Fort Worth. It seemed no amount of chicanery could shake the cowboy, and the Impala's steadily falling gas gauge mirrored Harvey's hopes for escape. When the needle dipped below E, he decided to try something desperate. At a busy intersection, he spun the wheel hard and reversed directions, swerving into a narrow gap in the oncoming traffic. Horns blared and drivers shook their fists, but he ignored them.

Heading in the opposite direction, Harvey whizzed past the El Camino and blew a kiss to Parker and Rose as he passed them. A few streets later, he pulled into a parking lot jam-packed with vehicles. The sputtering Impala coasted into a space between two massive trucks, hopefully hidden from the street, where the engine died.

Harvey released his white-knuckled grip on the steering

wheel. What he needed was to find a crowd and find it fast. He snapped the Pentax's shutter and advanced the film until the roll could be safely removed without exposing it. The task completed, he pocketed the film and went around to the trunk. He stowed his camera equipment inside, took out his emergency duffel bag, and headed for the nearest building to change clothes and lie low until nightfall.

Harvey found himself walking toward what appeared to be an old Southern mansion with a long balcony supported by white columns. In front of this odd structure was a made-to-order crowd in a line so long it wrapped around the mansion twice. People of every age and every description, rich and poor, young and old, queued up for something called The Village Opera House.

Harvey's heart leapt within his breast. An opera here, among the pagans? What performer might inspire such a crowd? *Great God, it must be Janet Baker.* Well, whoever it might be, he'd apparently found an oasis in the desert, the balm he'd been dreaming of to ease his troubled mind.

As he neared the entrance, wondering how he might bypass the line, the doors of the Opera House burst open. Happy crowds spilled out, their eyes dazzled by the afternoon sun, their expressions—what? Joyful? Jubilant? Harvey settled on beatific and was convinced he'd finally hear Janet Baker in the flesh.

In the confusion of milling bodies, Harvey slipped into the Opera House without paying for a ticket. Once inside, a wave of blessed air conditioning washed over him. The duffel bag slipped from his grasp, his body swaying with relief and pleasure. The crowds flowed around him, giving the disheveled Harvey a wide berth.

"Are you okay, sir?"

To Harvey's left was a middle-aged woman with thick glass-es, which seemed to magnify the impish spark of her green eyes. She wore medical scrubs and had a pager clipped to her waist. A surgeon, perhaps?

A dark-haired teenaged boy stood beside the woman. Like her, he wore thick glasses above the same button-nose. There was a Polaroid camera around his neck, and he had a long broom handle, minus the bristles and painted bright blue, tucked into his belt like a sword.

"I'm perfectly fine, madam," Harvey replied.

"I'm a doctor," she said, as though this statement meant he could trust her implicitly. Her gaze kept darting to Harvey's right cheek. "You looked like you might fall down."

The boy crinkled his nose. "He stinks, Mom."

In the boy's face and stature, Harvey recognized the telltale features of Down's syndrome, and the private detective felt a sudden swell of empathy despite the boy's comment. But for the glasses, here was Stanley in miniature, with a camera and broomstick.

The woman's face paled at her son's words. "That was very rude of you, Dennis."

Harvey laughed for the first time in days. "It's also very true. Your heatwave caught me unawares, I'm afraid. I'm Harvey Lisch."

Now why had he said that? He had aliases upon aliases when working in strange cities, and yet in an unguarded moment, he'd spoken his real name—at least, the name he'd adopted after discarding Harold Gordon "H.G." Lipper.

The woman smiled. "Diane Sanders. This is Dennis."

"Hello," Dennis said. He held up his Polaroid and snapped a photo of Harvey.

"Please excuse my son," Diane said. "Dennis, we don't take pictures of strangers without asking permission."

Harvey blinked away the purple spot dancing in his vision. "We're no longer strangers, Dr. Sanders."

Diane cleared her throat and said, "Please, not on my day off. Call me Diane."

"Diane, the pleasure was mine. And you may call me Harvey, should we meet again."

James A. Hearn

"Harvey," Diane repeated sheepishly.

"And you can call me Dennis," the boy said. "Here's a gift for your birthday, Harvey." The boy handed the private detective the Polaroid before saying goodbye and melting into the crowd with his mother.

Harvey felt deeply touched by the gesture. Stanley was always doing goofy things like that, things to cheer him up. And when was the last time anyone but Stanley had given him a gift? Harvey honestly couldn't remember.

"Oh my God," Harvey said as he looked at his ink-stained face in the photo. That blasted pen again! Diane had noticed but had the good manners not to comment.

With a sigh, Harvey pocketed the photo and looked around to get his bearings. He was in a lobby, but this wasn't like any opera house he'd ever visited. Behind a glass counter, teenagers sold popcorn, candy, and soft drinks to the crowd. This wasn't an opera house at all, he realized, but a one-screen movie theater.

False advertising strikes again. Well, whatever was playing, it had to be better than hiding in his Impala in triple-digit heat. Harvey picked up his duffel bag, found a bathroom, and went into a stall to change his clothes. He exchanged his sweaty suit for a Hawaiian shirt, khaki shorts, and sandals.

At the bathroom mirror, he washed the smudge from his face and took a long, hard look at himself. *Stanley, you've never been more right; I'm a real mess, all the way around. I'm a selfish, greedy snob.* Stanley had lived his short life caring about others; since his brother's death, the only person Harvey had ever cared about was himself.

Harvey took out his shaving kit and set it on the counter. There was no hot water, but he made do. Soon, the mighty walrus mustache—an affectation he'd maintained since college to separate himself from the crowd—was swirling the drain.

Good riddance.

As a final touch, Harvey sprayed a fog of antiperspirant

156

beneath his shirt, then tossed the suit and the duffel bag in the garbage. The suit reeked, and it wasn't worth enduring its presence another instant. Sinatra might've worn it while singing "Luck Be a Lady," but the only luck Harvey ever had in it was bad.

Back in the lobby, the line for concessions was thinning out. Harvey bought a bucket of buttered popcorn, a Coke, and Milk Duds, then went inside the theater and found two open seats on the aisle in the front row. It was the biggest crowd for a movie he'd ever seen, and he felt safe.

Harvey munched his popcorn and drank his Coke, enjoying the space afforded by the empty seat next to him. He wondered if someone might take the seat, but no one did. Maybe he smelled too strongly of Right Guard instead of a dead skunk?

The lights dimmed and the coming attractions rolled, starting with *Close Encounters of the Third Kind*, a science fiction feature by the guy who'd directed *Jaws*, Steven something-or-other, with music by "eleven-time Academy Award nominee" John Williams. Whoever he was. Harvey hadn't seen a movie since *The Godfather*, but the commercials alone about the great white shark were enough to keep him from dipping so much as a toe in any ocean. Next came a James Bond flick, *The Spy Who Loved Me*.

Midway through the last coming attraction, a Charlie Brown movie, a familiar voice said, "Harvey? Is that you? You look...different."

Harvey turned to see Diane and Dennis standing in the aisle. The doctor was holding her pager, a pained expression on her face. Dennis, as before, had his Polaroid camera and broomstick-sword.

"It's me," Harvey said. "I, ah, changed out of my work clothes. What's the matter?"

"My pager went off. I have to go to the hospital, and I don't want to leave Dennis alone on his birthday. Would you mind terribly if he sat with you?"

"Not in the slightest," Harvey said in all honesty.

Dennis clapped his hands with delight. "Oh boy! I get to stay to see a movie about a real space princess."

"Remember what we talked about, son?" Diane said. "Movies aren't real. They're make-believe."

Dennis adjusted his glasses, a very adult gesture. "It's not real up here, Mom." He tapped a finger against his left temple, then placed his hand above his heart. "It's real in here." With that, the boy seized the bucket of popcorn from her hands and took his seat.

"How old are you today?" Harvey asked.

"Sixteen."

"Happy birthday. Here, have a box of Milk Duds on me."

Dennis thanked Harvey for the candy. The familiar 20th Century Fox ident began to play, signaling the start of the film.

Diane put a hand on Harvey's arm. "Thanks for allowing me to keep my birthday promise. He's seen it ten times, but he still loves it."

Harvey nodded in understanding. Stanley had been the same way about his favorite shows and comic books; it was impossible to get too much of a good thing.

As other patrons asked for quiet or called out, "Down in front!" Diane bent close and whispered, "If you'd be so kind, would you read the opening credits to Dennis before they fly away?"

Before the credits flew away? What kind of movie was this? "Certainly."

Diane withdrew her hand—it left a lingering warmth on Harvey's arm that felt good—and she disappeared up the aisle.

Dennis tugged on Harvey's sleeve and whispered, "Read it."

On the screen, Harvey saw ten words against a backdrop of brilliant stars. He said, "A long time ago in a—"

The words were lost in a dramatic fanfare of brass, a rousing theme in the same key and style as the ident that had preceded it, but with the sweeping majesty of Gustav Holst's "Mars, the

Bringer of War." To Harvey's delight, the composer was utilizing a full orchestra and was clearly a classically trained maestro at the height of his powers. He listened, open-mouthed and enthralled, as the theme built in power.

"Read," Dennis implored.

The yellow words were slowly scrolling up the screen, the top line already almost too small to be legible. Quickly, Harvey read the introduction to his friend, feeling himself a boy at the old Flash Gordon serials Stanley had loved so dearly. This *Star Wars* film wasn't the opera Harvey had hoped for, but it was the next best thing: it was a *space* opera.

For two hours, Harvey and Dennis had the time of their lives. In the film's final scene, Harvey once again felt triumphal music crash over him like a warming ocean wave, this time a brassy overture punctuated with percussion that would've made Sir Edward Elgar himself envious. He sat transfixed before the movie screen, his mind swimming with visions of an exploding spherical space station destroyed in the nick of time by a ragtag rebellion. Though a villainous dark lord had escaped—there must always be a sequel, after all—a princess had been rescued, an evil empire defeated, and a galaxy saved.

Harvey's breath caught as the princess, a resplendent vision in white, stood on the dais of what looked like a throne room. This young woman had proved to be no damsel in distress; in the tradition of Maid Marian, Dale Arden, and Wonder Woman, she was a heroine in her own right at a time when the world desperately needed heroism.

Below the dais, rebel soldiers stood in formation on either side of a central runway while three champions made their way forward. There was the orphan-turned-hero, a boy from a backwater planet who'd always dreamed of adventure; beside him, the pirate and wise-cracking scoundrel with a price on his head and a heart of gold. Trailing behind the humans was a seven-foot alien completely covered in hair, wearing only a bandolier across one shoulder. The creature roared, and the assembly snapped to attention as one, as if obeying his command.

The princess smiled at her rescuers, and Harvey smiled back at her, imagining she was bestowing a gold medal upon him and not them. The youth beamed proudly, while the pirate gave the princess a mischievous wink. To one side, the camera flashed to the two robots who'd started the adventure—including the little blue guy who'd been shot in the final battle! Now fully repaired, the blue robot emitted a series of nonsensical beeps and chirrups.

Harvey and Dennis laughed. What was he saying? Did it matter?

Not at all. In fact, not a word was spoken by any character during the ceremony, save for a parting growl from the bear-like alien; but no words were necessary. It was the perfect ending to a perfect movie.

The audience cheered, and the credits rolled. As Dennis played with his makeshift lightsaber between the screen and the front row, Harvey was transported to his childhood home in Brooklyn, where two brothers zoomed around the front yard in a cardboard spaceship. The soundtrack perfectly matched the movie *and* his memories, forming an intense personal connection beyond the framework of its story. As the score of any great opera should.

On the screen, Harvey read this:

Music by
JOHN WILLIAMS
Performed by The London Symphony Orchestra

Harvey recalled with excitement Williams was the composer mentioned in the coming attraction for *Close Encounters of the Third Kind,* the Academy Award nominee who'd composed *Jaws.* Well, it might be worth watching a shark eat people if Harvey could hear more of Williams's work. Here was the music he'd been missing since New York, an act of genius masquerading as the soundtrack for a space movie.

The houselights snapped on, revealing Diane in the aisle. "What'd you think?"

Harvey Lisch got to his feet, but for a wonder felt no pain shooting through his back nor malaise clouding his spirit. For the first time in many years, he felt genuinely...*good*. "Stanley would've loved this movie."

Diane blinked in confusion. "Who's Stanley?"

Harvey shrugged. "Stanley is just Stanley." He said to Dennis, "Young man, thank you for sharing your special day with me."

In answer, Dennis thrust his blue broomstick into the air, a Jedi in training.

Diane held up a hand. "Why don't you join us for dinner? My treat."

Harvey was about to politely refuse, but he was arrested again by her impish eyes. "I'd be delighted. Where to?"

"The Ol' South Pancake House down the street."

"It's my favorite," Dennis said.

"Breakfast for dinner," Harvey mused. "Why not?"

They followed the crowds outside. The sun still blazed in a sky of molten gold, but the shadows of evening were lengthening. In the parking lot, Harvey spotted the El Camino creeping along with the windows down. Parker and Rose were scanning the crowd, their gazes momentarily meeting Harvey's own before passing right over him.

The disguise had worked. Harvey would return to Houston, hand the photos to Elmer Gaddis, and enjoy a nice payday. The businessman's goons would do away with the small fries who'd tried to swim with sharks, and the world would be a better place with two less drug runners.

But Harvey heard the lie within his heart. These two were babies, not hardened criminals, and might yet walk a different path if given half a chance. He put a hand in his pocket, his fingers brushing Stanley's photo before emerging with the roll of film.

As the El Camino was about to leave the lot, Harvey put his fingers to his lips and whistled shrilly. The car stopped. Parker and Rose, evidently recognizing him, got out but did not approach.

"Diane, wait here with Dennis," Harvey said. "I have some unfinished business with these two."

The doctor grabbed his arm in alarm. "Are you sure? They look like tough customers."

"Nothing I can't handle, my dear." For reasons Harvey couldn't explain, it felt natural to call her that, this woman he'd known for less than a day.

Dennis tapped his shoulder. "Take my lightsaber."

Harvey tousled the boy's hair. "You keep that and be my backup." He walked through the crowds toward his pursuers, trying to project more confidence than he felt. About ten feet away, he stopped and tossed the roll of film to Parker, who caught it deftly.

"That's for you," Harvey said. "I took your pictures for Elmer Gaddis; I don't work for that thug anymore."

Parker blanched, while Rose's hand instinctively took hold of her boyfriend's. "Elmer?" they said in unison.

"I see you've heard of him. He doesn't know your names and faces yet, but he's very interested in meeting you."

Parker pulled out a tattered wallet. "How much do you want for not giving him the goods?"

Harvey chuckled, but not with derision. "Nothing. The film is as free as the open road, which I suggest you take to get as far away from Texas as possible. I give you your lives; don't waste them in evil pursuits."

Parker stuck out his hand. "You're all right, Mr. Cross-word."

"Yeah," nodded Rose. "And you cleaned up nice, too."

Harvey shook the cowboy's hand. "Be good."

The young people climbed into the El Camino and drove away. Diane and Dennis came to stand beside Harvey.

Diane slipped her arm into the crook of Harvey's elbow. "I'm not sure what that was about, but I think you did the right thing."

Dennis's Polaroid snapped a photo of his mother and his newest friend. He handed the snapshot to Harvey and said, "Happy anniversary."

Harvey thanked Dennis for the snapshot and thought, *Out of the mouths of babes oft times come gems.* "Who's ready for some pancakes?"

COLD COMFORT
Andrew Welsh-Huggins

It took me nearly an hour to reach her house, a two-story white Colonial off Elmwood Ave., or nearly three times what the drive should have been. I was lucky the cops didn't stop me: we weren't supposed to be on the roads at all yet. They'd cleared the major arteries and some of the main thoroughfares, but most of the streets were still days away from rescue. Even Rochester only had so many plows for a snowstorm that big. They were saying it might have been as bad as the '66 blizzard, back when I was still on the force, or the monster that hit Buffalo a year ago. As far as I was concerned, one month into 1978 and winter storms of the century were already blending together. But either way, the woman on the phone had sounded desperate, her husband missing after the snow struck and something about doubling my normal rate, and I decided to risk it.

"Goodness, you made it," Marcia Trimble said, opening the door almost immediately after my gloved knock. I had the impression she'd been waiting there the whole time, keeping an eye out.

"Sorry I'm late. Roads are still bad."

"I can only imagine. Please, come in. Coffee?"

We sat in her living room, her on the couch, me in an armchair beside a coffee table. Mrs. Trimble was mid-forties, pretty in a favorite aunt kind of way, wearing a set of oversized plastic glasses emphasizing a pair of worried brown eyes and bundled up in what looked like at least two sweaters. We had barely settled when a trio of stairstep boys in the ten to fourteen range burst into the room, yelling at the top of their lungs. Something about something called Pong and whose turn it was. Seeing me, they stopped in their tracks and gaped.

"Are *you* the cops?" the oldest-looking boy said.

"Don't be silly," Mrs. Trimble said in a calm voice that belied the white of her knuckles as she gripped her coffee cup. "This is Mr. Hollister. He's just making sure your dad's okay."

"Like those other guys?"

"Not exactly. Just give us a few minutes, please."

"Do you have children?" Mrs. Trimble said, smile as fixed and frozen as the glittering drifts outside her house, after the crashing and yelling migrated upstairs.

"A daughter. She's three. She—my ex has her full-time. But I see her as often as I can."

"A girl. Wouldn't that be nice?"

"These other guys. Someone else is looking for your husband?"

She pulled herself out of whatever dreamscape the thought of a daughter inspired. Good thing she hadn't met my spitfire, Jenny.

"From Lowell's office. They said they were worried, after I called so many times. Wondered if they could help."

"Nice of them," I said, but privately wondered what I was doing here in that case.

"You'd think so. But it just made me more worried."

"Why don't you go over everything again."

A crash upstairs interrupted her. When it wasn't followed by reports of actual murder, she began talking. As she explained earlier, her husband, Lowell Trimble, worked as an accountant in the corporate offices at the Midtown Mall building downtown. The afternoon the storm hit, he called and said he was leaving early to make it home. It was already so bad out, with whiteout conditions throughout the city, that his wife asked him to consider waiting or to find a place to stay the night. But he insisted and told her not to worry.

"He didn't make it home."

She nodded. "I assumed he'd either been stranded or found shelter someplace. You're hearing all these stories—people stuck in movie theaters, in bank lobbies. Hotels jammed, of course. But then I didn't hear anything the next day. I tried his office, but no one answered. Eventually, I reached his boss at home, and he said Lowell left right after talking to me. I tried to keep my cool, but the boys, and everything...I assumed I'd hear something the next day—yesterday—but nothing. So now it's been days."

"And the men from his office?"

"They came by this morning. About an hour before you—I thought they were you, in fact."

"What about the police?"

"They took a report over the phone. They told me he was probably just someplace where he couldn't call. I don't think they took it seriously, but I guess they're overwhelmed."

I had her describe the route her husband would have taken home. There were plenty of places—shops, businesses, and the aforementioned hotels—along the way where he could have taken shelter. There were also plenty of apartment buildings and streets lined with houses buried in drifts it would take days to clear.

"There's no one"—I paused, carefully considering my words—"whose place he might have stopped by? Someone on the way he might know?"

Before she could reply, she was interrupted by another crash upstairs, this time accompanied by angry shouts.

Ignoring the din, Mrs. Trimble said, "You're asking if he has a girlfriend, aren't you?"

"Just trying to cover all the bases here. No offense."

Yet another crash, followed by the sound of something breaking.

"None taken. But I bet you're thinking"—she glanced up the gray carpeted stairs—"who could blame him, right? A house like this to come home to every night?"

"Not at all," I lied.

"Lowell's a good man," she said with a sigh. "He's loyal, maybe to a fault. Sometimes I wish he showed a little more gumption. But he's a good provider. And faithful," she added with emphasis.

"No behavior out of the ordinary recently?" I said, still focused on the possible mistress. A dollar for every faithful spouse I'd caught straying, and I could retire by forty.

"Not that I can think of. Home on time. Quiet evenings once the boys settle down. Mass on Sundays. Well—"

"What?"

"Work's been a little busy lately. He's done some paperwork after dinner a few nights a week. That's a little unusual, but it was a busy last quarter and he had catching up to do."

"What kind of paperwork?"

"I'm not sure. Statements and invoices, I think. Seemed like Midtown was doing well. 'So much money,' he said a couple of times. He got a little extra, for all the work, which we could use, honestly. So, I didn't mind."

I sat back and considered the situation. *So much money.* Unless Lowell Trimble was talking about the price of flowers and jewelry for a high-maintenance side piece, he did indeed sound like a hard-working stiff unlikely to be stepping out on his long-suffering wife and instead just trying to keep his head—and his company—above water. Which raised more dire scenarios, especially in this weather. I told her I'd do my best to find him.

"That's all I can ask."

She handed me a pair of recent photographs and an envelope with my retainer check. Right on schedule, the boys pounded back downstairs and demanded lunch. As we rose, the trio began thumping each other randomly.

"There won't be any lunch if you keep hitting each other," Mrs. Trimble said.

"It's the only way we can get your attention," the oldest complained.

Eager to leave this Donner Party fun behind, I told Mrs. Trimble I'd be in touch and beelined for the door. Outside, I gasped as my lungs contracted and the cold and wind stung my eyes. Random flurries sliced sideways, dusting the top of the massive drifts lining the street, some topping me by two feet.

I struggled up the street to my Cutlass, which I'd parked in front of a hydrant—the only clear space on the street—offering up a prayer no one would be by to ticket and tow me. I paused, seeing a car in the distance, hoping it wasn't a cruiser on the prowl for people just like me, blocking the plows from their appointed rounds. But I was in luck, and it just sat there, either stuck or hoping to bag my illicit spot as soon as I was gone. I pulled away from the curb and inched my way west down Elmwood to Clinton, then headed north into the city.

Working my way along the icy streets, I went over the outcomes involving Lowell Trimble and settled on three possibilities. First, the worst but most obvious, was that he was dead, likely frozen in his stranded car between work and home, the vehicle hidden by a drift that piled up overnight like something out of *Alive*, which coincidentally was sitting on my nightstand at this very moment. Perfect reading for the Rochester winter that year.

Second, Mrs. Trimble was either lying or naïve or some combination of both, and her husband was in fact shacked up with a lady friend someplace. Or a man, for all I knew. I'd stopped assuming anything on that front—or caring—after a few visits to my brother's apartment in Corn Hill, where I realized he was doing more than splitting the rent with his roommate. A storm like this was perfect cover for some illicit time beneath wool blankets. A lawyer I knew in Buffalo had told me that the previous year, in the aftermath of what they were already calling the Great Blizzard of '77, he personally handled three divorces stemming from that very scenario. The 'Any port in a storm' defense, he called it, not that it did his clients much good.

Third, but least likely, in my opinion, Trimble was alive but stuck someplace with a bunch of other miserable commuters waiting for the plows to reach their location. The problem was this option begged the question of why he hadn't contacted his wife. Playing devil's advocate, the reasons could be legion, from downed lines to overloaded circuits to some gentlemanly instinct kicking in to let people with more urgent communication needs cut in line ahead of him. A little voice in the back of my head told me three days was a long time to go without any effort to reach out. But then I thought of his three sons and all those crashes along with the random thumping—"It's the only way we can get your attention"—and decided maybe I could justify the logic. Just because you're not having an affair doesn't mean you wouldn't mind an unscheduled break now and then. Maybe.

Because, possibly because of the book on my nightstand, I just couldn't put Door No. 1 out of my head.

To my amazement, Midtown Mall was actually open, though the two-level enclosed shopping plaza was empty as a western ghost town. The only store with its lights on was a Spencer's Gifts, which made me smile; it had to be the least useful business in the snowed-under city right now. Good for them. The only people I spied were an elderly cleaning lady and a pair of maintenance men sitting by the fountain. I watched as the two-story Clock of Nations chimed noon, the pods opening and the dioramas of each country spinning about, eerily playing to a crowd of four as though nothing was amiss. When it finished, the figures safely back inside their pods, I set off to find

Midtown's corporate offices.

At first, I thought I was out of luck. The door to the upper-level suites was locked, and no one answered my knock. I was weighing my next option—tracing Trimble's predicted route home, checking for likely shelter options along the way, along with buried vehicles—when to my surprise the office door opened a crack and a woman peered out with a secretary's bearing and skepticism in her eyes.

"Help you?"

I gave the age-indeterminate Black woman the run-down and concluded by digging out a card from my wallet and handing it to her.

After studying it for a moment, she said, "Ever met James Garner?"

"No, ma'am. I mean, he's an actor, whereas I'm—"

"Nice man. Came through on a publicity thing one time. Told him I preferred him as Maverick. He just smiled and said he gets that a lot. So, what may I do for you?"

A few minutes later, I was settled in a chair beside her desk. She introduced herself as Shirley Simpkins, secretary to Midtown's assistant facilities director. I explained my mission and my theories about Trimble. She appeared to be the only person in the office because she paused several times to answer the phone, raising a finger each time to interrupt me.

"I'm with Mrs. Trimble on the girlfriend," she said when I was finished, and she had a minute between calls. "Skirt chasing up here is something you have to see to believe. I tell the other girls never go into the break room alone. And God forbid you have to work late. But Lowell wasn't like that."

"Which means—"

"He's either dead, God forbid, or stuck someplace."

The phone rang again, and she informed one more caller that yes, Midtown was open, and no, no one was available to speak to them at the moment.

"If he's dead, I'm sorry to hear it," she said, after she hung up. "Nasty way to go for such a nice man. That blizzard last month? Brother-in-law of one my cousins was shoveling snow over in Erie, had a heart attack, fell over, and froze to death not ten feet from his front steps. Wouldn't wish that on anybody. Except the problem with that theory—a good problem—is that it's been three days. You'd think someone would call it in by now. Which leaves him sheltering someplace. But if that's true, I find it hard to believe he wouldn't call. Even 7-Elevens have phones."

"Good employee?" I said, grasping at straws. "No problems on that front?"

"As far as I know. At his desk at nine, out the door at five. No complaints."

I mentioned the evening paperwork. That seemed to take her back a bit.

"Things don't seem that busy here," she said. "Between us, Eastview Mall's eating our lunch. But he's definitely good with numbers. I'll give him that."

"I can imagine. Not every company would be so concerned about a missing employee." I explained about the Midtown managers who stopped by Mrs. Trimble's before me.

"Now, say that again?"

I repeated the story. She frowned and furrowed her brow.

"She say what they looked like?"

I realized I hadn't asked her to describe the men. "Why the frown?"

"It just doesn't sound right, is all. I mean, I'm the only person I've seen here in three days. I need this job, so I'm coming to work even if there's a glacier rolling down Genesee Street. I know I talked to Mrs. Trimble when she called the first time. And I know she talked to Mr. Trimble's boss. But I have no idea who that would be, and I think I'd know if somebody sent out a search party."

* * *

I was still mulling this development as I stepped outside, gulped at the cold that shriveled my lungs, and unlocked my car. If the two men who beat me to Mrs. Trimble's by an hour weren't from Midtown, who were they? Obviously, somebody who wanted to find Mr. Trimble badly enough that they lied about themselves. Pulling back onto the empty, snowy street, I realized the discrepancy raised a fourth option regarding Lowell's disappearance: could he be hiding from someone? At first blush, it seemed unlikely. I'd tracked down plenty of people who went on the lam by faking their deaths, lying about a business trip, or making up a sick relative. But those folks almost always made their run when the weather was decent. Not during one of the worst blizzards in recent memory, when snow from the last storm was still being cleared. The winter of '78 was already shaping up to be one of the snowiest in Rochester history; with travel restricted, drifts as high as barn silos, and temperatures plummeting, it would have been easier to disappear during a midwestern tornado outbreak.

That's what I told myself for ten or so minutes, which is when I first spotted the tail.

I realized right away how sloppy I'd been. I'd seen maybe ten cars that morning. And I could tell that the dark, wide-bodied Lincoln creeping behind me, one and sometimes even two blocks back, was the same car I'd spotted up the street at Mrs. Trimble's house earlier that day, mistaking it for a police cruiser. They must have followed me from there to Midtown. Which meant someone had eyes on her house. Which confirmed that someone else wanted to know where Lowell Trimble was, fitting perfectly with the idea he, in fact, didn't want to be found and had used the storm to make an escape. The question was, in this game, and in this weather, who would freeze first, the cat or the mouse?

I thought about stopping in the middle of the street and having a conversation then and there with his pursuers. Cut to the chase and figure out what was going on. My .38 was in the glove compartment, and I figured I could handle myself. Except that might also scare them off. And I didn't want to do that, since discovering who else was hunting Trimble without tipping my hand seemed as good a way as any of digging up clues to his whereabouts.

Plan B, losing the tail on snow-covered streets, was out of the question. In these conditions, and with downtown essentially empty, you'd have better luck outrunning the lunar rover on the Sea of Tranquility. In the end, I settled on Plan C, driven partly by an idea forming in the back of my brain, and partly because breakfast was now a long time ago. I carefully made my way across downtown, being sure the trailing car stuck with me, until I arrived at Nick Tahou's on West Main. I parked a full block up from the restaurant and tromped back through the snow with no effort at surreptitiousness. Not surprisingly, the diner was the most crowded place I'd seen so far that day.

Inside, I took a seat at the counter and ordered a red hot, a white hot, fries, and coffee. As I waited, I glanced through the front window and watched as my tracker stopped two car lengths behind me. I half expected the doors to open and my surveillance team to reveal themselves. But no. They stayed put, intent to wait me out despite the cold.

As I formulated my next steps, luck fell into my lap. Or me into theirs. Just as my order arrived, I was distracted by the sound of laughter up front. I looked and saw two girls at the cash register, waiting for change as they shrugged on thick winter coats. One of them carried a backpack that said Eastman School of Music. I left my stool and approached before they could leave.

"Excuse me."

They both turned and gave me the eye. The more petite of the pair, with a pale face, upturned nose and black hair pulled into a tight ponytail, frowned at my appearance. The other, an older-looking redhead with a readier smile than her friend, waited expectantly.

174

"Do you go to Eastman?"

"Uh, yeah," Ponytail said, uncertainly, glancing at her companion.

"Long walk," I said.

"I guess."

"Not so bad," the redhead said. "We were starving, and this was the only place open. Why? Want to give us a ride back?"

"Possibly. But I've got a favor to ask first."

"Which is?"

"See that car out there?" I gestured out the window at the Lincoln.

"What about it?" the redhead said.

"Couple of my buddies are sitting in there, waiting for me to bring them lunch."

"So?"

"So, I'll give you twenty bucks each to deliver the food yourselves." I paused. "Thirty if you leave your coats here. Hats too."

"Are you nuts?" the first girl said. "It's freezing out there."

"My friends like pretty girls, and it's easier to see how pretty you are with your coats off."

Ponytail blushed and frowned at the same moment, and at first, I thought I'd lost them. But then the redhead said, "Forty. But I promise I'll smile a lot."

"Nancy," the first girl protested.

"Ease up, JoAnn. Studio fees aren't cheap. We have a deal?"

"Deal," I said.

Fifteen minutes later, I watched as the girls stepped outside with boxes of takeout in hand. They paused, shivering violently as the wind whipped their hair over their eyes, then slowly advanced to the Lincoln. I waited until each was positioned on either side—driver's and passenger's windows—and snuck outside behind them. As they explained their mission to the car's no-doubt confused occupants, I knelt behind a snowdrift and recorded the sedan's number and dealership info from the license plate holder. Finished, I stayed low and half crab-walked back inside. A minute later, the girls joined me. We stood together, rubbing our hands to warm up.

"They say anything?"

"They were suspicious," Nancy said. "But it helped that they liked my sweater. It being pretty and all."

I grinned at that. Then I had them describe the men. Big, dark-haired, clean-cut. Could have been anyone in the city.

"Thanks a lot," I said, peeling bills into the girls' hands. "You did me a big favor."

"We're not going to get in any trouble, are we?" JoAnn said.

"You'll be fine."

I helped them on with their coats and told them to hop in my car. Right on cue, the Lincoln pulled out a few seconds after we took off. But this go-around, I timed a light at Clinton, ran the red just ahead of an approaching plow—whose driver let me have it with the horn—and left the sedan behind. On the short drive to Eastman, I let slip without explanation that I was a private eye on a job. JoAnn absorbed the news as if I said I'd personally sold properties at Love Canal. But Nancy said it sounded super interesting.

"There you go," I said, pulling to the curb of the music school main entrance a minute later.

"You like classical music, Mr. Hollister?" Nancy said, turning to me. JoAnn was already on the street.

"Call me Jerry. I wouldn't say it was my style, if I'm being honest."

"Bet I could make you like it. I've got my master's recital next week." She pulled a flier from her backpack, found a pen, and wrote down her number. "You never know. Give it a try."

"What do you play?"

"Clarinet," she said. "It's a reed instrument. I put the tip in my mouth and blow."

* * *

Clear of my tail, I made it as far as the Greyhound station. I parked as best I could, went inside, found a pay phone, and called Mrs. Trimble. I asked her to describe the two men who visited her ahead of me that morning. She gave a description that more or less matched the pair that JoAnn and Nancy entertained in the freezing cold. I thanked her and told her I'd be in touch.

Any other time than one of the snowiest winters in Rochester history, the next step would have been easy. I had a cousin at the city DMV who'd been known to bend the rules and look up plates for me from time to time in exchange for a six of Genny Cream. But surprise, surprise, he wasn't answering the phone. I also knew a couple of cops who would have run it for me, but they were night shift guys, and I was guessing they had more important things to do, like welfare checks or digging frozen corpses out of snowdrifts.

So, I did the next best thing and called the dealership listed on the Olds' plate holder. As luck would have it, a girl answered after the seventh ring.

"Amalfi Motors. We're closed today. How may I help you?"

"Yeah, it's Piers Paul Read, down at parking enforcement. Hoping you could help me out."

"We're closed, like I said."

"Fortunately, I'm not looking to make a purchase," I said. "The thing is, we towed a car off Lake Ave. this morning, blocking the street. Plows couldn't get through. We're trying to notify the owner, but the DMV is snowed under like everybody else. License tag says they bought it from you. Any chance I give you the plate and the car info, you might be able to help me out?"

She asked what kind of car, and I told her. "I dunno, Mister. We sell a lot of black Lincolns. I'll do what I can." I could hear the snapping of gum as she spoke. One of the remaining bills in my wallet said she was also twirling her hair with a pencil. "What's the plate?"

I told her, then waited so long I started looking over my shoulder in case my traveling companions had somehow tracked me to the station. Overhead, a scratchy speaker announced the 2 p.m. to Syracuse was leaving in five minutes. I fed two more quarters into the machine before she returned to the line.

"You're in luck. Or maybe not."

"Why wouldn't I be in luck?"

She ignored the question, and said, "That particular car was purchased last fall."

"Okay. By who?"

"There's no name on it. It's registered to a company."

"Which is?"

She paused. "Telesca Meats and Perishables, Inc."

Oh shit, I thought.

Maybe the name wouldn't ring a bell for the average Rochester resident. But I recognized it right away. Anyone in law enforcement or even nibbling around the edges knew the name Telesca. As in Dominic "Donny" Telesca. As in, head of one of the three crime families currently dividing up Rochester's share of drugs, prostitution, protection rackets, and distribution of boxes that fell off the backs of trucks. As in a guy rumored to be behind one and possibly more of the car bombs that led to some fatal indigestion in the Blue Gardenia parking lot up in Irondequoit. Outside the family, Telesca was not somebody you wanted to associate with unless you had a generous life insurance policy. Definitely not someone you wanted to cross. And now two of his men were trailing me, presumably to draw a bead on Lowell Trimble. But why?

I walked over to the waiting area, parked myself in a hard plastic seat, and fired up my post-lunch Winston. I was down to three a day since I coughed up part of a lung the year before chasing a guy up Cobb's Hill and realized my addiction was becoming an occupational hazard. Taking a drag, I picked up a well-thumbed copy of the *Democrat and Chronicle* and thought things through.

First, I considered the paperwork Lowell Trimble was doing at night, plus the fact Mrs. Trimble said he was making a little extra, which came in handy. How handy, I wondered. Next, I recalled the mild surprise expressed by Shirley Simpkins, the Midtown secretary, that Lowell had so much office work he needed to take it home.

So, on the one hand, Trimble was a man who needed money, but who also kept secrets. He had somehow got himself tied up with Dominic Telesca or the very least one of his loan sharks. If he was as good an accountant as his wife and Mrs. Simpkins said he was, I could imagine thousands and thousands of reasons—and maybe millions—why his bookkeeping might be useful as a commodity in trade for somebody like the mafioso. *So much money.*

On the other hand, Lowell was, by all accounts, a family man. Nine-to-five job, home on time, dinner with the kids and TV with the Mrs., a little bit of paperwork at night—which now made a lot more sense—then bed. Rinse and repeat. Not an exotic guy. Faithful and loyal. Someone who liked his routines.

All this had me thinking that in the disappearing game, Trimble's version of going big might look pretty small to other people. He'd be like the guy who boasts about his trip to Paris, Madrid, and Rome without mentioning he spent most of his time on a tour bus. I rose from my chair, called Mrs. Trimble again, and told her I had two more questions. She balked at the first, about their finances, until I insisted it was important.

"Things got tight last summer," she conceded at last. "We had to loan money to my brother, and then my car broke down. The boys needed braces. And then the basement flooded. And that was just July."

So that answered that. The Trimbles needed some extra income and Lowell found a source, which unfortunately put him in the debt of Donny Telesca. Odds were he was then given two choices when he couldn't pay it back, and he decided that helping cook the Family books beat the alternatives he was offered. Until he realized the mess was in and decided to skip town mid-blizzard while the skipping was good.

"Second question. Where do you vacation?"

"What in the world does that have to do with Lowell?"

"Just humor me."

"Well, if you must know, we don't. Except occasionally to Tampa. Lowell has a cousin we can stay with, so it's halfway affordable."

"Nowhere else? Mexico? South America, maybe?"

"Goodness, no. We never go places like that," she said, a little wistfully. "Lowell doesn't even like going to Canada."

With a little prodding, she gave me the name of the cousin—Maggie Lettner—and her numbers, work and home. It took the last of my quarters, but a few minutes later I had Maggie on the line, and I introduced myself as the branch manager at Tampa First Third National Bank on Bayshore.

"Mr. Trimble left his driver's license here this morning. I found this number on the check he deposited. Maybe you could pass a message along?"

"Lowell?" she said after a long pause. "Are you sure?"

I assured her I was. The line went quiet. I was pretty sure I heard a gulf breeze rustling the leaves of sun-kissed palm trees in the background. Then the muffling noise of a hand placed over a receiver blocked my daydream. I heard Maggie say something to someone without catching the words, followed by a distinctly male response. Too many moments later, she returned to the line.

"You have the wrong number," she said, and hung up.

The first flights out of the reopened Rochester airport took off the following day. I wasn't sure if the "expenses" portion of my

180

arrangement with Mrs. Trimble covered such an expedition, but with Donny Telesca in the mix, I decided the money was worth it. I packed a small bag, stuck my Berretta inside a pair of shorts, and checked the suitcase all the way to Tampa. With the tarmac squeezed between foothill-sized snow piles, the takeoff made me think of departing an Antarctic research station. The trip took most of the day, including a delay at LaGuardia where runways were still being cleared, but by late that afternoon I was in a rented Buick with the windows down and the sun on my face. According to the chipper stewardess aboard my New York to Tampa flight, on landing, it was exactly seventy-nine degrees warmer than when I departed Rochester that morning.

I came close to checking into my motel before heading to Maggie Lettner's, but decided against it at the last minute. I was glad I did. As I pulled up outside a row of Hyde Park condos a street over from the beach, I saw three things of concern, right in a row.

The first was a black Lincoln parked outside Maggie's unit. Not the same one in Rochester, mind you. But there's such a thing as a company car. Which meant somehow, Donny Telesca had made the same calculations as me. The second thing was a woman standing in the open doorway of a two-story white stucco Mission Revival building at the address I had for Maggie, her hand over her mouth. The third was two guys who could have been cousins of my friends up north, except for their tans. They wore perfectly tailored suits with matching bulges on the left side of their lapels and were walking up the sidewalk with a pale-faced and terrified Lowell Trimble sandwiched between them. Whether he was headed for a return trip to Rochester or a faceplant in a swamp was a question for another day. For now, I had to act fast. But how?

In that moment, I flashed to the three-boy wrecking crew in the Trimbles' living room, one more snow day away from a full-on *Lord of the Flies* meltdown.

There won't be any lunch if you keep hitting each other.

It's the only way we can get your attention.

"There you are, you sonofabitch," I shouted.

Before Trimble's minders could react, I took two steps forward and punched Trimble in the face. I'm not the scrapper I was right out of the Army, but I still had a little arm strength left. I felt his nose break as I connected, then watched the blood bloom as he sagged between the two men.

"The fuck—" the handler on the left said, losing his grip on Trimble as the accountant dropped to the ground, face between his hands. I took advantage of Goombah No. 1's confusion by kicking him between the knees. As he tried to recover, I pulled out my Beretta, hooked my left arm around Trimble, and pressed the gun against the left side of his head.

"Either of you guys move a muscle and I'm painting the sidewalk with this cheating bastard's brains."

"You have no idea who you're dealing with," Goombah No. 2 said in an unnervingly calm voice as he reached inside his suitcoat.

"Maybe I do, and maybe I don't. Either way, he's all yours in about five minutes. But first, he and I are going to have a little conversation about my wife and some receipts for a Don CeSar penthouse I just found." Without another word, I force-marched Trimble up to Maggie Lettner's door, pushed him inside, and slammed the door behind me.

"Call the cops," I gasped, just before the pounding began.

I did my best to apologize to Trimble, although truth be told, I didn't have much of an opportunity after our first encounter. Thanks to the explanation I sputtered out to the local gendarmes, who arrived just in time to prevent permanent damage to Maggie's front door—not to mention Lowell Trimble and me—I was soon talking with the FBI and the ATF and a covey of AUSAs up from Miami. My quick trip to Tampa stretched to four days, and Trimble was still there when I left, singing and singing and singing. Back home, there wasn't much business being conducted at Telesca Meats and Perishables, Inc., which remained closed for operations until further notice. As did Amalfi Motors. Mrs. Trimble was relieved to hear her husband was alive, although the circumstances were cold comfort at best. She'd probably be alone with those boys a while longer, the way things were going.

Two days after arriving home, with temperatures warming and most streets passable again, I remembered the concert that red-headed, clarinet-playing Nancy mentioned. She sounded surprised when I called and said I'd be there, but then added it would be nice to see me again. She warmed up even more after I suggested we could go out to dinner afterward and mentioned Top of the Plaza at Midtown.

Late that Sunday morning, I was rifling through my closet trying to find a clean pair of pants that weren't jeans when the phone rang. Mindy, my ex, was on the other line.

"Where are you?" she said impatiently.

"At home."

"You're supposed to have Jenny today. Or did you forget? Again?"

I try not making a habit of disappointing two women in the same day. Which was why, with a little bribing involving a bag of candy orange slices and the purchase of a new doll, I found myself in a small performance room at Eastman that afternoon with Jenny beside me. To my surprise, she listened intently to the music, even humming along at one point, as she periodically fed candy to her doll when she wasn't grabbing yet another slice for herself.

As for me, I tried to focus on the music and not the pursing of Nancy's lips on the clarinet's reed as she played or the low-cut, close-fitting black concert dress she wore that emphasized all the things I was guessing had distracted Donny's Telesca's trackers the previous week. Images of a romantic candlelight dinner with a bottle of wine and dessert of one kind or another back at my apartment danced before my eyes, then dimmed quickly as she walked up to us at the reception afterward.

"Jerry, you came," she said with a smile, and then, eyes dropping, added, "with your...little sister."

Reluctantly, I corrected her and introduced Jenny. "My ex and I share custody," I said, putting extra emphasis on *ex*. "Signals got crossed. Sorry."

"No problem," she said, disappointment briefly crossing her face. "But, no Top of the Plaza, I'm guessing?"

"Maybe not today."

Then, to my surprise, Nancy knelt before Jenny. "I bet you're hungry, though, aren't you, sweetheart?"

"I'm starving," she growled.

"You monster," Nancy said, standing.

"She just ate half a bag of candy."

"No excuses. So, what are we are going to do about this?"

"Rain check?"

"Nice try." She thought for a second. "I bet Nick Tahou's is still open."

"Really?"

"Really?" Nancy said, taking my arm and Jenny's hand. "I hear all the guys take their pretty girls there."

STAYIN' ALIVE
Alan Orloff

FADE IN

Jerry Hanford sat at his desk sorting his bills into three piles: "Pay Now," "Pay Later," and "Bill? I never got any bill." Unfortunately, pile number three dwarfed the other two piles combined. Trying to balance your checkbook when there wasn't enough money was like trying to balance a cue ball on the top of your noggin after polishing off a six-pack in an earthquake.

If gas prices got any higher, he'd be doing a lot more walking. Unfortunately, Hanford didn't have much faith in peanut farmer Jimmy Carter to turn things around.

A rap on his trailer door startled him, and he almost knocked the answering machine off his desk. Didn't get too many visitors and even fewer clients these days. "Just a minute," he called as he slid his gun from the top drawer of his desk. Keeping his weapon at his side, he walked over to the door and opened it.

A young woman stood there, twenty-five years old, tops, expression wavering between embarrassed and terrified. Blond, trim figure, baby blue eyes. Yellow blouse, tight white hip-hugger bell-bottoms. A little too much make-up. Aspiring actress, odds were. 'Course in this town, that was a safe bet. "Are you Mr. Hanford? The private investigator?"

"That's right. Jerry Hanford. What can I do for you?"

"I need your help."

Hanford sized her up. "I'm afraid I don't work for free."

"I can pay."

"Then come in." Hanford opened the door wide. "Come right on in."

The girl's name was Linda Stanton, and—no surprise—she'd been in LA for about a year, trying to break into the biz. She and a roommate rented a tiny place in Van Nuys in a neighborhood full of body shops and barbed wire.

As she settled into an old loveseat, she noticed an 8 x 10 glossy in a cheap frame hanging on the wall. "That's Tim Warner, right? From that detective show, *The Bickford Files*?"

"It's *The Bickford Cases*, and yes, it is."

"Wow, I love him. Such a warm smile. Do you know him?"

"Actually, I do. I'm a technical consultant on the show." Hanford should have negotiated a better contract but, he had to admit, it was pretty cool to be called out to a shoot to answer the occasional question, even if he was only getting a hundred dollars per diem. It wasn't quite as cool that Warner kept calling, wanting to shadow him as he investigated a case. The last thing he needed was a narcissistic actor getting in the way. "In fact, they sort of took a few things from my life and put them in the show."

"Right, Bickford lives in a trailer, too, doesn't he? I guess it only make sense his is a lot nicer. And on the beach, rather than miles away, like yours. But I guess that's show biz, right?"

Hanford flashed a tight smile. "So, Linda, how can I help you?"

"My friend is missing."

"Oh?"

"Yes. Susan and I were supposed to go out dancing on Friday, and she never showed. I tried calling her on Saturday and then on Sunday, too. Even went over to her pad, but she wasn't there. I'm afraid something bad has happened to her."

"Are you sure she didn't just go away for the weekend?

Forget to tell you? Spur of the moment thing? Maybe she met a guy?" Hanford had seen this a hundred times. Hell, Susan probably woke up, realized she'd never make it as an actress, and hopped on the next Greyhound back to the farm.

"No, that's not Susan. She's very reliable. We go out to the discos every Friday and Saturday night. I'm not ashamed to say we love being part of the happening scene."

"Where the beautiful people boogie?"

"Yes, something like that. It's just…show biz is such a tough business and when you're out on the dance floor, grooving, and everybody is getting down, you kind of forget how hard it all is, you know?"

Hanford didn't really know from experience. His dancing days were long behind him—two bum knees and a distinct lack of rhythm—and disco music wasn't his thing. He didn't know a Bee Gee from a bumblebee. "Any idea what might have happened?"

"Well, I've been racking my brain trying to think of something, but all I could come up with was…" She twirled a length of her blond locks around a finger.

"Was what?"

"Nothing concrete. Just a feeling. We've been hitting this new disco lately, Boogie Starz. On Sunset. Last Saturday, Susan was dancing with this dude, and afterward, she seemed like a totally different person. I got some weird vibes. I asked her what happened, what this guy said to her, but she shrugged it off. Twenty minutes later, she was back to being fun-loving Susan. I know it doesn't sound like much, but it's all I could think of."

Linda was right. It wasn't much at all. "If you're so worried, why don't you go to the police?"

Linda swallowed, lowered her gaze into her lap. "I met Susan when I first moved out here. At an audition. We dug each other and started doing things together. But every time I asked about her past, she clammed right up. So, I stopped asking. I got the feeling she was running from something—or some-body—and I'm not sure she wasn't running from the fuzz. I'd just feel horrible if I got them involved and Susan ended up in trouble with the man." Linda raised her head, stared at Han-ford with those blue eyes and Midwestern freckles. "Please, you've just got to help me."

"Listen, Linda, you seem like a nice girl, so I'll level with you. Most likely, your friend is off on a bender someplace or she fell head over heels for someone—maybe a creep calling himself a movie producer or something. *Most likely*, she'll surface in another day or so, a little embarrassed, but none the worse for wear. I'd feel guilty taking your money if that were true."

"Well, it's my money, isn't it? And I understand what you're saying, but I want to hire you. I'm sure you have bills to pay." She glanced around his trailer to emphasize the obvious. "This is how business works, right? I pay you, and you provide a service." She nodded once, twice, as if matters were all settled. "So, will you take my case, Mr. Hanford?"

Business *was* business. "Yes, I'll do it. But only if you call me Jerry." He gave her a tight smile.

Linda exhaled. "Oh, thank you. I know you'll find her. You just have to."

"I'll do my best," Hanford said. "I charge two-hundred fifty a day, plus expenses."

Linda's face dropped. "Two-fifty? I, uh, I didn't know it would be that much." She opened her purse, dug out her wallet, started counting, mouth moving as she added up what she had. She handed over a wad of bills. "Here. Two and a half days' worth."

He felt a little like a heel, taking this girl's money for what promised to be a non-case. But there was always that one-in-ten chance something serious *had* happened to Susan. "Thank you. I'll try to work fast. Now, I have some more questions."

* * *

Hanford pushed through the doors of the Boogie Starz disco. No bouncer to deal with, no line of John Travolta wannabees. Of course, it was only a few minutes past six o'clock. He figured he'd have a better shot of talking to some of the employees before things got rolling.

The focal point of the club was clearly the dance floor. Gleaming wood parquet. Not one, not two, but three basketball-sized mirrored disco balls hanging from the rafters. Mirrors on the wall. An L-shaped bar ran along the entire length of one wall. About fifty tables crowded the other end of the cavernous space.

Currently, only a handful of customers were seated, completely ignoring the lone couple on the dance floor doing The Hustle.

He approached the bartender, who was slicing lemons and limes at one end of the bar. About Hanford's height, he sported shoulder-length hair and a thick mustache. He wore a black silk shirt, unbuttoned to mid-chest, and a thick gold rope necklace. Only a white bar towel draped over one shoulder set him apart from a typical customer.

"Evening. What can I get you?" The bartender set down his knife and wiped his hands on his towel.

"What's your name?" Hanford smiled, showing off some teeth.

"They call me *Rod*." There was a wink in his voice.

Hanford wondered if that line ever worked. "How about some information?"

The bartender's eyes narrowed. "If you want a drink, I can fix you right up, but I'm not much of an information source."

Hanford withdrew a photo of Susan that Linda had given him. Held it up to the bartender. "Seen her in here?"

Rod examined the photo for a second while Hanford examined him. Thought he caught a glimmer of recognition.

"Never seen her before. Why, she in trouble?"

"She's missing." Hanford leaned closer. "Heard she came in

here often. I'm not looking to cause any trouble. Just trying to locate her. Put her friends at ease."

"Missing, huh? That's heavy. Sorry, man. I don't remember her."

"Is there anything I can do to help refresh your memory?"

Rod glanced around, then back at Hanford. "Bartenders rely on tips to make a living, you dig?"

Hanford removed a wad of bills from his pocket. Peeled off a ten. Placed it on the bar but kept two fingers on it. "Memory starting to come back?"

Rod rubbed his temples. "Starting to…but not quite."

Hanford added a second ten to the first. "Now?"

"Yes, I do seem to recall a few things." Rod gripped the bills and yanked them out from under Hanford's fingers. "Name's what, Sarah, right?"

"Susan."

"Yeah, that's right. Susan. Came in with her friend, a hot blond chick named Linda. Piercing blue eyes. Real brick house. Anyway, they never had to buy any drinks, know what I mean? Always had dudes trying to pick them up. Seemed friendly, but not *too* friendly. I usually saw them leaving the place with each other, and only each other." Rod shrugged. "I don't pass judgment one way or the other. Free world, right?"

"When did you see them last?"

Rod pursed his lips. "Memory's getting a little hazy again."

Hanford forked over another ten. "This is it, so you might as well tell me everything. I know how much you value a satisfied customer."

"Right, right. Week ago, Saturday, I think. Arrived their usual time, between nine and ten—when most people come—left around one, maybe. Pretty sure they left alone."

"Did you see anyone harassing them?"

"Naw. The usual. Guys would buy them drinks. Dance. Flirt. Realize it wasn't going anywhere, then move on. New guys would step up to the plate, take a swing. How it is, man.

Everybody's putting on the moves, everyone's doing the hustle. And why not? We're young, we're beautiful, and we're in LA. It's a dream, man!"

"And you've got a front-row seat."

Rod looked taken aback. Slapped the bar. "This is just a gig. To pay the rent. As soon as I get my big break, I'm outta here. I'm gonna be a star and you can say you knew me when."

Hanford gave Rod one of his cards. "Well, star, if you think of anything else, give me a call. And good luck. It's a tough, tough business."

A man with an unnatural tan and a perm had oozed his way from the other end of the bar. "I've got it from here, Rod."

"Sure." Rod quickly put away the sliced citrus and tipped his head at Hanford. "Check you later." Then he stalked into the lounge area to clean some tables.

Once Rod was out of earshot, the man extended his hand to Hanford. An enormous gold pinkie ring reflected light as if it were a disco ball. "I'm the owner, Bobby Edelstein."

Hanford shook Edelstein's hand, careful not to smudge the ring. "Jerry Hanford."

"Well, Jerry, I noticed you and Rod having a little conversation. Money changing hands. If that was a drug transaction, you need to tell me. Can't have our bartenders dealing, can we?"

"Nothing like that. Just wanted some information."

"The kind you pay for?" Edelstein laughed, and it was as unnatural as his tan. "Maybe I can help. I usually know what's going on around here. And you won't have to pay me a dime."

"Sure." He pulled out Susan's photo again, showed it to Edelstein. "Know her?"

"She's a peach. Her friend too. Regulars like them who really make this a great place."

"She's missing."

"Missing? That's terrible." Edelstein tapped his chin, and for a moment, Hanford thought some of the spray tan was going to rub off on the guy's fingernail. "You know, I don't think I saw her this weekend, now that you mention it."

"Her friend said they were supposed to be here on Saturday, but she never showed."

Edelstein exhaled. "That's it?"

"What do you mean?"

"A girl doesn't show up one night and now she's missing? No ransacked apartment? No eyewitness who saw her get abducted? No abandoned car by the side of the freeway? Get real." Edelstein's tone had decreased a couple of notches on the friendliness scale and increased on the volume scale.

"You're probably right, but I'm investigating, nonetheless." Hanford offered a perfunctory smile, slid the photo back into his pocket. "See anybody bothering her?"

"Look, pal, we see anybody bothering anybody, we tell them to buzz off. I run this club right."

"Is there anyone else who might have a clue? House manager maybe?"

"Frankie Topaz's the guy who runs the club, day-to-day."

"Mind if I talk to him?"

"Knock yourself out. But it's Monday, so he's off tonight. Sharp guy. I'd be lost without him. Everybody loves Frankie."

"Know how I can reach him? Phone number?"

Edelstein grinned, showing off two perfect rows of capped teeth. "You can reach him here, tomorrow."

Thanks for nothing. "Then I guess I'll see you then."

"Sure, sure." Edelstein *clinked* the bar a couple of times with his pinkie ring. Shook his head. "You know, I love 'em, these bright-eyed enthusiastic girls, with their big hair and their big smiles and their big boobs, but so many of them come out here chasing a fantasy. Trying to get into the biz, think they'll get discovered by some big movie producer here at the club. After a few weeks or months, they realize that, while they're hot in Topeka or Springfield or Phoenix, this is Hollywood, baby. Bumfuck hot isn't anywhere close to Hollywood hot. Out here, smokin' hot chicks swarm like locusts. And don't you just love that?" Edelstein paused, smiled conspiratorially at Hanford, who didn't return the sentiment. "'Course, I don't have to tell you. Handsome devil. Bet you got the babes crawling all over you, huh? A private *dick*. Yeah, I'll bet."

Hanford didn't see the need to punch this guy's lights out, although he wouldn't have minded. But you never knew whose cooperation you might end up needing in an investigation. He swallowed his wise-ass retort and simply said, "Thanks."

Then he turned around and headed for the exit, eager for some fresh air. He'd almost made it to the door when he heard someone calling out, "Hey, mister."

He stopped, and a woman came up to him, breathless. "I, uh, saw you talking to the bartender. Asking him some questions."

"Yes?"

"I noticed the picture you showed him. Reflected in the mirror."

"Do you know her?"

"Are you a boyfriend or something?"

"No." Hanford studied this woman, tried to figure out her angle. "A friend of hers thinks she's missing."

"Friend named Linda?"

"So, you do know her?"

"Buy me a drink, and I'll tell you what I know. My name's Cindy."

As Rod said, everyone was doing the hustle. "Look, no offense, but unless you have something I might find useful, I really don't have the time."

"I do. But I sure am thirsty." She licked her lips theatrically. Everyone's an actor, too.

Hanford sighed. "Okay, sure. Let's get you a drink." He turned back to the bar, but the woman grabbed his arm.

"No, not here. There's a coffee shop not too far. This place is full of creeps, and it totally sucks."

* * *

After the waitress took their orders: coffee and pie for both, the woman started talking. "I know Linda and Susan from the club. We'd sit together, dance together. Look out for one another, too. When Susan didn't show up, I didn't think much about it, but Linda was kinda upset. I just figured…"

"That she found something else to do? Guy, maybe?"

"Exactly. At first. But now…"

"Now what?"

"Now that Susan is officially missing, maybe there's something to what I've been thinking." With one hand, Cindy patted her hair, which was feathered like Farrah Fawcett's.

The waitress served them their coffees and two slices of pie: peach for Cindy and pecan for Hanford. He forked a piece into his mouth. Not the worst he'd ever had, but it wasn't House of Pies. "Look, Cindy, let's just cut to the chase. I'm going to be done with my pie in about ten minutes, so if you have any idea what might have happened to Susan, now's the time to talk."

"Last Thursday, I saw Susan talking to Frankie Topaz, the club manager. Almost like they were arguing. Then Frankie took Susan by the arm, and they left. Right out the front door."

"Thursday, huh? Did they come back?"

"He did, about an hour later. Alone." Cindy slurped some coffee. "At the time, I figured it wasn't any big deal. He's a real piece of work; thinks he's God's gift to woman. I just figured she told him she wasn't interested, and he wanted to discuss it outside. But now that she's missing…"

"You think this Topaz had something to do with it?"

She shrugged. "I dunno. But I guess it's worth checking out. I mean, you're the detective, right?"

Hanford eyed her. "Let me ask you a question. If you think the club sucks and everyone there is a creep, why do you keep going there?"

Cindy took a minute, wiped a tear from one eye. "I got no

place else to go. At least there, I feel like I'm somebody, you know?"

Hanford didn't, not in the least.

They finished their pie and coffee and Cindy left to return to the club. Hanford didn't want to wait until tomorrow to talk to Frankie Topaz. He dug a dime out of his pocket and fed it into the coin slot of a payphone at the diner. Dialed a familiar number.

Two rings and the call got picked up. "Detective Porter. Whaddya want?"

"Hello, Porter. Jerry here."

"Oh, Christ, what good deed am I being punished for now?"

"Is that any way to greet one of your closest and dearest friends?"

"No, it isn't, but it's how I'm greeting you. Lemme guess, you need a favor. Or three."

"Why that's very kind of you to offer." Hanford put some cream and sugar in his voice.

"Just get to it, Jerry. I'm busy here. Trying to keep the city safe for you private citizens."

"And your efforts are much appreciated. I need an address on a Frankie Topaz."

"Frankie Topaz? That his real name?"

"This is Hollywood. So, I doubt it."

"Who is he, and what did he do?"

"Probably nothing, but I need to check him out. Club manager at a place called Boogie Starz."

"Disco on Sunset? Got a buddy in vice says there's a lot of drug dealing going down there. Been on their radar for a while, but they haven't been able to bust it up yet. That what you're investigating? Drugs? Seems out of your wheelhouse. Aren't you more of an insurance fraud kind of guy? Guy stepping out on his wife, perhaps?"

Hanford paused, waiting for Porter to get all his barbs out of the way. Silence. Had Porter tired of the game? "Well? Address?"

"You know, this is always a one-way street. Whenever I want some information, you hold out on me."

"You want a tip? Stay away from the ponies at Santa Anita," Hanford said.

"Funny. You owe me. And right now, you owe me so much I could repo your trailer."

"It's all yours."

"No, thanks, I don't have enough money to pay for the renovations. Hang on, I'll get you that address. But Jerry?"

"Yeah?"

"Don't do anything I wouldn't do, okay?"

"Do I ever?"

After Hanford got Topaz's address and said goodbye to Porter, his next call went to Tim Warner, TV star. "Tim, this is Jerry Hanford."

"Hey, it's Mr. Shamus. What can I do for you?"

"You know how you've been wanting to ride alongside me as I work a case? Get some real-world experience to make your portrayal more realistic? Well, if you're not busy now, I could use some help."

"You got it, sport! Tell me where and when, and I'm there."

"Meet me at my trailer in forty-five minutes. And wear some dark clothes, okay?"

"Oh, boy. This is gonna be a blast!"

Jerry sighed. *Actors.*

Hanford parked his gold Pontiac Firebird in front of his trailer and hopped out. Before he could get to the door, two guys dressed in slacks and sport coats stepped out of the shadows. One was ugly; his buddy was uglier. The sport coats did a poor job of hiding the thugs' bodybuilder physiques. From the misshapen noses and scars on their faces, Hanford figured they were washed-up boxers whose skills narrowed down their job prospects considerably.

"You Hanford?" Ugly asked.

"Who's asking?"

"We'll take that as a yes," Uglier said. "You stuck your nose into things it don't belong in. Now it's time to stick your nose out."

"I don't have any idea what you're talking about."

Ugly sprang forward and slugged Hanford in the breadbasket. "Now, do you know what we're talking about?"

"Look, I think there's been—"

Before he could complete his sentence, Uglier buried a fist into Hanford's midsection. Hanford doubled over, then dropped to his knees.

"There's been no mistake. Butt out, or we'll be back."

"I'll be sure to roll out the Welcome Wagon," Hanford mumbled, but the two heavies had already receded into the shadows.

"Come in," Hanford called out from his trailer's couch. He'd been wondering who had sent the goons to deliver the message. Had it been Frankie Topaz?

Tim Warner strode right in. Six-foot-two, solidly built, head of wavy dark hair, and a model-perfect smile, it wasn't hard to fathom that all men wanted to look like Tim Warner and all women wanted to date him. Hanford didn't know any real PIs who looked like movie stars, but TV was TV and reality had little to do with it. Hanford had been shocked when a producer had come to him wanting to base the Bickford character on his life, but he hadn't hesitated saying yes and cashing the check, meager as it was.

"This place looks exactly like a run-down version of my trailer," he said. "The one on the set, I mean. I live in a mansion in the hills." He noticed Hanford holding his gut. "Hey, what happened to you?"

Hanford told Warner about the two guys roughing him up.

"That really happens? I mean, it happens to me in every episode, but I thought that was just lazy writing."

"Doesn't usually happen to me." Hanford winced, just thinking about it.

"Sorry, I didn't mean to sound so…" He washed the glee from his voice. "Are you okay?"

"I'll live. Right now, we're going to pay a visit to a guy named Frankie Topaz."

"Okay. Why?"

Hanford explained the situation, and when he was done, Warner looked like a kid at Christmas. "This is exciting. Do you think we'll be *teaching him a lesson*, if you know what I mean?" Warner pounded a fist into his palm. "I've never done that in real life."

"It's not nearly as fun as it seems. Hard on the hands. And you really can't risk taking a shot in the face. America would hate to see that precious mug get damaged."

Warner ran the back of his fingers along his granite jawline, as if he was seeing how close his shave was. "I guess you've got a point. Still, we can talk tough and try to intimidate him, can't we?"

"Sure. Let's talk the truth out of him." Hanford rose and retrieved his gun from the desk drawer.

"Whoa," Warner said. "You're not planning to use that, are you?"

"I sure hope not. But it pays to be prepared."

Hanford drove to the address Porter had given him for Topaz. A well-kept bungalow in Los Feliz. There was a single car in the driveway and a light shone through one of the two front windows. Hanford parked two doors down from the house under a streetlamp and killed the engine.

"What's our play?" Warner said.

"First of all, we're not playing around." Hanford locked eyes with Warner for a beat. "It's still before ten, so why don't we just walk up to the door and talk to him?"

"That's it? No fake story? You know, saying you're from the power company or something?"

"No fake story."

"How about if you barge in while I cover the back? In case he runs."

"No barging. No covering the back. At least not yet. Remember, for all we know, Linda is mad at Topaz and just trying to get him in hot water. For all we know, maybe he's a stand-up guy. So, we're going to be nice and polite and respectful. Until we know the score. Then we'll see."

"And that's why you brought the gun?"

"Forget about the gun. We're playing this straight."

Warner's face sagged. "Okay. Fine."

"Hey, being a real PI isn't so exciting."

"I'm starting to get that picture."

Hanford and Warner got out, crossed the street, and ended up on Topaz's porch. No other people were outside, and the only evidence of life in the neighborhood was the faint sound of a neighbor's TV.

Hanford used the knocker to rap on Topaz's door.

A moment later, a voice from within. "Who is it?"

"I spoke to Edelstein at the club a little while ago, and he told me to talk to you." Straight enough.

"Oh, yeah?" The door remained closed. "Talk about what?"

"I think it's something you probably don't want your neighbors to hear."

There was silence, followed by a scuffling sound, followed by the door cracking open, followed by Topaz peering out. "Who are you?"

"My name's Hanford and this is…" Hanford trailed off, leaving it to Warner whether he wanted to use his real name or not.

"Tim Warner." The TV star smiled his TV star smile.

"Holy smokes, what are you doing here?" Topaz's demeanor did a one-eighty, going from suspicious to adoring in two seconds flat. "Come on in!"

Hanford and Warner followed Topaz into the living room. "Care for a seat?"

"No, thanks. We don't want to take up too much of your evening," Hanford said.

"Not a problem." Topaz faced Warner, even though Hanford was doing the talking.

"Okay, good. I'm trying to locate—"

Topaz interrupted. "Tim Warner, in the flesh. Is this research for your show or something? Doing an episode at a disco?"

"Um, yeah, something like that, I guess."

Warner hadn't stopped smiling since Topaz had opened the door, and Hanford wondered if always being "on" was an occupational requirement for TV stars.

Hanford snapped his fingers, trying to get Topaz's attention. "Look, Mr. Topaz, I just have a few questions."

Topaz finally broke his attention away from Warner and faced Hanford. "Sure. Sorry. Shoot."

Hanford took Susan's picture out of his pocket and showed Topaz. "I'm trying to locate this woman. Do you recognize her?"

"I...uh, no, who is she?" Topaz sputtered. His face had paled two shades and his breathing had quickened. Hanford noticed Topaz's eyes cut to the back of the small house, but he didn't have to be a trained PI to notice that. Hell, Hanford figured even Warner must have seen the change come over Topaz.

"Okay, okay. Let's have the truth. We know you know her, and judging by your reaction, you must have some information on her whereabouts."

"Never saw her before."

"We have a witness who saw you arguing with her. Last Thursday night. At the club, and then you left with her. You returned to the club, she didn't. That's the last anyone's seen of her."

Topaz shot another quick glance toward a hallway leading to the bedrooms. Hanford would have loved to play poker with him. "Can you guys excuse me for a minute? I think I need to, uh, check on my sick mother." Without waiting for an answer, Topaz rushed off, leaving Hanford and Warner standing in the living room.

"Okay, Tim," Hanford said. "Now you can go cover the back. Topaz's going to make a run for it with Susan."

"She's here? How do you know?"

"'Cause I'm a PI. Now get going. Out the front and around the back. Just block their way. I'll make sure they don't get past me."

Warner didn't have to be told again. He raced out the front door. Hanford figured it would take a minute or two for Topaz to get Susan and gather whatever stuff he thought they might need for hitting the road.

Hanford made it to the hallway, just in time to see Topaz come barreling out of a bedroom, one hand holding Susan's, the other hand clutching a duffel bag. When Topaz saw Hanford, he turned left toward a back door at the end of the hall.

"We're not here to hurt you, Topaz," Hanford called after him. "Susan, either."

Topaz released Susan and grabbed for the doorknob, flung the door open. Warner was standing there, a huge grin on his face. "Going somewhere?" he said, delivering his line like it was the last snippet of dialogue before the commercial break.

Topaz stopped, glanced back at Hanford. Frantic eyes like those of a cornered animal. "Why are you here?" Next to him, Susan appeared even more terrified, if that was possible.

"Susan, your friend Linda hired me to find you. She was worried when you disappeared."

Susan exhaled. "You're not going to hurt me?"

"Wasn't planning to." Hanford gestured at Topaz. "Is he holding you against your will?" Hanford didn't think so, based on how Topaz was reacting, but he needed to make sure.

"Against my…? No, of course not," she said. "Frankie saved me."

"Good. Then maybe we can all sit down and talk about this."

Susan explained that she and Topaz had been seeing each other on the sly for about a month. She stopped by the club early last week, looking for Topaz in the back-office suite, and accidentally saw Edelstein involved in a shady deal involving a couple of suspicious characters and packages of white powder Edelstein removed from a hidey-hole under loose floorboards. Susan quickly scampered off, thinking she hadn't been seen. A day later, Edelstein had put out the word—through Topaz—that he wanted to meet with Susan to discuss a few things about a new customer loyalty program he was thinking about starting.

It sounded legit to Topaz, so he didn't think much about it. But last Thursday, when Topaz told Susan that Edelstein wanted to talk to her, she fessed up to what she'd seen. That's what they were discussing—it wasn't really an argument Cindy had witnessed. Finally, Topaz persuaded Susan to go into hiding at his place until they figured out what to do. Topaz knew what his boss was capable of and wanted to keep Susan safe.

"What are we going to do now?" Susan asked. "Frankie says Edelstein will kill me to keep me quiet."

"And if she rats him out to the cops, he'll find a way to kill her, too. Edelstein has long arms." Topaz sighed. "Maybe we should go to South America."

Hanford had an idea. "I have a better idea. We can nail Edelstein, so Susan won't even have to testify. We just need some evidence."

That night—at three-thirty in the morning, to be exact—Topaz used his key to let Hanford and Warner into the club. They kept the lights out, guided only by the flashlight in Hanford's hand and an illuminated Miller Lite sign behind the bar.

"Tim, why don't you check the bathrooms to make sure nobody's passed out in there. We'll meet you in the back office."

Warner veered down a side hallway toward the restrooms. Topaz and Hanford entered the club proper, headed for the office. Before they made it, a voice called out. "Freeze right there. Make a move, and I'll shoot."

A bank of lights flickered on above the bar, and Rod the bartender stood there, police special aimed right at Hanford.

"Breaking and entering is a crime, you know."

"I work here," Topaz said.

"Not anymore you don't." Rod sneered. "Good thing Mr. E. asked me to watch over the place. Guess he had an idea what was gonna happen, huh? Too bad I had to shoot the burglars. I'll be sure to act real sad when the cops get here. It'll be a performance to remember."

Rod pulled a phone out from behind the bar and dialed a number, keeping the gun trained on his captives. "Mr. E.? Rod here. You were right, they came. Got 'em under control. Yes. Yes. Okay, ten minutes. Yes, sir." Rod hung up. "He'll be here shortly. You're gonna wish you never got involved with this."

Out of the corner of his eye, Hanford noticed Warner creeping up on Rod from the shadows.

Topaz took a step forward. "Put the gun down, Rod. You're not going to shoot anyone. When Mr. Edelstein gets here, we'll hash all of this out."

"Dream on," Rod said.

Topaz took another step forward, and Rod jerked the gun in Topaz's direction. Then Warner came rushing at Rod from the other side. Rod whipped around. Hanford joined in the melee, and he lunged at Rod, too.

The gun went off, and chaos ensued.

* * *

Hanford sat on a chair in Edelstein's office, hands behind his back, a strip of duct tape around his ankles. From the main area of the club, he heard the door opening. Then footsteps, then a voice called out, "Rod, you here? Where are you?"

The footsteps got louder, the door to the back office swung open, and Edelstein strode in. When he saw Hanford sitting there, his eyes went wide. When he saw the floorboards pried up and the drugs and money piled on his desk, his eyes grew wider. "What the hell is going on? Where's Rod?"

"He took the others out back." Hanford squirmed in his chair, hands still behind his back. "You have quite the drug operation going here, don't you? What else are you into?"

Edelstein raised his chin slightly, beamed. "I'm good at many things."

"Running numbers? Prostitution?"

"Why not? Someone has to make money keeping people happy. Like I said, I'm good at many things."

"You weren't so good at killing Susan."

"The game's not over yet. If I set out to kill someone, I will."

"Done it before?"

"You have no idea." Edelstein delivered the line dripping with action-movie-star bravado.

Hanford nodded and raised his voice. "Okay, I think we've got enough evidence. With the drugs and the incriminating comments, the cops should be able to make a good case."

"What are you talking about?" Edelstein said. "You're going to be dead in ten minutes. Soon as Rod is finished dealing with the others."

Hanford brought his hands out from behind his back. Leaned over and pulled the duct tape off his ankles. Stood.

Warner stepped out from behind the door, holding Rod's gun, which was now trained on Edelstein. "We heard every-thing. You're going to jail, buddy. For a long time."

"Fuck you," Edelstein said to Warner.

Warner reared back and slugged Edelstein in the jaw, and the man fell to the ground like a deadweight.

"Shit!" Warner shook his hand out, as if that would reduce the pain. "That hurts like the devil."

"Told you." Hanford clapped Warner on the back. "We make a pretty good team, don't we? Now, go help Topaz keep Rod subdued. I'll call the cops. They have some trash to take out."

Hanford set the tray of tacos in the middle of the picnic bench at Casa Tacos. "Ladies, dig in."

Linda grabbed a taco and placed it on a paper plate in front of her. "Jerry, thank you again for all your help. Without you, I'm afraid Susan might have been..."

"Yes, thank you so much for saving my life." Susan took a taco for herself and started picking off some shredded lettuce.

"I think you're being a bit dramatic, but I'm glad I could be of service," Hanford said, around a mouthful of taco. He glanced up from his meal and saw Tim Warner approaching. "Here's someone else you should thank."

The girls turned around and their faces lit up when they saw Warner.

"Oh, hi, Tim." Linda fluffed out her hair with her hand. She patted the bench next to her. "Have a seat!"

"Got a break in the shooting schedule." He plopped down next to Linda and helped himself to a taco. "Nice to see everyone in a happy mood."

The two girls focused all their attention on Warner and began peppering him with questions. About being a TV star, about other actors he'd worked with, about his mansion in the hills. Warner soaked it all in, smiling the entire time he told his wild show biz stories.

Nobody cared about the real-life PI, par for the course. Hanford snatched the last taco and smiled entirely to himself.

FADE TO BLACK

EVERYBODY WAS KUNG FU FIGHTING
William Dylan Powell

Houston, Texas 1978

"How many?" asked the ticket lady. She sported round, oversized glasses and an enormous Afro, leaning out of the ticket box to see inside the gold Ford Elite. But the car's interior was all shadow and smoke.

"Five," said the driver, not looking at her but scanning the drive-in's ocean of cars.

"Five dollars, please," the woman said.

"Jungle Boogie" played on the car's radio as the man handed over a five-dollar bill and took his tickets.

"Enjoy Chopsocky Saturday."

On the big screen, *Five Deadly Venoms* was projected fifty feet high—Lo Mang and Wei Pai battling to the death as fists and feet flew. The Elite crept up and down the lines of parked cars like a bull shark. Windows down, the men heard the on-screen action come and go from the speakers clipped to each car.

"Thought you'd find my weak spot," said the man on screen, his lips moving out of sync with the sound. "But still, you've failed."

The driver of the Elite stopped behind a two-tone brown Oldsmobile Cutlass. The men poured out and surrounded the Olds. "Jimmy Chin," one of the men said. "You're a thief and a coward. Come out and face us."

On screen, Lo Mang was being placed in an iron maiden, his screams falling on deaf ears.

A young Asian man stepped out of the Cutlass, bag of buttered popcorn in hand. "Derrick Lau? Is that you?" he said, squinting through the darkness. "What kind of jive y'all talkin' man?"

"Shut up, fool." The man flicked open an expandable baton. "You crossed the line. Now it's time to pay."

Gene lit a cigarette, took a drag, and set the pack and lighter on the table, which was covered with half-eaten roast duck, Mandarin pancakes and spring onions. "Look, I've got my license now. At six clients you're groovin'."

The waitress set Dan's *Tsing-Tao* on the table.

Dan loosened his tie. "Okay, Lew Archer, do you have six clients?"

"I just got my license last week," Gene said, tapping his ash into the nearest plate.

"Would you like a job?" Dan said.

Gene blinked. "What? A PI job?"

"No," Dan said. "A real job. Offshore. One month on, one month off. Ridiculous money, and you'd be great at it. Basically, just problem solving."

Gene held out his hands. "What have I been saying? I'm starting a business, growing a client base. How am I going to do that if I'm turning wrenches offshore?"

Dan took a long pull of his beer and leaned forward. "Goddamnit, Gene. You owe me a lot of fucking money. And you owe my sister more than that after y'all's clusterfuck of a marriage."

Gene rubbed his forehead. "Look, this thing is going to work. I can feel it. But not if I change the plan every few months. Just be patient."

"Jesus Christ," Dan hissed. "I'll be your boss's boss's boss. Pay me back in a month and buy a house for cash at the end of the year. What the fuck is there to talk about? You still going to meetings?"

Gene took a drag on his cigarette, glaring at Dan. He exhaled. "Yes, I'm still going to meetings. Look, thanks. Really. But I'm a grown ass man. I gotta square my life my way."

The waitress appeared with the check. "Who's the lucky winner?"

Dan drained his beer, slamming the bottle onto the table and standing. His face was red as sweet-and-sour sauce. "Give it to the grown ass man over here," he said, tossing his napkin in his chair. "The grown ass man who'll be at our Galveston heliport in forty-eight hours for deployment if he knows what's good for him."

The waitress was in her seventies, gray hair in a bun. She wore a mustard-yellow blouse, polyester slacks, and an orange ascot. She handed Gene the check and raised her eyebrows.

He sighed. "Ma'am, I'm sorry, but I can't cover that. When my doofus ex-brother-in-law invited me, I just assumed..."

Gene had been eating at Hong Kong Palace since Sandy divorced him, and he'd never seen the old lady smile. Not once. In his mind, he saw her pick up the red phone by the hostess station and call the cops. Cops meant charges. Charges meant no PI license. But, instead, she took Dan's place in the opposite chair.

"You're a private investigator, right?" she said.

Gene nodded. "Yeah. Gene Kuykendahl." Gene reached out his hand and she shook it.

"Maggie Chang," she said. "Pleasure."

"Likewise."

"One year now you've come every night. Ordered the cheapest menu items and read all those private investigation books.

Get your license yet?"

"Uh, yeah. Last week."

"Perfect. Come, take a ride." Despite her age, she hopped off the chair with the agility of a child and smoothed out her slacks.

"Excuse me?"

"C'mon. You're on a case."

"Just like that?"

"You got $82 dollars to cover the Space City Peking Duck Special?"

Gene swiped his keys off the table. "I'll drive."

The caramel tan Plymouth Volare was the only thing that had survived Gene's gambling, a loan shark named Big Bubba Valentine, and his ex-wife, Sandy. It had a dent in the hood after an unfortunate incident at Gilley's, and a cracked windshield.

Smoke erupted from the slant six as he cranked the ignition. Maggie Chang directed him from Hong Kong Palace and down the street. The heat was oppressive, the Volare's underpowered air conditioner struggling against a coastal breeze that felt like it was blowing from the back of an overloaded clothes dryer.

"We're looking for lions," Maggie said. "Hundred dollars now, two hundred when the lions come home."

"Lions? Like, live lions?"

"Yeah, you have a whip handy? No, dummy, stone lions. From the kung fu school. Somebody stole them."

Maggie pulled a pack of Chunghwas from her purse and lit one. "We reported it to the police, but you know." She shrugged.

After Maggie pointed Gene down Leeland and over a few blocks, they pulled up to a brick building with a glass storefront. "My brother and I bought this place for a song when we moved from California ten years ago. Built in nineteen twenty-five. Maintenance is a nightmare, but it's paid for."

"It's a great old building," Gene said, shutting the car off as they hopped out and walked to the entrance.

"Used to be a soda shop back in the day. Then it was a jazz hall, then a dance club. Today, it's a Wing Chun school."

"Wing what?"

"Wing Chun. Kung fu. You know, like Bruce Lee?"

"Ah."

Inside, Gene saw men in white T-shirts and black cotton pants punching, kicking, and doing various exercises. A few plonked on wooden dummies or hit punching bags.

Just outside the front door, Maggie gestured at the ground. "Well, Perry Mason, here's the crime scene."

Gene looked around. "Where?"

"Some detective," Maggie said, pointing at the ground.

On either side of the door, Gene now noticed two dark rectangles where the bricks were a rich maroon. Elsewhere, the brick was pink, faded, dirty, chipped, and cracked. The patches looked around two-by-four feet.

Gene knelt and inspected where the lions had been. "Perry Mason was a lawyer. Paul Drake was his investigator."

"Whatever," Maggie said. "When a new school opens, your master paints the eyes of lions guarding your door. So, they can always watch over you. Dig?"

Gene stood, wiping his hands. "How tall were these lions? They must have weighed a ton."

Maggie put a hand to her waist. "About like so. Yeah, weigh a lot for sure. Must have brought a pickup or something."

The front door flew open. A slim man in a white T-shirt stepped out. He had shaggy black hair and was out of breath, hands on hips.

Maggie said something in Cantonese and gestured at Gene.

Gene smiled and extended his hand. The two shook.

"This is Derrick Lau, my nephew. Derrick, this is Gene. He's going to find our lions."

"Nice to meet you," Derrick said. Then he said something

else in Cantonese, pointing at the spots where the statues had been.

Maggie rolled her eyes.

"Do you have a copy of the police report?" Gene said. "That would help me catch up more quickly."

Derrick looked at Maggie, whose eyes narrowed.

"Fine," Derrick said. "Make it fast, though. We do kung fu here, not Kojak. You dig?"

As they walked inside, Maggie said: "Derrick thinks he already knows who stole the lions."

"Who?"

"Iron Mantis Fist Society," Derrick said.

Sweat popped from Gene's forehead as soon as they stepped into Cheung's Martial Arts, where it felt twenty degrees warmer than the summer heat outside. He removed his fedora, wiping his forehead. None of the students paid them any attention as Gene followed Derrick and Maggie into a small office. Traditional Chinese music played from speakers in the ceiling. The plonk-plonk-plonking of men hitting the wooden dummies echoed through the space, which Gene thought cramped for a gym now that he was inside. Those who talked whispered, as though in a library.

The office held a small brown couch, a metal desk with piles of papers and a glass case containing bottles and jars. Derrick opened a desk drawer and pulled out a pink can. "Tab?"

Maggie sat on the couch.

"Is it cold?" Gene asked, wiping his forehead again.

Derrick smiled. "Air conditioning makes you weak." He took a folder off the desk and handed it to Gene. "I want that back. Sifu needs to see it when he returns next week."

"And who is Sifu, exactly?"

"Sifu Cheung," Derrick said. "Our teacher. This is his school."

"Sifu means like master," Maggie said, lighting a cigarette.

How can she smoke in this heat? Gene thought.

"Sifu is in Hong Kong," Derrick said.

Gene scanned the police report. "So, he was gone when the theft occurred?"

Derrick nodded. He opened his Tab and dropped the pull top into the trash. "Never would have happened if he were here."

"That's not the only thing that wouldn't have happened." Maggie said, taking a draw off her cigarette.

Derrick glared at her, then looked at Gene. "Look, this was all Jimmy Chin. We worked it out. Far as I'm concerned, it's done. I'll replace the lions before Sifu gets back."

"What makes you think this Jimmy guy took the lions?"

Derrick took a sip of his Tab. "Man, he's always talking trash about the Wing Chun style. Not to my face, you dig, but out in the street. You know what a praying mantis is? An annoying little bug."

Gene looked at the police report again. "You left around midnight and the lions were here, then gone when you came in the next day around noon?"

"Yep. Two days ago."

"Mind if I look around?" Gene asked.

Derrick shrugged, drinking the rest of the Tab and throwing the can into the trash. "Free country. Now, if y'all don't mind, I've got work to do."

Maggie stood.

"Thanks for your time," Gene said, shaking Derrick's hand again.

"No sweat."

"Bullshit," Gene said. "Everyone in here is sweating."

Gene followed Derrick into the main room. There wasn't much to the place, mostly empty space with framed photos and Chinese prints on the wall. A rack of sticks and swords stood in the corner. In the middle of the room near the ceiling was a clock built into the wall. A recessed rack of shelves sported trophies, metals, and trinkets. A tiny decorative fountain sent the calming sound of trickling water throughout the room.

A man and woman stood chatting by the fountain. Maggie joined them and waved Gene over.

"Mary, this is Gene Kuykendahl, private investigator. He's going to get our lions back. Gene, Mary Fung, and Matt Yu."

"Hello," Gene said, nodding. A drop of sweat fell off his forehead and onto the hardwood floor.

"Mary is Sifu Cheung's Disciple," Maggie said.

"Nice to meet you," Mary said. Gene thought she seemed sad and a bit detached, her expression blank and voice robotic.

"I don't know anything about kung fu," Gene said, "other than the movies. Disciple means you're good, huh?"

"That's one way to look at it," Mary said.

A few feet away, Derrick began pounding a punching bag. The building shook.

"It means she'll learn everything Sifu knows," Matt said. "Hey, come workout with us. You can protect yourself while you're doing all that PI jive."

"Yeah," Derrick said, pounding the heavy bag. "We'll make a man out of you."

"We'll see," Gene said as Mary Fung excused herself and walked over to a wooden dummy, her ponytail flopping back and forth as she struck the polished wood.

"Her fists must be pretty tough after hitting on that thing," Gene said to Matt.

"Oh, it's not about that," Matt said. "In Wing Chun, the goal is to dominate the center of your opponent." Matt stood in front of Gene, placing a fist in front of his chest. "These cats on the wooden dummies are practicing various hand and foot positioning to take the centerline. Feel me?"

"Must take a lot of time to learn," Gene said.

"Yeah," Matt said. "*Kung fu* translated actually means work time. Gotta put in the work to get the skills."

"Interesting," Gene said. "I didn't know that. I'm going to poke around a bit."

"Later, gator."

The first door he opened revealed just a toilet and sink. Opening a second door, the smell of vinegar radiated from a small closet with a mop, broom, and bucket. The only other door was thicker and clearly the back door.

The door led to a small alley, pocked by mud-filled potholes. A gold Ford Elite and a black Datsun 280Z with racing wheels were parked next to a pair of metal garbage pails. It was a longshot, but he lifted the lid off the nearest can. Again, Gene smelled vinegar. A pile of rags covered the bottom. The other can held only a dead flower bouquet, which he inspected. Tulips, mostly, the card attached mostly disintegrated. The only legible word was "congratulations."

Maggie Chang stepped out of the back door, lighting another cigarette. She and Gene walked around the building as they talked. At the entrance, they stopped where the lions had been. Gene looked up and down the street.

Either side of the school held vacant lots, but across the street stood a strip mall with a dry cleaner, a bank, and a dentist. The signs were in both English and Chinese. Gene took out a handkerchief and wiped his forehead.

"You know," Gene said, "some random person probably just pulled over and threw them in their truck. Hell, they could be at a frat house."

Maggie Chang dropped her cigarette onto the pavement and mashed it with her espadrille. "Really? This is what my $82 Space City Peking Duck special bought me? And my hundred? A 'guess we'll never know' attitude?"

Gene's face reddened. "I'm just saying random, stupid crime happens. Not everything is Sherlockian." *But she has a point*, Gene thought. *If this is the line of work that will help rebuild my life, and maybe even allow a little self-respect, I have to give my all.*

He took a deep breath and looked around again. That's when he noticed the camera.

"That bank," Gene said. "Think their security camera works?"

"What am I? Maggie the Mind Reader?"

"Right. C'mon, let's ask."

Gene held the door for Maggie as the two went inside Hang Seng Southwest Bank of Houston. He heard no English as the tellers served customers from behind a counter. Cantopop music played overhead.

A woman in a gold beret and jumpsuit sat by the front door watching a chunky black-and-white television. On screen, JR Ewing was having a serious discussion with Bobby and Sue Ellen. The subtitles were in Chinese.

"Excuse me," Gene said. "Could I speak to the manager?"

Maggie lit another cigarette.

The woman looked up from the TV for a split second but didn't respond and went right back to watching.

"Uh, miss?" Gene said. "Sorry to disturb you, but could I have a moment?"

The woman ignored him all together. On screen, Bobby Ewing's office was under construction as he tried to work.

"Hey," Maggie said. "Lemon tart." She walked around the desk and turned off the television. "This man is asking you a question."

The woman's forehead wrinkled. "Can I help you?"

"Yes," Gene said. "My friend was the victim of a burglary two days ago. We'd like to see outside security footage from out front that day. Thursday."

"Mr. Lee isn't here," the woman said, clearly pleased she couldn't help. "He is the only person authorized to share such a thing, and he's fishing. In Corpus Christi."

She reached to turn on the television, but Maggie cleared her throat. "When are you expecting him?"

"Tomorrow," the woman said.

"Fine," Maggie said. "Have him call Mr. Kuykendahl as soon as he returns. This is urgent."

Maggie looked at Gene.

The woman looked at Gene.

"What?" Gene said.

"No business card?" Maggie said.

Gene shrugged. "You're my first client."

Maggie tore a page from a *Have a Nice Day* notepad on the woman's desk and handed it to Gene. "Write your name and number down for the nice lady."

Gene wrote down his information. The teller let the paper fall on her desk and turned her TV back on without another word.

Smoke erupted from the Volare as Gene cranked the engine. The Groove Line was on the radio singing "Heat Wave." Despite the swelter from the summer sun, the interior of the car was still cooler than inside Cheung's Martial Arts. Gene backed out and dove into stop-and-go traffic. "So, what's with this other kung fu school?"

Maggie rolled her window down and rested her arm on the door. "Iron Mantis Fist Society."

"Right. Think there's any truth to what Derrick said? That guy take the lions?"

Maggie slid on oversized round sunglasses and stared back at him. "I don't know."

"There's bad blood between the schools?"

She shrugged. "Kung fu schools always talking jive about one another. There's an old saying that a kung fu master will beat a karate master, but one karate master can beat five kung fu masters at once. You just wait for them to kill each other."

Maggie looked at her watch. "I have to get back. Some friends are picking me up for a show at the Alley. *Echelon*."

Gene nodded, turning on Chartres Street. "So, Derrick took

matters into his own hands?"

Maggie frowned. "I don't like it. He caught Jimmy Chin at the movies and beat him with a club. He's still in ICU, no visitors. My brother's gonna be furious."

"Is that common? Actual fighting between schools?"

"No," Maggie said. "Back in the day, people would challenge rival masters. If they won, they'd prove their kung fu was better and take all the students. But today? Everyone stays in their lane."

A farm truck cut Gene off at Leeland, running the light. Gene mashed the horn. A middle finger shot from the window of the truck, waving back and forth.

"Nobody stays in their lane around here," Gene said.

The Iron Mantis Fist Society wasn't a secret lair from a Bond movie like the name implied, but rather a small, wooden-framed house just off Dowling Street. The time was past eight when he'd dropped Maggie off, eaten a complementary bowl of Crossing the Bridge Noodles, and hit the streets again. A dozen cars were parked in front.

The smell of cigarette smoke and the sound of music strengthened as Gene walked to the entrance. A mural on the building featured dragons, praying mantises, and fighting Shaolin monks. The closed double front doors featured a painting of a lion on each door.

Smoke spilled out from around the doors. Gene was about to knock when they flew open, toppling him onto the walkway. A skinny kid who'd been hurled out of the building lay alongside him.

A long-haired, elderly Asian man stood in the doorway smoking. He wore black cotton pants without a shirt. A jagged scar like lightning zig-zagged his chest.

"What did I say?" said the man. "Don't keep weight on your front foot. If you're going to keep doing that, I'm going to keep making you look like an asshole."

The kid stood, brushing off his pants and limping back inside. The shirtless old man slapped him on the head as he passed, then squinted at Gene. "What's happenin' my man? You sellin' vacuum cleaners or something?"

Gene got to his feet, brushing off his corduroys.

"Sorry," Gene said. "Didn't mean to intrude."

The man turned and went back inside, leaving the doors open.

Gene followed. It looked a little like Cheung's Martial Arts, with racks of weapons and framed photos. But it felt more like a clubhouse—a giant praying mantis painted on the polished concrete floor. About fifteen students in all black practiced the same techniques in lock step—punching, kicking, and making mantis-like hand gestures. Sweat poured off their faces. Black Sabbath's "War Pigs" played from a stereo in the corner and the room was thick with cigarette smoke.

"Let me guess," said the old man, leaning against a wall. "You saw *Drunken Master,* now you wanna learn kung fu. No beginner class until Saturday." The man waved Gene away as though he were an opossum that had wandered in from the bayou. "Go. This ain't open casting, baby."

"Actually, I'm here to talk about Cheung's Martial Arts."

One of the students on the front row shot Gene a glance between punching and kicking.

The instructor's eyes narrowed. "Who the hell are you?"

"Private investigator," Gene said. "Maggie Cheung hired me to find the stone lions taken two days ago."

The instructor shook his head. "Nobody here knows what happened to those lions. Derrick Lau is a dolt. Cheung can't control his students and now the whole thing will be a tragedy."

Taking a draw off his cigarette, the man walked to a framed photo showing five unsmiling men in front of a temple. "Cheung is an all-right cat," he said, stabbing at the photo with his cigarette. "I've known him a long time. I respect him, even if the Wing Chun style is inferior to the Iron Mantis Fist."

"When you say tragedy," Gene said. "You mean what happened at the movies?"

"James Chin is a solid kid. Studies kinesiology at Rice. Now he's having seizures. That ain't right."

"He's your student who got attacked at the drive-in?"

"He's my student who got *ambushed* at the drive-in by a man *with a weapon*. Five on one. Girlfriend terrified in his car." The instructor shook his head. "Lau is a punk."

He turned back toward his students. "Stay low," he told the group as they practiced. "Remember, low center of gravity. Low center of gravity. Don't make me show you why."

"That is a tragedy," Gene said.

"Well, yeah," said the instructor, "James is in bad shape. But the tragedy I meant was Master Cheung."

"What do you mean?"

He shrugged. "I got a student in the hospital. I know Derrick Lau went rogue, but there's no other way my man. I'll give Cheung a few days for jet lag when he gets back."

"I'm sorry, you lost me," Gene said. "Give him a few days for what?"

"The death match, of course."

Death match. The phrase rattled around in Gene's brain as he steered the Volare up Dowling toward Navigation. *Should I call the police?* Gene thought. *I could ask Sandy to help.* But what could the police do until after the fact? His hands were sweaty on the Volare's hard plastic steering wheel as he pulled into Sunny Horizons Apartment Homes.

The crickets in the apartment's patchy brown lawn droned on as Gene retrieved his mail from a rusty lock box. He thumbed through the envelopes as he walked toward his apartment. Water bill. JCPenney flier featuring a comely woman in bell-bottoms vacuuming maroon carpet. A postcard declaring *Vote for John Luke Hill for Governor* and *Say No to Nuclear Power!*

He opened the front door and flicked on the dim yellow lamp. Tossing his keys onto the table next to the ashtray, he kicked the door shut behind him and gasped.

A man in a black hood, mask, and cotton pants stood in his living room, hands out like knives.

"What the fuck?" Gene said, grabbing the heavy ashtray. He turned to swing at the intruder, but the shadowy figure struck Gene's hand, the ashtray falling to the carpet. His hand numbed with pain.

"Halloween's not for two months yet," Gene said, shaking his hand. "And I'm out of Zagnuts." He reached to unmask the attacker, but the figure parried, Gene grabbing nothing but air.

"Wassah!" cried the man, driving a series of punches into Gene's stomach, chest, and face. The room spun as Gene felt his body crumple, the floor rushing up to meet him.

Gene's lungs fought for air. He landed face-down, the coarse blue fibers of the shag carpeting rough on his cheek. His stomach lurched, the Crossing the Bridge Noodles almost crossing back the other way. The ashtray in front of him lost focus as the shadow man stepped over his broken body and fled. Gene closed his eyes, the droning of the crickets outside carrying him into dark, comforting nothingness.

The knock rattled Gene's head. Swinging his legs over the side of the couch sent a wave of pain throughout his body. "Coming," he croaked. "Hold your horses." The steak he'd put on his eye earlier now lay on the floor.

Daylight blinded him as he opened the door.

"Jesus, what happened to you?" Dan asked.

"My first kung fu lesson," Gene said as his eyes adjusted. He squinted at his Timex: 2:34 p.m.

Dan leaned in and sniffed.

"I'm not drunk," Gene said. "I got jumped. What's up?"

Dan held up a thick envelope. "Onboarding papers. Tax forms, next of kin, life insurance…"

Gene reached for the envelope, but Dan held it out of reach. "Ah, ah, ah. That's not all."

Dan turned and walked away. "C'mon, Rocky. Get that eye of the tiger working and follow me."

Gene stepped into the afternoon sun, the humidity like a rice cooker. He licked his busted lips and tasted blood as he followed Dan to the parking lot.

Dan stopped and turned around, smiling. Next to him stood a black Pontiac Firebird Trans Am, complete with gold phoenix decal and dealer's sticker still on the windshield.

"Mag wheels, T-Tops, performance package and, most importantly, a 403 cubic inch V-8. Bootleggers still use these things to run moonshine."

"I don't get it," Gene said.

Dan shrugged. "Signing bonus."

He tossed the keys to Gene, who winced in pain as he caught them.

"Yours free and clear after sign-on. Let's face it, that old shit pile has one foot in the grave." He jammed a thumb at Gene's old Volare.

Gene opened the Trans Am's door and sat. The interior smelled like new leather and carpet. In the mirror he caught a glimpse of himself—one eye purple and swollen almost shut. He started the engine, the V8 roaring to life. Rod Stewart's "Do Ya Think I'm Sexy" played on the radio.

"I appreciate this," Gene said, shutting off the engine. He got out slowly. "Really. I'm lucky to have this kind of opportunity."

"Don't answer now," Dan said. "Fill out the paperwork and come to the helipad tomorrow even if you turn me down." He held out the envelope. "Please. This could change your life."

Gene nodded, taking the paperwork. "I'll give it some thought."

"Uh…" Dan said. "Do I need to be worried about you?" He pointed to Gene's face.

Gene shook his head. "Nah, my first PI case isn't going great. Do people get their asses kicked offshore?"

"Absolutely," Dan said. "Just not when their former brother-in-law is the Vice President. Two o'clock tomorrow at the Hexagon helipad. Galveston. Paperwork in hand."

Gene heard his lime green kitchen phone ringing as he walked back into the apartment. "Hello?"

"This is Gloria from Hang Seng Southwest Bank of Houston."

"Who?"

The woman sighed. "The lemon tart at the bank, genius."

"Oh, right. How are you?"

"Just peachy," she said. "Mr. Kuykendahl returned and has copies of the security tapes at our front desk. He told me to say the system uses a new technology called a Video Cassette Recorder and that if you don't have one you could review the footage here."

"Thanks," Gene said. "I've got one. Sort of." But the woman had already hung up.

The weather was sweltering but sunny, and Gene removed the Trans Am's T-tops. KC and the Sunshine Band's "I'm Your Boogie Man" playing as he gunned the engine. The wind whipped around him as he weaved through traffic, first to the Hang Seng Southwest Bank of Houston and then the Houston Police Department's downtown station.

"My God, what happened to your face?" Sandy said.

Gene touched his eye. "I wish you could see the other guy."

"Really?"

"Yeah, like in a lineup or something. Sorry to barge in but I need a favor."

The twenty-eight-story HPD headquarters bustled with people coming and going, phones ringing and the *click-click-clacking* of typewriters. In the hallway a man in rust-color bell-bottoms and a red hat with an oversized feather wrestled two uniformed officers.

"This for your PI business?" Sandy asked.

"Dan told you?"

Sandy nodded. "Coffee?"

"Sure."

They stopped in a breakroom where Sandy poured scorching tar-like coffee into two Styrofoam cups.

Coffees in hand, they got on the elevator where Sandy hit the ninth-floor button. The elevator chimed as it climbed.

"You don't approve either?" Gene said. "The PI gig?"

"What?" Sandy said with a shrug. "I didn't say anything."

"Yeah, but that look. You get this line in your forehead."

"Oh, Jesus," Sandy said. "I'm not your wife anymore, you don't need my approval."

When the elevator opened, she took the lead. "This way."

"Ah, that's right. I forgot. For you, marriage means dictatorship. Everything must be approved by *mein Fuhrer*."

She opened a door and turned on the light in what looked like a classroom. Rows of school-style desks stood in front of a hulking gray television with a silver block of buttons and dials beneath it. Sandy stopped and put her hands on her hips.

"Yeah, and for you, marriage is fucking anarchy whereby you never know—"

Gene held up a hand. "Sorry. That was shitty. Really. Sorry. I'm just having a bad day. Thanks for doing this."

Sandy glared at him for a moment before turning on the television. She powered up the VCR and inserted the bank's tape. He couldn't tell if the room was cold or if it was just them.

On screen a blurry, black-and-white image of the parking lot of the Hang Seng Southwest Bank of Houston appeared along with the road and a view of half the Cheung's Martial Arts building. In the bottom corner a time stamp clicked up hours, minutes, seconds, and microseconds in white block letters. You couldn't see the entrance or the lions from that angle, only the road and part of the building.

"Our AV nerd says these VCRs are catching on and one day people are going to rent movies in their houses instead of going out."

Gene snorted. "Who the fuck wants to go to a movie at their house?"

Sandy took a yellow pad and pencil out of her satchel.

"They don't know what time they were hit," Gene said. "But according to one of the owners, he left at night, and when he came back Friday, the lions were gone."

The time stamp at the bottom read 5:32 p.m. last Thursday.

"What kind of car does the owner drive?" Sandy asked as she fast-forwarded the tape.

"A gold Ford Elite."

At 11:47 p.m., the shape of a Ford Elite cruised past the school. "There's the owner leaving," Gene said.

The two sat in front of the TV watching cars come and go, fast-forwarding through most of the footage until cars approached—Sandy scrawling down plate info of each passing car.

"Wait, go back," Sandy said. "Did you see that?"

"What?"

At 3:14 a.m. a car slowed as it approached the school, rolling past the view of the camera.

"Look how everything reflective gets lighter just for an instant." *True*, Gene thought. A street sign reading McKinney Street and a group of mailboxes lit up just after the car passed. *Brake lights*, Gene thought, *just off camera*.

"Looks like a Cutlass," Gene said. "Two people in it."

"Is that a ponytail?" Sandy asked, pointing to the passenger.

At the end of the tape, Sandy tore a sheet out of her legal pad. She had a list of seven cars and their license plates, plus Derrick Lau's Ford Elite.

She stood, "All right. I'll go run these."

"I owe you," she said.

"As usual."

The deadbolt in back of Cheung's Martial Arts was an ancient Yale. After a few minutes, the lock gave with a *thud*. He knew this was a gamble. Knew if he got caught, he could kiss his private investigation career goodbye. But he had to know he was right.

Gene stuffed the lock picks into his pocket, opened the door and flicked on a red flashlight. The inside of the building was still hot, even at almost midnight. The fountain sat unplugged and silent. The instructor's office, bathroom and supply closet all shared brick with the exterior wall, as did the back wall. But the east side of the building...

Gene faced the east wall. The swords in the rack glowed crimson. Photos and knick-knacks cast long shadows as he walked up and down the wall, knocking. Solid brick. The art deco style clock in the wall read 11:41 p.m.

There were no switches or plugs or sconces. He went to the bookshelf. If this were a Hardy Boys novel rather than a real-world felony in progress, there would be an old leather-bound book somewhere that did the trick. But there were no books on the shelf, only trophies and metals, small jade buddhas and a few framed photographs. One by one, he lifted each up, moved it around and looked beneath—glad he'd worn gloves. The top shelf was more than eight feet high.

Remembering the supply closet, he fetched an empty bucket. Flipping it he stepped up and inspected the trophies on top. Nothing unusual. On a whim, and since he'd explored everything else on the wall, he moved the bucket under the clock. Stepping up he used his finger to swirl the clock forward. A tingle ran across Gene's scalp when he felt a click as the hands reached midnight.

He heard a latch release to his right and, shining the red light on the bookcase, saw it swing out like a door. "Yes!" Gene hissed. "Yes, yes, yes. I knew it. I fucking knew it."

Leaping off the bucket, he ran to the bookshelf door and opened it wider. Four red eyes glowed back at him in the reflection of his flashlight. The stone lions snarled in the shadows, all teeth and claws yet silent and still.

Clap.

Clap.

Clap.

Gene turned.

The lights flicked on. Derrick Lau entered the room from the office and crossed his arms. "Gotta hand it to you, that was a good guess."

As Gene's eyes adjusted to the light, he tried to swallow, but his throat felt like sandpaper.

"But for a detective, you sure can't take a hint."

"And for a warrior, you sure can't lose gracefully."

Derrick scowled. "You don't know shit."

"I know you were probably jealous when Sifu Cheung passed you over as Disciple in favor of Mary Fung. Someone sent her flowers congratulating her. I'm guessing it wasn't you."

Derrick took a few steps closer, the polished wooden planks creaking beneath his footsteps.

"I know some people use vinegar to clean hardwood floors. I'm guessing you used a dolly or something, and the wheels left marks. I'm just struggling with why."

Derrick waved his hand. "It's ridiculous. A girl as Disciple? Makes us look weak. If he'd chosen me, a rival would have never done this."

"Yeah, but the Iron Mantis Fist Society didn't do it. You

did." Gene lifted his shirt. "Wing Chun focuses on the center of the body." Black and blue bruises ran up Gene's stomach and chest. "So, it had to be someone here. And you seem to be the only asshole."

Derrick's face darkened.

I am going to die, Gene thought. But he kept talking.

"The age of the building, the space feeling off, and someone mentioning bootleggers to me yesterday. It all sort of just clicked—this was an old speakeasy. Sometimes they built them like this, with hidden rooms."

Gene pulled out the printout Sandy had given him. "Jimmy Chin stopped by the school the night the lions were stolen, but I'm guessing he wasn't stealing lions. I'm guessing he was dropping Mary off after a night out. She was the girl with Jimmy when you put him in the hospital. So, what, you're jealous of her because she was made Sifu Cheung's Disciple, and jealous of him because, let's face it, you like her, huh?"

Derrick stepped forward, hands out like knives. "Your bones will rot in that secret room!"

He leapt at Gene, reaching a paranormal height, black cotton uniform rustling as he flew—foot chambered for a flying sidekick.

Gene closed his eyes.

At the last minute, Gene heard another flutter of cloth, a wet smack, and a grunt of pain. When he opened his eyes, Maggie Chang stood before him, a small strand of gray hair hanging in front of her face. Derrick was on the ground, scrambling to stand.

"You young fool," Maggie said to Derrick. "Your pride has caused a lot of trouble."

"Old woman, you're going to die." Derrick launched himself at her, fists flying. Blow by blow, Maggie Chang adjusted her position, slapped the young man's fists just off-center and took big steps backward to stay just out of his reach. *Thwack, thwack, thwack-thwack* went Derrick's punches against Maggie's blocks.

Maggie's face was calm and expressionless. After blocking several blows, she grabbed Derrick's fist with perfect timing, stepping in between his legs and making an elegant sweeping motion with her arms.

Derrick flew backward, slamming his head on the hardwood floor. Blinking hard, he screamed in fury. Getting to his feet, he charged and swung wildly. Parrying like a bullfighter, Maggie tripped Derrick—who fell forward into the open bookshelf. His head slammed into one of the lions, going limp like a robot unplugged.

"Shit," Gene said. "We have to call an ambulance."

Derrick lay crumpled on the floor, blood pooling from his head.

Gene ran to the phone.

Maggie knelt at Derrick's side and stroked his hair, fingers coming away bright red.

Derrick moaned.

In a moment, Gene returned. "The ambulance is on the way. Thank you. You saved my life. You were...you were incredible."

"Of course," she said. "Sifu Cheung is my little brother. Who do you think taught him?"

"How did you even know I was here?"

"You tripped the silent alarm. I'm part owner. They called my house."

"Did you know about that secret room?"

Maggie shook her head. "No. But, truly, who cares about the lions? I see now it's the people in this family who need to do a better job of watching over each other."

Seagulls flapped around Gene, begging for a handout as he leaned against the Trans Am. Dan came out of the trailer that served as Hexagon's helipad office. "Well?" he said.

Gene held out the keys.

Dan let his head drop, then took the keys. "Really, man? You'd be great offshore. What can I say to change your mind?"

Nearby, a Sikorsky's turbines whined to a crescendo, blades chopping faster and faster as the helicopter lifted its nose and thumped away over the green-brown waters of Galveston Bay.

Gene shook his head. "Just because I can do something doesn't mean I should."

"What does that mean?"

"It means I just wouldn't have been into the job. It would have gotten me down, and I'd probably have started gambling again, and I could just feel the cycle coming on. But this? This I'm into."

"Getting your ass kicked playing private detective?"

Gene held up a small piece of stationery with Chinese writing. "Hey, I've got skills. My first case and I turned a death match into a wedding invitation for Jimmy Chin and Mary Fung."

Dan turned to look out over the water. "Well, I tried," he said, tossing Gene the keys.

Gene caught them, confused.

"Rockford had a Trans Am, right? Keep the Volare for stakeouts."

"No shit?"

"No shit," Dan said, turning to look out over the water. "Actually, I need to ask you a favor."

"What kind of favor?"

Dan rubbed the back of his neck. "What do you know about Worker's Comp cases?"

The two talked as Dan led Gene into the trailer. Another Sikorsky wound up its turbines and lifted off the ground, *thump-thump-thump*ing into the sun as Gene took out his notebook and bit the cap off his Bic pen. Ready to listen. Ready to get the facts. And ready to put in the work.

LAST DANCE
Bill Fitzhugh

San Bernardino, California
Thursday, July 19, 1979

I was in my office reading the paper that morning. The shit was hitting the fan in Nicaragua; one of Somoza's goons had killed a reporter from ABC, prompting Cyrus Vance to call for an inter-American peace force to restore order and democracy.

Closer to home, the Public Health Service was suggesting the US government stop spraying paraquat on the pot fields in Mexico, their reasoning being that nobody had died from smoking pot until we started spraying it with the herbicide.

Meanwhile, President Carter announced a sweeping proposal to eliminate forty years of regulations on the trucking industry. Naturally, this had the Teamsters and the American Trucking Association up in arms owing to the fact they were both making out like bandits under the current set of regulations for which they had paid good money.

I was turning to the sports page when the door creaked open. This guy stood there for a second before he said, "I'm looking for the investigator..." he jerked a thumb toward the name on the door, "...uh, Bennett?"

"Congratulations," I said. "You found him on your first try. I'm Hunt Bennett." I gestured at the chair across from my desk.

The guy didn't seem to appreciate my humor, but he came

in, anyway. He glanced at the walls like he was trying to find investigator credentials or something to make him feel better about his choice. He was around fifty, wearing checkered Sansabelt pants, a collared shirt half unbuttoned, loafers, no socks. If I'd had to bet, I'd say he didn't belong to a gym.

After he sat down, I said, "What can I do for you?"

He pulled a pack of cigarettes from his shirt pocket and slipped a wallet print from the cellophane. He flipped it onto my desk like dealing a card. "I think she's cheating on me." He didn't sound broken-hearted about it so much as pissed-off.

Either way, it was good news for me. Cheaters keep me in business. The cheated just pay the bill. Some of the cheated come in crying about lost love, but that wasn't this guy. Some just want out of a marriage without paying alimony. This seemed entirely possible. Some of them want to take it out on the cheating spouse or on the third party. Some want to take it out on both. These all seemed equally plausible.

I tend not to care which of these describes a client, but I can usually tell—and when it looks like there might be violence, I do my best to warn the potential victims. The one time I didn't, a guy ended up in the morgue; granted, it was my client, not his wife, who turned out to be quite a good shot, but still, I'd rather not have to answer a lot of questions down at the station like I did that time. So, I try to give a heads up when appropriate.

I looked at the photo. She was pretty in a rough-around-the-edges kind of way, and more than a little younger than him, young enough to be his daughter, in fact. All things considered, I could see why she might be tempted to step out on this guy, but that wasn't my concern.

I pulled a new client form from the drawer. "Name?"

He paused before he said, "Uh, Vivian. Viv Harris."

I looked up, surprised. "Your name is Vivian?"

"That's *her* name," he said.

"Oh. I need your name first."

"J.C. Dunbar."

I wrote it on the form. "And Mr. Dunbar, you want proof, one way or the other about the cheating."

"That's something you do, right?"

"That's one of my specialties," I said. "So, let's start with place of employment..."

"Hers or mine?"

"Surprise me."

"The cosmetics counter at Harris Department Store."

"How about you?"

Another pause before he said, "Self-employed."

"Okay." I gestured for some elaboration.

"I do a little of this, a little of that," he said. "I'll be paying cash, if that'll cut this short."

"Fine. How about an address?"

"What do you want that for?"

"It makes it easier to do a stake-out if I know where to park."

He gave me an address and a two-hundred-dollar retainer. He left without signing the new client form or giving me much more information, so I'd have to get that on my own. I fully intended to follow the woman, get some incriminating photos if possible, and get paid the rest I was owed. But first I was going to get some background on Mr. Dunbar. I like to know who I'm working for.

Taking a dim view of humanity, as I'm prone to, I assumed the worst about Mr. Dunbar and called my friend at the County Probation Department. He said J.C. Dunbar wasn't currently on parole but only by six months. He'd done a stint in county for aggravated assault. The victim was a young woman. He gave me Mr. Dunbar's last known address, which was not the same as Vivian's.

"You know if he's married?"

"Used to be," my friend said. "Woman named Theresa Wiggins. Says here they divorced in '76."

None of this surprised me. Dunbar hadn't been wearing a

ring, and he didn't have a tan line from one recently removed. And he never actually said he was married to Vivian, just sort of implied it. But you don't have to be married to be jealous or to hire a private investigator, so none of that mattered.

What *did* matter was the fact he'd been cagey about it.

Before he left, Mr. Dunbar told me he was going out of town the next day on business and wouldn't be back until the following Tuesday. He figured if Vivian was groping for trout in peculiar rivers, as they say, this weekend was as likely a time as any for it. It made sense to me.

I drove over to Harris Department Store to get eyes on my target. Watching from the dress department, adjacent to cosmetics, I saw her there, bagging up some powders and lipstick for a customer. I got close enough to see her name tag, just to confirm it was Vivian.

She got off at five-thirty, and I followed her to the address Dunbar had given me, an apartment building on West Valley Boulevard. Thirty minutes and a change of clothes later, she was on the move, dressed for dancing. I guess you'd call what she was wearing a jumpsuit, but it wasn't the kind of jumpsuit mechanics wear. This was a slinky and fashionable one-piece outfit with bell-bottom legs and frills at the collar and a zipper in the back. I couldn't help but wonder how she got out of it when it came time to pee.

I tailed her burgundy Olds Cutlass to a TGI Fridays where she met a girlfriend for a couple of drinks, Harvey Wallbangers from the looks of it. Around nine-thirty, Vivian and her friend paid their tab and headed uptown to The Asylum, San Berdoo's hottest disco.

A couple of years ago, after Saturday Night Fever came out, you had to circle the block three times to find a parking spot before you stood in line half an hour for the privilege of paying a ten-dollar cover to get inside for a taste of the glitz and glamor. But it looked like that moment had passed. There was plenty of parking now and no line at the door.

I gave Vivian and her friend a minute before following them in. I grabbed a seat at the bar and scoped things out. If you drew a line from the bar to the dance floor to the elevated DJ booth and back to the bar, it was a perfect triangle. There were small tables at the edge of the dance floor and faux leather sofas along the walls. Vivian and her friend were seated at a two-top halfway between the dance floor and the bar.

There was a wall of lights behind the dance floor and some spots overhead. It was hard to distinguish where the fog machine discharge ended and the cigarette smoke began but the effect with the strobe lights was entrancing.

I thought the DJ was pretty good too, matching the beat from one song to the next so the energy kept growing. When he mixed from "I Will Survive" into "We are Family," the crowd threw their hands into the air and cheered. The lights pulsed to the beat, and you could feel the bass throbbing through your entire body.

I ordered a scotch rocks and kept an eye on Vivian to see if a boyfriend showed up. When I got my drink, I noticed a guy slip a couple of twenties onto the bar then lean over to say something to the bartender. The bartender nodded, filled a glass with water from the soda gun, then wrote something on a cardboard coaster. He put the glass on the coaster and scooped up the cash. I watched as the customer drifted away with the most expensive glass of tap water I'd ever seen.

When the DJ mixed into "Bad Girls," Vivian and her girl-friend jumped up and raced to the dance floor. They looked like they were having plenty of fun without benefit of boyfriends.

Over the next hour, Vivian danced with a couple of different guys but always returned by herself to the table with her friend. Meanwhile, the same bartender continued selling expensive glasses of water in addition to cocktails at more reasonable prices. I noticed the water customers all ended up at the DJ booth soon after leaving the bar. I couldn't quite put together what was going on, but I didn't think they were up there making requests, at least not for songs.

A man in his sixties came in from a door by the end of the bar, which I assume led to the stockroom and back office. He spoke to one of the waitresses before sauntering down the bar, schmoozing with customers. When he got to me, he smiled and said, "Having fun yet?"

"Yeah, not bad."

A waitress brought the man a club soda with a lime wedge.

We struck up a conversation. It turned out he'd owned the place for twenty years. "It used to be smaller," he said. "Half this size." He pointed to the middle of the club. "There was a wall over there and nothing but a jukebox for music. A few years later, everybody wanted to hear live bands, so we tore the wall out and built a stage where the dance floor is now. Then, around '74 or '75 the tide turned again, and we took out the stage and replaced it with the dance floor and put in that wall of lights." He said the switch to disco was great for his business. "Crowds are just as big as they used to be but now I only have to pay Gig instead of six guys in a band."

"Gig's the DJ?"

"Yeah, Gig Stevens, a real pro," the guy said. "Knows how to control a crowd with the music. Gets them all worked up, then slows it down so they order drinks, then he does it again."

"So business is good?"

He wagged a hand in the air. "Not as good as a few years ago," he said. "Pretty sure disco's just about run its course, but hey, we've had a good five-year run."

"Maybe it's just a blip."

"Nah, it's more than that," he said.

"What makes you say so?"

"Did you see that story in the paper last week where the White Sox had to forfeit a game against the Tigers?"

"No, I guess I missed it."

"Some radio DJ did this promotion called Disco Demolition Night. Told listeners if they brought a disco record, they'd get into the double-header for only a buck. The DJ was going to blow up all the records during the break between the games. They thought fifteen thousand people might show up if they were lucky, but fifty thousand showed up instead, drunk, stoned, and agitated about disco. After the DJ blew up the records, the fans stormed the field, which now had a huge crater in it from the explosion. Sox had to forfeit the game."

"Oops."

"Yeah," the man said. "I'm telling you, that marks the beginning of the end for disco."

"Yeah, well, it's nice of the gods to send such an obvious sign."

"No kidding. Even Gig knows it," the man said. "He gave me notice earlier this week. Said he's heading for Hollywood, getting into the movie business."

"I guess that's too bad for you," I said. "Looks like you've got a nice thing going here."

The guy shrugged all nonchalant, and said, "One thing I've learned owning a bar: the only thing that's constant is change."

"So what's next? Back to live bands?"

"Not sure, but I just read an interesting magazine article about this club outside Houston, owned by some country singer. I can't think of his name."

"Like a honkey-tonk sort of thing?"

"Sort of," he said. "But updated. The place is huge and so are the crowds, according to the article, thousands every night. Hell, there's even a rodeo arena outside the place. That's how big it is."

"I can see how that would work in Texas, but..."

"Yeah, I know what you're saying, but think about it," he said. "Discos started in New York and San Francisco. But they didn't stay there, right? There's a disco in every city in the country now. And let's face it, San Bernardino ain't exactly Miami Beach, am I right?"

"I see your point," I said. "Fads come and go."

"You know what I think it is? It's a backlash to all this," he said, gesturing at the glitzy crowd. "The big city slickers acting like they're celebrities in their John Travolta outfits, with the gold chains, flashing lights, and all the drugs-on-the-dance-floor decadence. I think it's played out, and it's time for the next thing."

"And you think it's...cowboys in the city?"

"Why not? Urban Cowboys," the guy said. "In fact, I think that was the title of that magazine article I read."

I was about to ask him about the overpriced tap water deal when he waved the bartender over and told him to give me one on the house. He gave me a pat on the back and told me to have fun before he drifted into the crowd. Nice guy.

When the bartender delivered my drink, a guy slid in next to me and put a few twenties onto the bar. I acted like I wasn't paying attention as the bartender pulled a cardboard coaster and wrote something on it. Out of the corner of my eye, it looked like '1D 2DB', something like that. The customer took his glass of water and the coaster and headed for the DJ booth.

My guess was drug deal in some sort of code. I figured 1D was maybe a dime of coke, though I suppose it could have just as easily been one Demerol. The 2DB could mean two Quaaludes, because they don't call them Disco Biscuits for nothing. Based on the small glass tubes near the dance floor, I guessed Gig was selling poppers too.

I had to admit it was a pretty smart set up, keeping the cash and the drug exchanges separated and having the coasters to balance the books at the end of the day. Gig and the bartender must have been raking in some serious cash with a few hundred potential customers under one roof every night. Most of the drug dealers I've known would be loath to walk away from such a sweet setup. Then again, maybe Gig was smarter than most and he'd stashed all the cash he needed to ease his transition into the higher cost of living in LA.

By the time the club closed, Vivian's friend had hooked up

with some guy and split. I trailed Vivian outside and headed for my car. I saw her talking to Gig in the parking lot for a minute. Then she got in her car and drove off. I was about to shift into gear when Gig pulled in behind her, driving a shiny new Trans Am, the one with the big Firebird painted on the hood. I wondered if Gig was the guy I was looking for.

I followed them to an apartment building over on Belmont Avenue and drove past as they pulled into the lot. Then I circled back to see which apartment was Gig's. Parking across the street, I saw them go into the last apartment on the right. I grabbed my camera and was going to see if Gig had forgotten to close any of the curtains when a Chevy Caprice pulled up. The driver got out. He was wearing a baseball cap, and he had a large flat box in his hand.

It was a pizza delivery.

I wasn't sure what to make of that. If Vivian and Gig were lovers, I would have expected them to be struggling to get her out of that slinky jumpsuit and stumbling toward the sofa. Instead, Vivian opened the door, fully dressed, and started talking to the pizza guy. Then she invited him inside and closed the door behind him. I wasn't sure what to make of that, either.

I figured he'd be back out in five, but twenty minutes later, he was still in there. So, I grabbed my camera and crossed to the apartment but I couldn't see a thing, all the blinds were shut tight. Back in my car, I waited another thirty minutes before Vivian came out, followed by the pizza guy, who hopped into his Caprice and drove back the way he came. Vivian waved goodbye to Gig, got in her car, and headed back to her place.

I followed. By the time we reached Vivian's apartment, it was nearly three in the morning, and I didn't think there would be any boyfriends showing up at that hour. I planned to give it thirty minutes to see if she turned off the lights before I called it a night and headed home.

It was warm out, and I had my window down. I could hear the traffic rolling by in both directions on I-10, a steady, droning white noise. A few minutes later, I was rubbing my tired eyes when I heard the unmistakable sound of a gun cocking awfully close to my head. This was followed by a woman's voice saying, "Put your hands on the steering wheel, creep."

I did as instructed and said, "There's no need for a gun."

"We'll see, won't we?" Vivian poked my head with the .38. "What're you doing out at here at three in the morning?"

"Minding my own business," I said. "You?"

"I don't care much for stalkers," she said.

"Stalkers? You got it all wrong."

"Shut up," she said. "I saw you lurking in the dress department at Harris this afternoon, and I saw you tailing me to Fridays, and I saw you at The Asylum. You might as well just introduce yourself if you're going to be that obvious."

"Are you serious?"

"Listen, mister…whatever your name is."

"Bennett."

"Listen, Mr. Bennett, people have been underestimating me all my life." She poked me again with the gun. "As you can see, it doesn't really pay off."

"I'm just disappointed I—"

"Awww, don't start feeling sorry for yourself," she said. "It's not so much that you suck at your job. It's just that very little gets past me."

"Well, thanks, that makes me feel better," I said. "But why would I be stalking you?"

"Same as all the others," she said. "You saw a few of my films, you fell in love—or more likely lust—and figured all you needed to do was show up and—"

"You're in the movies? I thought you sold cosmetics."

"That's just my day job," she said. "I'm an actress."

"No kidding?" I was genuinely surprised to hear this. And my curiosity was definitely piqued. "Have you been in anything I've seen, like…I don't know, *Rocky* or *Bad News Bears* or, oh, maybe *Saturday Night Fever?*" I gestured at her jumpsuit. "I see you've got the outfit, and you're a really good dancer."

"You're serious?"

"Totally. I mean, I'm not a real film buff, you know. I don't go to foreign stuff with subtitles and shit, but I see my share of movies."

Vivian lowered the gun. "Maybe you're not a stalker after all."

"Like I said."

She aimed her gun at my camera. "So maybe you're a different kind of creep, the peeping-Tom-with-a-camera type."

"What? No, actually, truth is, I'm a private investigator, which I guess technically doesn't mean I'm not a creep, but I like to think I'm an okay guy."

"And you're following me? Who hired you?"

"I'm not at liberty to say."

"Oh, please," she said with a laugh. "It was J.C. Dunbar, assuming you're telling the truth. Who else could it be?"

"I couldn't really say."

"Listen, Mr. Bennett, if you want to see my movies, you're going to the wrong theaters," Vivian said. "You need to get over to the Pussycat."

It took me a moment to figure it out. But then it hit me. And it all made sense. A young girl from a broken family runs away from home and ends up in the nearest city, in the case, San Bernardino. She runs out of money and finds herself out on the streets where she's spotted by an older guy on the prowl, a guy like J.C. Duncan. He tells her she's beautiful and gets her something to eat, then something to drink, then gives her some drugs to make her feel better. She asks what he does, and he says he's a film producer who can make her a movie star. All she has to do is a little screen test, maybe a nice love scene or two, all very tasteful, he assures her. Next thing you know, she's addicted to the drugs the old guy uses to control her. It's a story as old as porn itself.

"Ohhh," I said. "You're a...porn actor?"

Vivian rolled her eyes. "Adult films, yeah, but what I really want to do is direct. And produce. There's a fortune to be made, and I plan to make it. Well, me and Gig. He's my business partner."

That explained that. "Just out of curiosity," I said, "What was the deal with the pizza guy over there?"

"Oh, just a story element," she said. "You know, plot. Girl orders a pizza then realizes she doesn't have the money on hand when the pizza arrives. The delivery guy is understanding, and he's good looking and sparks fly, so, you know, they have sex. Basic storytelling, really."

"So, you guys were...filming in there?"

"Film..." she said it like it tasted bad. "You sound like that dinosaur, Dunbar. Film's dead. It's over. The future is videotape."

"Who is Dunbar to you, exactly?"

"He produced my first few films, but he's a fucking creep, plus he's violent," Vivian said. "And like I said, he's a dinosaur. He's still shooting on sixteen millimeter for Christ's sake. What did he tell you? I'm his daughter and he was worried I was hanging out with the wrong crowd?"

"He implied you were his girlfriend, and he suspected you were cheating on him."

"First of all, gross. Second, he's right, in a way. I'm dumping him as my producer. Gig and I are moving to LA to start our own production company. I don't plan to spend the rest of my life in front of the camera with my legs spread. That's J.C.'s plan, not mine. That asshole's living in the past. Me and Gig are heading for the future."

"Meaning?"

"Like I said, videotape. Market research shows videotape's going to dominate the home market in the next five to ten years, everything from home movies of the kids to studio films for rent to watch on your television. Trust me, every house in America will have a videotape machine within five years," Vivian said. "For low budget producers, tape's a no brainer. No film development costs, high-speed duplication's cheap and easy. Adult movies on video is going to put the Pussycat theaters of the world out of business in five years, ten at the most. You'll be able to watch at home! And me and Gig are setting up offices on the ground floor."

I had to admit, Vivian's research was impressive. It certainly convinced me. I bet there were a lot more guys who wanted to see porn than were willing to risk being seen coming out of a Pussycat theater. If they could rent a videotape to watch in the comfort of their living rooms? I think Vivian had seen the future.

"So, you say Dunbar likes to get tough?"

"More and more," she said. "When I refused to do something in one of the movies a month ago, he broke a couple of my ribs and promised to do worse if I didn't start cooperating." She shook her head. "I'm done with that asshole. He hired you to find who I was working with so he can try to intimidate us. Well, that ain't gonna happen. Gig was in Vietnam. It's gonna take more than a fat man with a bad attitude to scare him. Besides, we're all packed up and heading out of here on Monday. J.C. gets back on Tuesday and comes to my place, all he's going to find is an empty apartment with some real estate brochures about renting a place in New York."

"Smart," I said. She was impressive. She had ambitions and a plan. Maybe she was acting, I don't know. But she was easier to root for than a man who hits women.

Vivian said, "So what're you going to tell Dunbar?"

"I'll tell him the truth," I said. "I followed you to Fridays and The Asylum and then saw you share a pizza with a couple of friends, then you went home alone. Case closed."

"I appreciate that," she said. "Hey, listen, the real reason I noticed you at the department store is…you're a pretty good-looking guy. Ever thought about being in a movie?"

"What, like being the pizza guy?"

"Actually, I'm thinking a private investigator plot would be great," she said. "You know, a hot lady goes to see a handsome PI about her cheating husband and the next thing you know…"

"Happens all the time."

She laughed as I started my car and put it in gear.

"Take care," she said.

As I pulled away from the curb, I waved goodbye and said, "Good luck."

A few months later, I was driving uptown to meet with a client. I was listening to the Top-40 station. They were playing something new that caught my ear. I'd never heard anything quite like it. I turned up the volume. It had an unusual beat, and the vocalist wasn't really singing so much as he was speaking the words to the beat. The DJ said it was a song called "Rapper's Delight" by The Sugarhill Gang and it was on its way up the charts.

A few blocks later, I was passing near where The Asylum was and noticed the sign was gone, replaced with a new one that said: Wild Bill's Rodeo Lounge. I pulled in for a closer look and saw some guys unloading a big crate from a truck. They popped it open in the parking lot and there, for the first time in my life, I saw a mechanical bull.

Six months later *Urban Cowboy*, starring John Travolta, opened in theaters on its way to earning $47 million worldwide and kicking off a nightclub fad that lasted about three years.

Not long after that, The Pussycat Theater chain declared bankruptcy.

It turned out the guy was right. The only thing that's constant is change.

Photo Credit Amber Bracken

MICHAEL BRACKEN is the author of several books, including the private eye novel *All White Girls*, and more than twelve hundred short stories in several genres. His short crime fiction has appeared in *Alfred Hitchcock's Mystery Magazine, Ellery Queen's Mystery Magazine, Espionage Magazine, Mike Shayne Mystery Magazine, The Best American Mystery Stories 2018, The Mysterious Bookshop Presents The Best Mystery Stories of the Year 2021*, and in many other anthologies and periodicals. A recipient of the Edward D. Hoch Memorial Golden Derringer Award for lifetime achievement in short mystery fiction, Bracken has received two Derringer Awards and been shortlisted for two others. Additionally, Bracken is editor of *Black Cat Mystery Magazine* and has edited several anthologies, including the Anthony Award-nominated *The Eyes of Texas: Private Eyes from the Panhandle to the Piney Woods* and the *Mickey Finn* series. Born in 1957, he experienced the sixties through the eyes of a child and still remembers stringing his own love beads.

ABOUT THE CONTRIBUTORS

ANN APTAKER's Cantor Gold novels have won the Lambda and Goldie awards. Her short stories have appeared in *Fedora II* and *Fedora III*, the *Mickey Finn: 21st Century Noir* anthologies, *Switchblade*, *Black Cat Mystery Magazine*, and *Punk Soul Poet*. Her novella, *A Taco, A T-Bird, A Beretta and One Furious Night*, is featured in season two of the *Guns + Tacos* crime fiction series.

N.M. CEDEÑO (nmcedeno.com) is a member of the Short Mystery Fiction Society and Sisters in Crime: Heart of Texas Chapter. Her stories have appeared in *Analog: Science Fiction and Fact, After Dinner Conversation, Black Cat Mystery Magazine, Black Cat Weekly*. and *Groovy Gumshoes*. Her short story "A Reasonable Expectation of Privacy" placed third for Best Short Story in the 2013 *Analog* Reader's Poll.

BILL FITZHUGH is the award-winning author of eleven satiric crime novels, including *Pest Control*, which was adapted into a stage musical in Los Angeles and as a radio drama in Germany. *The New York Times* put him in a league with Carl Hiaasen and Elmore Leonard, calling him "a strange and deadly amalgam of screenwriter and comic novelist." His latest, *A Perfect Harvest*, is the final book of the Transplant Tetralogy, following *The Organ Grinders, Heart Seizure,* and *Human Resources*. *A Perfect Harvest* is in development as a stage play at The Group Rep theatre in Los Angeles. He lives in Los Angeles with his wife and an entertaining menagerie.

JAMES A. HEARN (jamesahearn.com), an Edgar Award nominee for Best Short Story, writes in a variety of genres, including mystery, crime, science fiction, fantasy, and horror. His work has appeared in *Alfred Hitchcock's Mystery Magazine, Mickey Finn: 21st Century Noir*, and *Monsters, Movies & Mayhem*.

LAURA OLES (lauraoles.com) is the author of the Jamie Rush mystery series. Her debut mystery, *Daughters of Bad Men*, was an Agatha nominee, a Claymore Award finalist, and a Killer Nashville Readers' Choice nominee; she is also a Writers' League of Texas Award finalist. Laura's work has appeared in trade and consumer magazines, crime-fiction anthologies, and she served as a business columnist. She loves road trips, bookstores and any outdoor activity that doesn't involve running.

ALAN ORLOFF (alanorloff.com) has won two ITW Thriller Awards—including one for his short story, "Rent Due," from *Mickey Finn: 21st Century Noir*, Volume 1. His novel, *I Know Where You Sleep*, was a Shamus Award finalist, and his novel, *I Play One On TV*, won both an Agatha Award and an Anthony Award.

NEIL PLAKCY (mahubooks.com) is the best-selling author of the golden retriever mysteries and won a Lefty for his police procedural *Mahu Surfer*. A four-time finalist for the Lambda Literary Award, he is the author of more than fifty novels in mystery and romance.

GARY PHILLIPS has published various novels, comics, and short stories; worked in TV; edited several anthologies, including the Anthony-winning *The Obama Inheritance: Fifteen Stories of Conspiracy Noir;* and he co-edited *Jukes & Tonks*. *Violent Spring*, first published in 1994, was named in 2020 one of the essential crime novels of Los Angeles. The *Washington Post* said his twenty-second novel *One-Shot Harry* "...is fast-paced, tough, wry and smart."

WILLIAM DYLAN POWELL (texasmischief.com) is an award-winning author who writes crime stories, mystery fiction, and books about Texas. The author of ten books, his short fiction has been featured in *Ellery Queen's Mystery Magazine, Alfred Hitchcock's Mystery Magazine,* and *The Best American Mystery Stories 2018.* He lives in Houston.

STEPHEN D. ROGERS (stephendrogers.com) is the author of *Shot to Death* and more than eight hundred shorter works, earning among other honors two Derringer Awards (with seven additional finalists), a Shamus Award nomination, and mention in *The Best American Mystery Stories.* He's also a Distinguished Toastmaster who has performed stand-up comedy and led improv workshops.

MARK THIELMAN (markthielman.com) is a criminal magistrate working in Fort Worth, Texas. His short fiction has appeared in *Alfred Hitchcock's Mystery Magazine, Black Cat Weekly, Mystery Magazine,* and a number of anthologies.

BEV VINCENT (bevvincent.com) is the author of several books, including *The Road to the Dark Tower* and *Stephen King: A Complete Exploration of His Work, Life and Influences.* He co-edited the anthology *Flight or Fright* with King and has published more than one-hundred twenty stories, with appearances in *Ellery Queen's Mystery Magazine, Alfred Hitchcock's Mystery Magazine,* and *Black Cat Mystery Magazine.* He has been published in more than twenty languages and nominated for the Stoker, Edgar, Ignotus, and ITW Thriller Awards.

ANDREW WELSH-HUGGINS is the author of the crime novel *The End of the Road;* the Andy Hayes private eye series, including the Shamus Award-nominated *An Empty* Grave; and is the editor of *Columbus Noir.* His short fiction has appeared in *Ellery Queen's Mystery Magazine, Mystery Magazine, Mystery Tribune, The Best Mystery Stories of the Year 2021,* and other magazines and anthologies.

On the following pages are a few
more great titles from the
Down & Out Books publishing family.

For a complete list of books and to
sign up for our newsletter,
go to DownAndOutBooks.com.

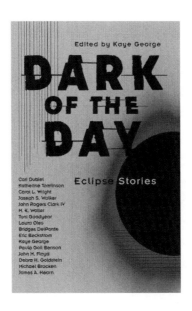

Dark of the Day: Eclipse Stories
Kaye George, Editor

Down & Out Books
April 2024
978-1-64396-395-2

An anthology of stories to celebrate the April 2024 eclipse in North America. These stories are located in various places and are even of various genres and themes. What they have in common, besides featuring eclipses, are that they are all written by brilliant authors and will all entertain you. Read them before the eclipse, to get into the mood, or after, to nostalgically remember it.

Contributors include Cari Dubiel, Katherine Tomlinson, Carol L. Wright, Joseph S. Walker, John Rogers Clark IV, M. K. Waller, Toni Goodyear, Laura Oles, Bridges DelPonte, Eric Beckstrom, Kaye George, Paula Gail Benson, John M. Floyd, Debra H. Goldstein, Michael Bracken, and James A. Hearn.

The Killing Rain
Left Coast Crime Anthology 2024
Jim Thomsen, Editor

Down & Out Books
April 2024
978-1-64396-362-4

The Killing Rain is collection of short crime fiction, ranging from the cozy to the hardboiled, with each story depicting the Seattle area as a real or imagine place.

It's in conjunction with "Seattle Shakedown" — the slogan for the 2024 Left Coast Crime conference, slated for April 10-14 in nearby Bellevue.

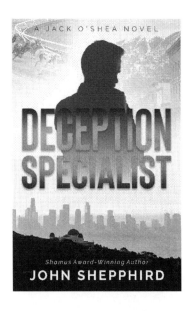

Deception Specialist
A Jack O'Shea Novel
John Shepphird

Down & Out Books
April 2024
978-1-64396-363-1

Reformed-swindler-turned-private-eye Jack O'Shea was first introduced in a series of short stories published in *Alfred Hitchcock Mystery Magazine*. The debut won the Shamus Award. The second in the series was a finalist for the Anthony Award.

Seeking redemption from his criminal past, Jack investigates a murder at a shadowy Northern California mountain college—a "visa mill" with ties to Silicon Valley. As he uncovers the truth, Jack's life of crime catches up with him. Nothing is as it appears.

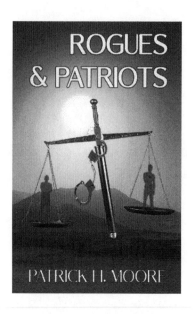

Rogues & Patriots
A Nick Crane
Patrick H. Moore

Down & Out Books
April 2024
978-1-64396-364-8

Patrick H. Moore's new novel *Rogues & Patriots* is Book Two of Moore's taut and topical three-volume series in which veteran LA PI Nick Crane finds himself locked in a life or death struggle with Miles Amsterdam and "the Principals," a terrifying group of aristocratic, right wing "super patriots."

With its well-drawn characters, non-stop action, and sharp, first person narration, *Rogues & Patriots* will leave the reader breathless and begging for more. Once again, Nick Crane stands tall as a world-weary PI everyman who takes on all comers in his battle to make America safe again for everyone.

Made in the USA
Middletown, DE
14 May 2024

54348161R00158